TIKI BEACH
PARADISE CRIME COZY MYSTERIES
BOOK 6

by
Toby Neal

"The way to right old wrongs is to turn the light of truth upon them." ~
Ida Wells

1

I WOULDN'T NORMALLY SPEND a Friday evening at a Japanese tea ceremony; I, Kat Smith, former Secret Service and current Postal Service, was tired.

I'd already spent the day manning the counter of Ohia's busy post office—but Pearl Yamamoto's invitation, printed on formal card stock no less, carried the weight of a summons.

The Red Hat Society ladies didn't make casual requests, least of all Pearl.

Upon arriving at Pearl's beachfront house in Ohia, each of us Red Hatters, including Josie, Edith, Clara, Opal, Rita, myself, Aunt Fae, and Ilima, had been issued a delicately patterned cotton kimono to wear and a *zabuton* cushion to sit on. The normally boisterous group was subdued by the formality of the occasion as we filed out onto the deck.

Tiki, my formerly feral, one-eared tortoiseshell cat, had also been invited—she was a favorite of Pearl's, and she sat beside me on her very own little pillow. I never would have believed my ornery feline could act like such a lady.

And then, Tiki extended a leg and leaned down to lick her privates.

The rhythmic shushing of waves on coral sand below Pearl's deck provided a backdrop to the clink of delicate porcelain as Pearl arranged the tea bowls at the low round table where the other Red Hat ladies and I sat on her beachfront lanai. Kawika, her burly young aide, placed a bell beside her place should she need something, before gliding back into the house.

Late afternoon gilded the surface of the ocean beyond us and a warm breeze carried the scent of Pearl's prize gardenias, growing in a large ceramic pot nearby. I shifted on my cushion, the kimono clinging to my skin in the humid air, finally beginning to relax in the beautiful setting.

But then my stomach gave a loud growl. Tiki interrupted her intimate personal grooming to glare at me and hiss a challenge.

"Okay, Pearl, lay it on us." Outspoken Edith tugged at the sash around her plump waist. "You're darn lucky I can still sit on this pillow without a back support. The tea better be good after all this folderol."

"Hear, hear," agreed Opal. She'd attached one of her trademark crystal frog pins to her kimono; I winced as a sunbeam reflected off of it and hit me in the eye with all the potency of a laser.

"Patience, ladies." Pearl's tiny form, elaborately gowned and made up, was propped to sit with us in a detachable section of her electric wheelchair. The elderly Japanese woman's signature red hat featured a live bonsai orchid that bobbed as she moved, casting dancing shadows on the weathered teak floor of the deck.

"Watch how I fold the *fukusa*." Pearl's commanding voice cut through my distraction. Beneath the arching orchids of her headdress, Pearl's eyes held a sharpness that belied her age. "Every motion has meaning. Josie will interpret as I go."

All of us watched the precise gestures Pearl made with a colored silk napkin, and Josie's brown eyes sparkled as she translated the cultural nuances. "The folding of the square represents the four elements: earth, air, fire, and water. Each fold connects earth and sky, like the way we honor both *mauka* and *makai* in Hawaiian tradition."

Pearl then purified the tea utensils by wiping them down using the *fukusa*. She then added hot water from the iron pot into the tea bowl to warm it up. Her arthritic fingers moved with surprising dexterity as she soaked each side of her bamboo whisk by gently moving it through the water in the bowl. She then discarded the water into a waste water bowl and dried the bowl with a cloth. Then she added two large scoops of matcha into the bowl and added hot water. The morning glory pattern on her vintage kimono rippled as she demonstrated, each sleeve carefully tied back with a cord. "This bowl belonged to my grandmother's grandmother. It bears the marks of loving repair—*kintsugi*."

"*Kintsugi* is an art form practiced in Japanese culture," Josie said. "Making cracked things beautiful through the application of lacquer dusted with powdered gold in the broken places."

"Very important to understand both cultures, yeah?" Pearl nodded to us as she whisked ceremonial matcha, the green tea bubbling like seafoam. "Japanese tea ceremony, Hawaiian protocols —they're all about respect. Mindfulness." She paused, her weathered hands steady as she poured, then handed the first bowl to me. Our eyes met. "Sometimes, the old ways show us things the new ways miss."

A sudden gust of wind rattled the banana leaves screening the lanai's sides, sending chicken skin racing up my arms as she poured and passed out the rest of the tea. Tiki's fur bristled, and she came to press against my thigh. The cat's amber eyes fixed on something in the deepening shadows beyond the circle of women. Was somebody out there watching us?

After we'd all dutifully sipped our tea, Pearl rang her bell. Kawika reappeared, carrying a large tray of fancy tea cakes, cookies, and pastries. "Now that's more like it," Edith said, filling her delicate plate with goodies as Kawika held the tray for each woman to help themselves. "I was feeling peckish."

"Mmm," I agreed as I bit into a cream-filled eclair that burst in my mouth with sinfully luscious vanilla goo. "Delish!"

Once we were all served, Kawika set a fluted glass sundae dish filled with wet kitty food in front of Tiki—and she hopped back onto her cushion to partake of her treat with the rest of us.

Once we'd eaten, Kawika removed the extra dishes.

"Let's get to the main event," Pearl told him imperiously. "The real reason we're here."

Edith, who was an attorney, put on a pair of readers. She adjusted her witch-style Red Hat. "Do you have to be so theatrical, Pearl?"

"Heck yes." Pearl clapped her hands. "How often does a woman get to reveal her legacy to her closest friends? Kawika, bring out the blueprints."

I still had a few cookies and pastries to go and wasn't about to skimp on the good stuff. I rolled the goodies into one of Pearl's silk napkins and stuffed the whole caboodle into my bra, handily concealing my snacks under the loose-fitting folds of the kimono. After all, talk of "legacy" and "blueprints" with a bunch of old ladies was liable to require further sustenance.

Tiki finished her food and climbed into my lap. The twenty-pound cat spread herself over my thighs like a hot furry rug with teeth. I knew better than to argue with her space invasion. We both knew who was boss, and it wasn't me.

"Here, you see?" Pearl's crimson-painted nail traced the outlines of the blueprints Kawika helped her spread out over the table, placing a teacup on each corner to hold it down. "This's my property. I plan to leave it to the towns of Ohia and Hana as a cultural park and event venue. A traditional Japanese tea garden created around native Hawaiian plantings." The tiny yellow orchids on her headdress trembled as Pearl leaned forward, a crimson nail pointing to the key on the side of the plans that listed all the types of vegetation being used. "Endemic Hawaiian plants will create a sense of peace and preservation for all who visit."

Everyone leaned forward to study the plans, noting the careful integration of existing features like the beachfront house. From one end of the property, a natural spring (currently a ditch) fed into a series of pools. Ancient rock walls webbed through the property like veins, each carefully planted and artistically framed. Arched decorative bridges rose above the meandering stream. Raked sand areas were dotted with art and repose benches marked places to pause and enjoy.

"Wow, Pearl, it's beautiful," Clara said, long purple beaded earrings swinging as she pointed to a miniature temple reached by a flagstone path. "Where's all the money for this going to come from?"

"I've liquidated all my assets and stock already," Pearl said. "Development is set to begin next week. I'm not getting any younger, and I want to see this done before I go."

"And I've already filed the preliminary paperwork." Edith tipped up her hat, the better to show us a legal pad covered in precise notes. "The property will be held in a perpetual trust and protected from development." She gave Pearl a sharp look. "Though certain parties are already expressing . . . concerns."

"Those 'certain parties' who want to stop my legacy from going forward can pound sand." Pearl's voice held steel beneath its refined surface. "I have friends in interesting places, yeah? The governor himself knows about this plan and approves of it."

"As do we all, of course, Pearl," Clara said.

"We've talked extensively about how to incorporate the endemic plants into your traditional Japanese tea garden vision," Josie added.

"And I love this, too," Ilima Kaihale chimed in, adjusting the kukui nut lei she wore over her kimono. Not only was Ilima my hot pilot boyfriend Keone's mother, but she was also a powerful *kumu* (teacher) of various Hawaiian cultural arts and practices and well-known on the island. "It's very generous of you to gift Ohia with your property, rather than keeping it for your family."

"Oh, well." Pearl flapped a beringed hand. "My family is all gone but for a nephew who lives in Honolulu and does well enough for himself not to need anything from me."

"Then who are these . . . 'certain parties' who might object to your bequest?" I asked. My investigator 'spidey sense' was tingling. A valuable estate like this being donated to the public was bound to put someone's undies in a bunch.

Pearl sniffed and poured herself another cup of tea. "I prefer not to speak of such things at this celebration."

The sun had slipped lower, painting the ocean in shades of amber and rose as Pearl lifted her cup. The blueprints crinkled in the salt breeze, tugging at the fragile porcelain anchors holding down each corner.

Tiki leapt suddenly onto the table, hissing, her tail bottlebrush-thick and her one ear pasted back. "Tiki!" I exclaimed.

I reached for her but the cat dodged, weaving between the tea bowls with uncharacteristic clumsiness until she knocked into Pearl's teapot—the one with the gold repairs tracing its history. Pearl's fresh tea splashed across the plans as Tiki's tail lashed. The cat stood in front of our hostess and yowled—a sound I'd never heard her make before. She swiped at the tea bowl Pearl held, then darted off the table to leap into the deepening shadows beyond the lanai.

"I'll get towels," I said quickly. Pearl set down her cup and her hand shot out, gripping my wrist with surprising strength.

"Leave it," the older woman said, her eyes following Tiki's retreat. "Some things must run their course."

Our hostess returned her attention to the architectural plans, which we were all dabbing at with our napkins—except me, of course, because my napkin was already in use holding the pastries in my bra.

I got up to look for Tiki in the banana trees lining the deck as Kawika appeared with a pile of dishtowels. Pearl focused on the dry spot on the map in front of her. "The meditation garden will . . ."

She blinked rapidly, the orchids on her headdress swaying. "Will be …"

I hurried to her side, noticing the sheen of sweat on Pearl's upper lip, how her cheeks had gone pale beneath her makeup. "Pearl?" I reached for her, but before I could make contact, Pearl's eyes rolled back. She slumped sideways, taking the antique teapot with her as she fell out of her low chair. "Pearl!" I lunged forward, barely managing to catch her head before it hit the teak flooring.

The woman's frail body went rigid, then began to jerk and tremble—some kind of convulsion. A stroke? Porcelain shattered somewhere behind us as I held her.

"Call 911!" I yelled to Kawika, whose eyes were wide with alarm. He grabbed his phone out of his pocket, but Edith already had hers out and was speaking loudly into it.

"Oh, Ms. Pearl!" Kawika's slippers slapped against the lanai as he rushed to help. His hands shook as he helped me roll Pearl onto her side and hold her in place.

Edith's voice cut through the chaos, clear and steady as she spoke to the dispatcher, but when I glanced up and met her eyes, her free hand clutched her Kwan Yin pendant, the knuckles white with tension.

"Stay with us, Ms. Pearl. Stay with us," Kawika said, patting her back, rubbing her cold hands. I monitored Pearl's pulse with two fingers on her tiny wrist—it was thready and erratic under her papery skin.

When the trembling stopped, I checked for breathing—but Pearl's chest had gone still. Her pulse had gone to nothing. "Starting CPR!"

My training took over and I did the compressions, leaving the breathing part to Kawika. We could keep going longer that way.

Someone sobbed and the gathered Red Hats formed a circle of crimson toppers and worry around Kawika and me as we took turns working on Pearl. The scent of spilled tea mixed with the orchids that had shaken loose from Pearl's hat, now lying crushed nearby.

Five compressions. Pearl's ribcage was so dangerously frail I was afraid to press too hard lest I break her delicate bones.

Kawika breathed for her, his large frame dwarfing hers as he gently exhaled into her slack mouth.

Compressions.

Breathing.

Each second stretched into the next, thick as saltwater taffy being pulled and just as slowly elastic. In the distance, the mournful cry of ambulance sirens held the promise of relief.

A flash of tortoiseshell fur caught my peripheral vision. Tiki had returned. She crouched near the spreading puddle of tea around the broken pot, pawing at the scattered leaves. The cat's ears lay flat against her skull, and she made a low growl in her throat that raised the hair on my neck.

"Come on, Pearl. Hang in there." My back and shoulders burned with effort; I was getting ready to trade places with Kawika when the paramedics burst onto the lanai in a flood of urgency and equipment, shouldering us aside.

As they worked on Pearl, I found my gaze drawn back to those spilled tea leaves—but Tiki had vanished again. Hopefully she'd find her way home.

The waves kept their rhythm off in the distance, indifferent to the drama unfolding above the tideline. But their whisper now seemed to carry a different word: *hurry*.

The paramedics worked efficiently around Pearl's still form while I helped Kawika clear away the remaining tea things. On impulse, I scooped up a sample of the spilled tea leaves from Pearl's pot and took them inside the house. I found a ziplock bag and put them inside, wondering why I felt so compelled to do so.

Maybe it was because of Tiki's odd behavior. The cat sure seemed to think there was something wrong with the tea, and she'd prevented Pearl from drinking any more of it.

Back outside, someone had switched on the lanai lights, and the Japanese lanterns Pearl had strung for ambiance now seemed oddly festive against the gravity of the moment.

"I think we've got her stable enough to move," one of the EMTs said, holding up an IV bag. "Bring the gurney!"

His partner took off at a run, and I heard the two remaining personnel talking about calling a chopper to take Pearl to Oahu's more sophisticated intensive care unit.

The Red Hat ladies had gone back inside the house, and I joined them as Pearl was wheeled through the room. Edith, in full attorney mode, trotted after them providing insurance and contact information.

I paused to let the cavalcade go by. Near me, Opal dabbed at her eyes with a handkerchief while Josie patted her shoulder. Clara shook her head sadly. "I hope she pulls through this."

"We all do. And at least she was with friends," Josie murmured. "Doing what she loved. Maybe the excitement was too much."

Kawika brought in a large tray containing the tea things, and Josie waved him away. "Let me deal with those. You get a hospital bag together for Pearl, please."

"Good idea," Kawika said, and surrendered the tray. Josie gathered the special implements with shaking hands, carrying them toward the sink. I hurried to help her. We ran a sinkful of warm, sudsy water, and Josie carefully placed each piece into the deep washtub. "I'll just put these—wait a minute."

"Hmm?" I glanced up, trying to shake off the surreal feeling that Pearl would roll up in her fancy standing wheelchair at any second, cracking one of her sly jokes.

"Pearl's special tea blend is missing." Josie held up a lacquered tea caddy. "The one she was so excited about serving today. She keeps it in this and serves it with her grandmother's ceremonial scoop."

I frowned but was distracted by the red and blue lights from the end of Pearl's driveway flashing nonstop emergency warnings across the ceiling. Soon the loud wail of the siren as they departed drowned out any further discussion.

Pearl was on her way—hopefully to a level of care that could avert tragedy.

Once the ambulance was gone, I fumbled my phone out of the kimono's pocket.

My boyfriend Keone, as a pilot, was privy to the comings and goings at the airport. He'd know if the helicopter the EMTs had ordered was taking Pearl to Maui's local hospital or over to the intensive care specialists on Oahu.

"What's up, Trouble?" Keone's warm voice saying my private nickname was enough to bring quick tears to my eyes—that's how soft I was getting—a far cry from the tough Secret Service agent I'd been only a couple of years ago.

"Trouble is right. Pearl Yamamoto had us over for a tea ceremony and collapsed. Her symptoms seem like a possible stroke. Something neurological, though it could be a heart attack, I guess. We did CPR until the EMTs took her away. They called for an air evacuation, so they'll be headed for the Hana Airport. Can you find out where they're taking her? I'm hoping it's Oahu."

"Let me find out." The phone went dead immediately.

I liked that about Keone. He never wasted time with personal reactions or unnecessary questions—he took confident action.

I sank onto a nearby stool, holding the phone cradled in my hands.

Josie turned from the sink, a frown between her brows. "I think there might have been someone else at the tea party with us," she said. "Someone we didn't see."

"What do you mean, someone else?" I asked Josie, my investigator instincts perking up despite my exhaustion.

"Just before Pearl collapsed, I noticed movement in the banana trees. I thought it was Tiki at first, but . . ." Josie wrung out a cloth, her hands still shaking . . . "maybe I was wrong."

Speaking of Tiki, my cat chose that moment to nudge open the door that led onto the back steps. Her eyes were slitted, her ear back, and her kinked tail looked like a bottlebrush.

"Tiki! Where've you been, girl?" I gestured to her luxuriously padded carrier, awaiting our ride home. "I thought I'd have to let you walk all the way back."

Tiki stalked menacingly toward me. She kept up a low warning growl deep in her throat— the same sound she'd made before Pearl collapsed. In her mouth was a scrap of brown paper.

No, not paper. A large, dried leaf.

"That's not from Pearl's special tea blend," Josie said slowly, pointing to the leaf in Tiki's mouth. "I've never seen tea like that before." Josie was a local expert on Hawaiian plants and herbs and their uses; for her to be unfamiliar meant something.

Tiki let me take the leaf when I reached for it. I pulled out the ziplock bag where I'd stored my earlier sample. "Josie, can I get another bag for this?"

She rifled through a few drawers until she found a snack bag and handed it to me. I placed the new leaf in that and put it inside with the other sample. Using a handy Sharpie from a mug beside the sink, I marked the date, time, and where I'd collected the leaf samples from—giving full credit to Tiki for the latest one.

My phone buzzed and I picked up for Keone. "They're taking Pearl to Queens on Oahu," Keone said without preamble. "Critical care unit. Mom's already calling her contacts there to make sure Pearl gets the best team."

"Thanks, Keone. That's good; your mom knows everyone, and not just on Maui! Listen, something weird is going on with the tea Pearl served. Tiki's been acting strange about it and I collected some samples. Do you know anyone with access to a lab who could analyze it?"

"Yeah, and you know her too. Call our friend the detective, Lei Texeira over at Maui Police Department. Maybe she can get it processed through their lab." Keone paused; I could almost see the frown on his handsome face. "You thinking this wasn't natural causes?"

"I'm thinking my cat doesn't usually try to knock teacups out of people's hands." Through the kitchen window, I could see the garden where Josie had spotted movement. It was now completely dark except for the security lights and the lamps on the deck.

Kawika had reappeared on the deck; he was cleaning up the blueprints for Pearl's legacy that still lay scattered on the lanai, spotted with spilled tea. He stacked the little silk-covered pillows we'd used for our interrupted tea party; they were a poignant reminder of something festive that had gone badly wrong.

"Want to come over to my place?" Keone asked. "You seem stressed."

"I am. Doing CPR on a fragile elder friend is not something I ever wanted to experience again," I said. Josie patted me on the shoulder comfortingly as she left the now sparkling kitchen and headed out to rejoin her partner, Edith. "Appreciate that, but I think I'll just go home. I've got work tomorrow. Tiki and I both need some rest."

"I'll be here if you change your mind, Trouble. Love you."

After we hung up, I pulled out my phone again to look up Detective Sergeant Lei Texeira's number. I scrolled through my contacts until I found it; Lei picked up on the second ring.

"If you're calling about those speeding tickets, I already told Keone they don't disappear just because he's dating the postmaster," Lei said by way of greeting.

"That was one time, and we were chasing a thief," I bantered back. "You'd be doing the county a service."

"Uh-huh. What does my favorite Secret Service Agent turned postmaster sleuth need this time?"

I shifted the phone to my other ear. "You're not wrong, I need a favor. Pearl Yamamoto just collapsed at our Red Hat tea ceremony this afternoon, and something's not right about how it went down."

"Pearl? The tiny one who uses a fancy wheelchair? She's quite a character. I'm sorry to hear that." Lei's tone sharpened. "What kind of not right, exactly?"

I explained about Tiki's behavior and the strange leaf she'd brought to me. "I was hoping there was some way you might be able to get it analyzed?"

"Your one-eared furry detective strikes again, eh?" Lei chuckled. "Yeah, I can run your tea leaves through our lab here in Kahului. But I need proper chain of custody of the samples. You can't just mail them to me."

I thought fast. "Keone's flying his usual Monday morning run tomorrow. He could drop it off at the station for us."

"Of course, your partner at K & K Investigations is available for custom airline deliveries." I could hear the affection in her voice. "Fine. Tell your boyfriend to bring it to my office before nine. And Kat?"

"Yes?"

"If your cat's right about this, it's going to be my case. No playing detective this time."

"Would I do that?" I cast my gaze heavenward—and spotted a pair of geckos getting busy in the warmth of the overhead light fixture.

"Do you want a list chronologically or alphabetically?" Lei's voice softened. "I'll call you as soon as I have results once Keone brings me your mysterious tea leaves."

"Thanks, Lei. You're the best."

"I know. Oh, and Kat?"

"Yes?"

"Tell Pearl's family I'm keeping her in my thoughts and prayers."

I ended the call feeling sad as I remembered Pearl's words about how little family she had. Fortunately, she had our Red Hat community, her nephew on Oahu, and faithful, kind Kawika to look after her.

Through the kitchen window, I could see the other ladies

heading to their cars, their usual chatter subdued. The ziplock bag with its suspicious contents felt heavy in my pocket.

Kawika reappeared carrying the stack of silken sitting pillows. He opened a large cabinet and stowed them inside on a shelf. "Thanks for all the help with Ms. Pearl," he said. I told him where Pearl had been taken, and he nodded. "Yes. I'm on her access list, always. I was already notified. I'll lock up the house. You should change out of that kimono and get on home."

I'd forgotten I was still wearing it. "Thanks. I'll check on Pearl first thing tomorrow."

"We all will." Kawika managed a smile. "At least we know she's getting the best care on Oahu."

I changed quickly in the guest restroom and, when I returned to the kitchen, gathered up Tiki and stowed her in the carrier. Getting her used to that had involved many hours of training, treats, and outright bribery. Curled up on her fuzzy pillow inside, she was now acting perfectly normal—the drama queen.

But my cat might be onto something bigger than any of us realized. We'd soon find out when those tea samples were analyzed at Maui Police Department.

I DROVE the winding road to Hana in the dark, the air growing thicker with moisture as a light fog rolled in from the sea. Tiki curled up in her carrier in the passenger seat, occasionally letting out a mewing comment as we hit a guava in the road or I took a hairpin turn too fast.

Keone's cottage sat nestled in the shadow of his mother's much larger, sprawling plantation house, where the lights were still blazing. She was probably hosting family, or an impromptu community gathering. Ilima's home was unofficial headquarters for everything from hula practice to area crisis management, and tonight's events would certainly qualify.

But Keone's smaller place, perched beside it on a little knoll overlooking Hana Bay, beckoned with its quieter welcome. A single lamp glowed through the screened lanai, and his mother's old orange tabby, Mango, dozed on the railing among potted orchids that Ilima insisted on "lending" him.

Tiki had fallen asleep and I didn't want any hostility to get going between her and Mango, so I cracked the windows of my vehicle and left her inside.

The wooden steps creaked under my feet as I went up them and sneaked past Mango carrying the baggie of tea leaf samples. The familiar scent of plumeria from the tree that grew on one side of the cottage wafted around us as Keone opened the door before I could knock.

"Hey, Trouble." He was still in his pilot's uniform, the crisp white shirt unbuttoned to the navel to reveal his rather spectacular chest. That ridiculous shirt with its gold epaulets and navy braid was somehow unwrinkled despite a full day of flying. "Glad you changed your mind about coming over." His warm brown eyes softened as they moved over my frizzing hair and stressed-out face. "Need a hug?"

"Heck yeah." I loved that he still asked permission, though I'd come a long way from my touchphobic early days in the relationship. He looked, smelled, and felt like pure catnip for this feline lover as I stepped into his arms and nuzzled his neck with a sigh, then kissed him.

Something I haven't mentioned yet is that I'm a healthy six-foot-one in height. So is he. That's only one of the reasons that, as a couple, we go together as perfectly as bananas and peanut butter.

"You okay?" he asked.

"I am now."

After several moments of hugging, snogging, and general relationship bliss, I stepped over the threshold into his little cottage. He closed the door behind me, and I held up the ziplock bag, trying to ignore how my hand shook at the memory of Pearl's collapse. "I need you to take these tea samples to Lei at MPD tomorrow morning. She's agreed to have the lab analyze them for us."

"Done." He took the plastic bag from me and set it on the nearby table. Suddenly, a loud yowl made us jump—Tiki made her presence known, even from the car.

"Can I bring her in? She's been really upset all afternoon," I said. "I'll keep her in the carrier so she doesn't fight with Mango."

"Of course."

Soon Tiki was inside, fed, watered, and back in her carrier. I frowned as I addressed Keone, closing the door on Tiki.

"Pearl's like everyone's auntie, you know? If someone hurt her . . ." I shook my head, rubbing the chicken skin bumps that had risen on my arms.

"Hey." Keone tucked a strand of hair behind my ear, his fingers lingering against my cheek. "Let's get Lei's lab results first. Then we'll figure the rest of it out. Meanwhile, I was about to eat. Have some of my homemade chili and rice. You look like you need food."

"Trying to get me to spend the night, Mr. K?" I followed him into the kitchen. "Because you already know the way to this woman's heart is through her stomach."

"Is it working?" His smile gleamed like a Cheshire cat's as he took down a bowl from a nearby shelf and handed it to me. "Let's eat."

From the big house's open garage, someone's ukulele started up, the music distinct through the open window. Several voices joined, singing a familiar local melody. Ilima was leading another impromptu gathering, helping the community process the pure Hawaii way.

Once we were done eating, we headed for the shower —together.

Sometimes a girl just needed her pilot, her cat, a roomy shower, and a small Hawaiian cottage by the sea.

2

I WAS ONLY a little fuzzy and frazzled from a fun-filled (if sleepless) night doing the No Pants Dance with Mr. K when I arrived at work the next morning. Our delivery guy, Chad, had arrived at the P.O. early and was honking the mail truck's horn as I pulled into the lot at eight a.m. on the dot.

I was rather proud of myself for being able to make yesterday's clothes smell OK with a laundry freshener sheet in Keone's dryer.

"It's time you left a few things here," Keone had said, and I was still thinking on what he meant by that as Chad and I toted in the usual canvas bags and towering piles of mail-order boxes for sorting. The package delivery revolution had caught Ohia understaffed and unable to keep up most days, but we did the best we could.

My bright purple nitrile-clad hands moved on autopilot, sorting the mail delivery into our few and highly prized postal boxes. The familiar scent of paper, cardboard, and sniff-of-the-day tropical air freshener (today's surprise: guava) felt oddly comforting in their normalcy.

But nothing really felt normal after yesterday's tea party gone wrong.

Pua Chang, my coworker, came in at nine several mornings a

week so I could go off duty a little early. This was time I usually spent private sleuthing for K & K Investigations, my little side hustle with Keone. I'd be out at three p.m. today so I could follow up with all that had unraveled at Pearl's house yesterday.

According to Kawika, who I'd contacted first thing in the morning (Pearl's main health contact as her caregiver), she had made it through the night but was still in intensive care and being treated by neurological specialists.

This wasn't the first time I'd been on tenterhooks (whatever the heck that meant!) about an elderly friend's health status. So far, Keone and I had weathered serious crises with his mother Ilima (a terrifying stroke, mostly recovered), Edith (heart episode, fully recovered), and Opal's husband Artie Pahinui (diabetes, partially recovered.) Maybe that's what came of having friends in the over-seventy age bracket, but it didn't mean I was ever going to like that aspect.

I replayed yesterday's tea ceremony in my head as I took a break from envelopes to stack boxes and fill out matching call slips for them.

Had Pearl seemed different? Worried about anything? No. Far from it. She'd been excited and a little mysterious, but that went with her theatrical side.

But maybe the stress was what had caused her collapse. Maybe the tea just smelled wrong to Tiki. How embarrassing if the lab at MPD turned nothing up from my samples! I'd never live it down. I could hear Lei teasing me now. "Remember the time Kat brought in those tea leaves her crazy feral feline decided she didn't like?"

I cringed at this possible future outcome. "You better not be wrong about those tea leaves, Tiki," I muttered. "My butt is on the line here."

The back doorbell chimed precisely at 9:00 a.m.

"Good morning, Kat." Pua Chang glided in, elegant in a silk pantsuit that somehow defied humidity, stains, and her mundane job as a postal clerk. Her neat chin-length bob set off crystal hoop earrings that caught the morning light. "Such a tragedy about Pearl."

I nodded, throat tight, eyes on my task. "She's got the best care in Hawaii. Hopefully she'll pull through."

"My sources say it was a stroke." Pua always had her finger on the pulse of the 'coconut wireless' gossip hotline around here. She set her Chanel bag behind the counter with precision. "Helen at Sweet Dreams Bakery in Kahului mentioned something interesting from their bridge game last week. Pearl was talking about 'making things right' and 'before it's too late.'"

"Could've been about what she gathered us to discuss yesterday." I hefted another big square plastic bin of mail, welcoming the physical effort to ground myself. Campaign flyers spilled out over the broad mail table as I dumped it. "Mayor Santos: Building Our Future" competed with "Council Member Lee: Voice of the People" and "Vote Chang for Real Change."

"Not your cousin's campaign, I assume?" I pointed to the Chang flyer and managed a teasing smile. Pua was related to a large and infamous family that dominated organized crime in Hawaii.

"No relation. You know Chang is a common name here in the islands." Pua's perfectly arched eyebrows conveyed volumes of disdain as she gazed at the blocky print of the postcard. "My cousin Raymond, who's in politics, would have far better graphic designers." She flipped up the old-fashioned pass-through counter and headed over to pull back the reinforced shutters and unlock the lobby doors. On her way back, she straightened a display of priority mail envelopes that had been perfectly straight to begin with. "But about Pearl—you were there at her party, weren't you? Was there anything . . . unusual about what happened?"

"Of course. Pearl collapsed," I snapped. Pua was fishing, and I wasn't ready to talk.

The front doorbell jangling saved me from answering as Mrs. Agusto arrived for her daily morning P.O. box check. She yelled a greeting to Pua; apparently she'd forgotten her hearing aid again.

Was there anything unusual about Pearl's tea party? Besides *everything*?

A strange envelope addressed to *"The Keeper of Secrets" care of Pearl Yamamoto* caught my attention. No mail was ever delivered to her home, and this had her house's address on it. I flipped the card over, looking for a return address. Nothing. The paper was the same cream-colored stock Pearl always used. *Very* strange.

Pua had returned to continue her stream of consciousness on the events surrounding Pearl's collapse, and because of the envelope I'd lost the thread of it.

"—and, naturally, the development contract for her proposed Heritage Tea Garden remains unsigned," Pua was saying, adjusting the stacks of forms behind the counter. "One does wonder about the timing of her health emergency."

"Pua," I interrupted, studying the mysterious envelope. "Did Pearl mention expecting any important correspondence to you?"

"Correspondence? No, but she did seem preoccupied at last week's Historical Society meeting. And you know how meticulous she usually is about the minutes..."

"That's right. Pearl is the recording secretary for the East Maui Historical Society," I muttered, still studying the mysterious piece of mail.

Pua raised a brow at me, clearly restraining herself from commenting on my keen sense of the obvious.

I held the envelope out for her inspection. "Does the title 'Keeper of Secrets' mean anything to you?"

"That's not a title we use at the Historical Society." Pua came in beside me and tweaked the missive out of my gloved hand. She studied the card carefully, holding it aloft and backlit to try to see through the envelope, but the heavy paper was too thick. "Very dramatic."

"Do you know if it's used anywhere else?"

"If so, I'm not aware of it." She shook her head.

"Since this card is addressed to her home, I'm going to set it aside and hold onto it for her," I said. "Hopefully I can visit her in the hospital and deliver it in person."

"And satisfy your curiosity," Pua said. "They say curiosity killed the cat. And your name is?"

"Katherine," I replied, zipping out of the sorting area to stash the envelope in the inbox on my desk. "And I'm keeping this safe for Pearl. Nothing more."

Never mind how my fingers itched to get into that envelope . . .

3

The morning at the post office dragged on interminably. Even the unusual envelope couldn't distract me from my growling stomach —or my worry about Pearl. By the time noon rolled around, I'd sorted what felt like half of Maui's mail and was beyond ready for a lunch break.

"I'M HEADING NEXT DOOR," I called to Pua, who merely nodded without looking up from her meticulous organization of certified mail receipts.

The short walk to Ohia General Store took all of thirty seconds, but it was enough time for the humid air to make my already questionable day-two hair situation even worse. I combed the mass of brown locks back with my fingers as I opened the door. The familiar bell jingled as I entered, bringing with it the comforting scent of Artie's local-style beef stew—a reliable midweek special.

"Come for lunch, Kitty Kat?" Artie called from behind the counter. Despite being blind for many years, he navigated his domain with the confidence of someone who'd spent five decades in the same space. Using modern technology, he was even able to wait on customers single-handedly.

"It's me, Uncle Artie," I confirmed, making my way to the counter where a couple of vinyl-topped stools awaited. "And that stew smells like heaven."

"Coming right up." His weathered hands moved with practiced precision, ladling the thick stew into a ceramic bowl. "Opal said you might be stopping by today."

"I had a premonition I'd see you." As if summoned by her name, Opal emerged from the small stockroom, wearing a purple *muumuu* aglow with white hibiscus flowers. A black velvet scarf draped around her neck was fastened with an outrageously sparkly rhinestone unicorn that winked in the fluorescent lighting overhead. "Not that it was too far a stretch that you'd show up after all that went on yesterday."

"Right? What a thing that was," I agreed.

"How's Pearl doing today?" Opal took a stool opposite me. The runes she carried in her pocket made a sound like a rain stick as she arranged her roomy dress.

"No change from this morning," I said, accepting the bowl Artie slid across the counter with impressive accuracy. I dug into my stew. I only got a thirty-minute break, so I had to make it count. "She's still in intensive care. Kawika says the doctors are cautiously optimistic."

Artie shook his head slowly. "She'll recover. Woman's tougher than old leather."

I was heartened to hear him say that; both Artie and Opal were a touch psychic, though in different ways. "That's why the timing of her collapse doesn't make sense," I said. I waggled the spoon at him. "This stew is amazing, Uncle."

"Secret's in the timing," he said with a wink that still worked despite his sightless eyes. "And in knowing when to leave well enough alone."

Opal absently adjusted her unicorn pin, her pale blue eyes gazing at me intensely. "You look like you've got something on your mind besides Pearl's condition."

I swallowed a spoonful of stew before answering. "Pua Chang has been asking questions all morning. About the tea party."

"That woman," Opal clicked her tongue disapprovingly. "She's my friend and I love her, but she's always digging for gossip."

"She mentioned Pearl talking about 'making things right' at some bridge game last week." I studied Opal carefully. "And something feels off about the whole situation. I can't stop thinking about Tiki's reaction to that tea."

Artie's hands stilled on the counter. "Your cat's got better instincts than most people I know."

Opal jiggled the bag of runes in her pocket; they made a distinct dry rustling sound. "I've been thinking about it too, Kat. There was something . . . unusual about yesterday."

"Like what?" I set my spoon down, giving her my full attention. "I need your impressions of things."

"I was the first to get to her house. And . . . well, for one thing, Pearl seemed . . . a little nervous." Opal lowered her voice, though we were the only ones in the store. "And she had that little sandalwood box on the side table—you know, the carved one with the crane design?"

I nodded, remembering the ornate box from another visit.

"When I arrived early to help with the teacups, I saw her slip something inside it and lock it with a tiny key she wore around her neck. She was startled when she noticed me watching." Opal leaned closer. "And when she was pouring the tea, her hands were shaking. Pearl Yamamoto never has shaky hands, Kat."

"Did you see anything else unusual?" I asked, pushing the half-eaten bowl of stew aside.

"The phone rang just before everyone arrived. Pearl answered it in the kitchen, and when she came back, her face was pale." Opal shook her head, the unicorn pin catching the light. "I mean, paler than usual. She tried to hide it, but I've known that woman for forty years. Something frightened her."

"Her words were pretty defiant later on," I said. "That 'pound sand' phrase."

"I had the feeling she was talking herself into that," Opal said.

Artie slid a glass of water toward me with perfect aim. "You planning to look into this, Kitty Kat? Because if something happened to Pearl that wasn't natural—"

"I'm already on it," I assured him, thinking of the envelope in my desk and the tea samples with Lei. "But I need to be careful. If someone did something to Pearl . . ."

"Then they might not want anyone asking questions," Opal finished. "And she's vulnerable in a high-traffic place like the hospital."

The store's bell jingled, announcing a customer. Opal squeezed my hand before rising to attend to them, leaving me with a bowl of cooling stew and a glass of cold water.

I polished off the last few bites, the warmth settling my stomach even as a chill of unease ran down my spine.

Artie patted my hand silently; his was warm and calloused from many hours of guitar playing. "I have a feeling she'll be okay," he said. He went across the store and began unloading canned goods onto a shelf.

Opal returned after directing the customer to the small hardware section.

"Opal," I said, pushing my empty bowl aside, "would you cast your runes? See what they might say about Pearl?"

She didn't look surprised by my request. Her hand instinctively went to her pocket where she always kept the hand-carved kukui nut shell runes. She'd made them herself decades ago, polishing each shell to a warm glow before etching the ancient symbols with meticulous care.

"Artie," Opal called softly across the store to where her husband was rearranging canned goods by touch alone.

"Hmm?" He cocked his head in her direction, always attuned to the shifts in her voice.

"Would you mind turning the sign to CLOSED for a bit? Kat needs a reading."

Without hesitation, Artie navigated the familiar path to the front door. His fingers found the hanging sign and flipped it with practiced ease.

"Take your time," he said, sliding the deadbolt into place.

Opal unwound the black velvet scarf from around her neck, laying it across the counter with care. The fabric created a light-absorbing, intimate space between us. Her rhinestone unicorn pin, still attached, caught the overhead light as she leaned forward, sending prismatic reflections dancing across the ceiling.

"I haven't done a reading about something this serious since the last time you had a case," she murmured, reaching into her pocket. The kukui nut shells made a soft clacking sound as she withdrew them in their leather pouch. She poured them out and, cupped them in her weathered palms. Thirteen pieces in total, each one polished to a deep mahogany gleam, each one bearing a symbol that seemed to breathe in the dim light of the store.

"Focus your thoughts on Pearl," she instructed, closing her eyes and keeping her hands cupped around the shells. "Think on what happened yesterday, on what you feel in your gut about it all."

I did as she asked, concentrating on Pearl's face just before she collapsed, on Tiki's strange reaction to the tea, on the rustle in the vegetation alongside the deck.

Opal's lips moved in a silent prayer or invocation—I'd never asked which—before she cast the runes onto the velvet scarf with a practiced flick of her wrists. The kukui nut shells scattered across the black fabric, some clustering together, others landing far apart. One rolled off the scarf entirely, clattering to the floor.

"Oh," Opal breathed, her eyes widening as she surveyed the pattern. Her expression grew grave.

Artie had made his way back to us, his hands finding the edge of the counter. "What do you see, love?"

Opal touched three shells that had landed in a tight triangle.

"Secrets," she said softly. "Old ones. From before." Her finger moved to another shell that had landed upside down. "Betrayal. Something hidden being revealed."

I leaned closer, drawn to the patterns though I couldn't interpret them. "What about Pearl? Is she going to be okay?"

Opal's hand hovered over the shells, trembling slightly. "There's danger here. Not just for Pearl." She pointed to a shell that sat alone at the edge of the scarf. "This might be you. The seeker. But look—" She indicated another shell nearby. "This speaks of watching eyes. Someone knows you're asking questions."

"What about the one that fell?" I asked, noticing how Artie had grown very still.

Opal bent to retrieve the fallen rune, holding it in her palm for a long moment before placing it in the center of the pattern. "This one portends death," she whispered. "But whether it's already happened or is yet to come, I can't tell. Generally, when a rune falls out of the reading, it doesn't want to be included."

"Could be the death of a secret, or a way of life," Artie said. "And no death could mean Pearl will be fine. Eventually."

"Nothing is too straightforward with the runes," Opal said, her finger tracing a connection between the death rune and another. "This suggests that what's happening now has roots in the past. Something buried that won't stay buried."

"The Heritage Tea Garden," I murmured, remembering Pua's comment about the unsigned development contract. "Maybe this is about that."

Opal gathered the runes quickly, as if suddenly uncomfortable with what they revealed. "Be careful, Katherine," she said, returning them to her pocket. "The runes are clear about one thing —there's danger in digging too deep."

She must be serious if she called me Katherine. "But they also suggest that's exactly what I need to do, don't they?" I pressed.

Opal refolded her scarf, pinning it back around her neck with the unicorn brooch. "They do," she admitted. "Just remember that some secrets are kept for a reason."

Artie reached across the counter, his hand finding mine with unerring accuracy. "Watch your back, Kitty Kat. And maybe keep that cat of yours close by. Tiki's better than a watchdog."

"That she is." I thanked them both, promised to be careful, and headed for the door. Artie unlocked it for me, his milky eyes somehow still conveying concern. I gave him a spontaneous kiss on the cheek, and he patted my shoulder. "Come back by if you need some more stew."

As I stepped into the humid afternoon air, the envelope addressed to "The Keeper of Secrets" seemed to burn in my mind. Whatever was happening with Pearl went deeper than a simple health emergency—and I'd been pulled right into the middle of it.

AT PRECISELY THREE O'CLOCK, I locked my desk drawer, retrieved the mysterious envelope, and slipped it into my purse. While I trusted Pua to handle the afternoon mail rush, I didn't quite trust her not to snoop if given half a chance.

"I'm heading out," I called, tossing today's gloves into the rubbish. "See you tomorrow morning at the usual time."

Pua glanced up from helping young Windy Nakasone with a big Amazon package. The once unfriendly girl gave me a cheerful wave as she hurried out of the lobby with her box. We'd come a long way since the little rascal declared she was marrying Keone and I had to disavow her of that notion.

"Will you be following up on that business we discussed this morning?" A couple of customers were unlocking their boxes but her arched eyebrow conveyed her meaning clearly.

"Just some personal errands," I replied blandly. "Thanks for covering."

The knowing look Pua gave me said she didn't believe me for a second, but she nodded. "Give my regards to . . . whoever you might be meeting. And Keone, of course."

I slipped out the back door of the post office, my pulse quickening as I crossed from the building toward the familiar shack that had once been my home. Now the humble former postal worker's quarters served as the headquarters of K & K Investigations—a grandiose name for what was essentially me and Keone poking our noses where they didn't belong, occasionally for pay.

The wooden steps of the porch creaked underfoot as I moved off the big beach rock top step, a sound that brought back memories of my first days in Ohia.

The shack looked different now. Keone and I had replaced the rusted tin roof, fixed the sagging porch rail, and even hung a discreet wooden sign with our business name carved into koa wood. The coconut palm that had been growing in one of the gutters was now transplanted to a spot far enough away from the side of the shack to account for its eventual growth (and coconut-dropping hazard potential.)

I frowned; the small porch usually held our bikes, but those had been moved. Today the porch held a pair of mismatched Adirondack chairs and a small foldable wooden table holding two sweating glasses of iced tea and a manila folder.

Before I could reach for the handle, the door swung open and there he was: Keone Kaihale, aka 'Mr. K,' the first person I'd met in Ohia—in fact I'd met him before I arrived, as he flew the plane I'd come in on.

He filled the doorframe, all six-foot-one of him, wearing swim shorts and a faded aloha shirt that did nothing to hide his broad shoulders. His warm brown eyes crinkled at the corners as he smiled. "Surprise. My last flight was canceled today. You're right on time for today's investigation."

My heart did that ridiculous flutter thing the romance novels I'm addicted to never fail to mention. "Hey, hey, Mr. K," I replied. "I didn't expect you. Pua says hi."

Smooth, Kat, real smooth.

"Who cares about Pua." He pulled me in for a kiss that made me forget all about mysterious envelopes and suspicious tea for approximately five glorious minutes.

When we broke apart, I was breathless and momentarily disoriented. "That's one way to debrief," I mumbled.

Keone laughed, leading me to one of the chairs. "I thought we'd start outside," he said, settling into the blue chair. "It's too nice an afternoon to be cooped up in there."

I sank into the red plastic chair, gratefully accepting the iced tea. "Any word from Lei about our samples?"

"Not yet," Keone replied, taking the blue chair. "She said the lab's backed up with a drug case from Kihei side. But she promised to fast-track it as much as possible."

"I hope she calls soon. I might have made a fool of myself for hauling in those tea leaves because my cat got spooked." I took a long sip of the cold tea, savoring the mint Keone had added.

"I dropped the samples off myself this morning. Lei could tell I was serious about it. Tiki may be a cat, but I've learned to pay attention to her."

"So have I." More than once that formerly feral feline had been vital in solving a case. I reached into my purse and pulled out the cream-colored envelope. "I brought something interesting to show you. This came in the mail today, addressed directly to Pearl's home. She doesn't get mail there. Weird, right?"

Keone leaned forward, his eyes narrowing as he read the elegant script. "'The Keeper of Secrets, care of Pearl Yamamoto'?"

"No return address, and it's the same paper Pearl uses for her correspondence." I turned the envelope over in my hands. "I was going to hold onto it for when she recovers, but after Opal's rune reading . . ." I summed up the warnings Opal had shared from her own impressions of the tea party, and also what the runes had indicated.

Keone's brows drew together. "You think it might be connected to what happened?" He took the envelope, examining it carefully.

"Maybe? And given that Pearl's in the hospital and can't open it herself . . ." I let the implication hang in the air. "There might be a clue inside."

Keone raised an eyebrow. "Are you suggesting what I think you're suggesting, Postmaster Smith? Tampering with the U.S. mail is a federal offense."

"I know," I groaned. "And I feel terrible even considering it. But if there's something in there that could explain why Pearl collapsed —or worse, whether she was poisoned—don't we have a responsibility to look?"

He studied my face for a long moment before nodding. "I think we can justify a peek, under the circumstances." He stood up. "Come on. Let's do this properly."

Inside the shack, Keone filled the pot of the coffeemaker. The interior of our makeshift office was comfortably cluttered with our investigation materials—a table and chairs, a corkboard covered in notes and photos, a small desk with a monitor we could use with laptops, and file cabinets. The Murphy bed I used to sleep on was up and out of the way, revealing a fundraiser rag rug made by Aunt Fae which I'd won in a raffle.

"Steam is gentler than other methods," Keone said as he tugged on a pair of thin rubber gloves. "Less chance of damaging the contents or leaving evidence we tampered with it."

"Since when do you know so much about it?"

"The internet. I can pick a lock, now, too." He slanted me a mischievous glance.

But I felt the weight of my postal oath pressing down on me. "I could lose my job for this."

"I'm the one who's doing it. And we'll only be in trouble if someone finds out." Keone held the envelope over the rising vapor, carefully working his gloved finger under the loosening flap. "And since the addressee is 'Keeper of Secrets,' not Pearl specifically, there's some ambiguity about who it's really for."

"That's a pretty thin justification," I muttered, but I didn't stop him as slowly, methodically, he eased the envelope open, taking care not to tear the delicate paper. When the flap was fully lifted, he extracted a single folded sheet of thick, creamy paper and laid it on the nearby table.

"You want to do the honors?" he asked. "It was your find."

Guilt and curiosity battled within me—this was definitely crossing a line I'd never crossed before, even in all our other amateur sleuthing. My hands trembled slightly as I unfolded the paper using a capped ballpoint pen. The paper contained just three lines of the same elegant handwriting as on the envelope. I read aloud:

"The time has come. The garden reveals all. The crane will fly once more."

Keone and I exchanged puzzled glances.

"What the heck does that mean?"

"I don't know. But combined with Pearl's collapse and Opal's rune reading, it feels like a warning—or a threat."

"We need to reseal this," I said, my conscience kicking into overdrive. I took a picture of the note with my phone, then carefully refolded the paper using the end of the pen. Keone slipped it back into the envelope. "And I should put it back in my desk tomorrow."

Keone reached for a stick of glue from the office supplies. "We'll make it look untouched, and we haven't disturbed any prints in case that matters. But Kat?"

"Yeah?"

"I think we just stepped into something much bigger than a mysterious health emergency. I won't be surprised if Lei gets back to us that those tea leaves aren't what they're supposed to be." He slipped the envelope into an empty file and stuck it in the nearby cabinet. "You can take it back to the office tomorrow."

Whatever secrets Pearl was keeping, someone else knew about

them. And that someone had attempted to make cryptic contact with a woman who was in intensive care.

The distinctive sound of tires on gravel announced a visitor—not the gentle crunch of a cautious driver, but the confident approach of someone who knew exactly where they were headed, and they were pulling up in front of the shack.

There was no window at the front of the building, so Keone cracked the door to peer outside, squinting against the late afternoon sun. He broke into a smile.

"It's Mom," he said, his voice carrying that special blend of respect and fondness he reserved for her. "Hey, *Mamacita*," he called out to her. "What brings you this way?"

"Just popping by to see my two favorite investigators," she called back. I heard her car door slam.

Meanwhile, I shoved the file drawer that held the incriminating envelope shut with a metallic bang that seemed to echo in the small space. My guilty conscience was kicking into gear big-time.

A minute later, Ilima stood framed in the entrance, backlit by golden sunshine that created a halo effect around her impressive silhouette.

At sixty-five, she was a striking woman—tall and statuesque, with silver-streaked black hair pulled into a bun. Crowning her head was a *lei po'o* of purple orchids and ferns. She wore a traditional floor-length *muumuu* in a rich royal blue fabric patterned with subtle white ginger flowers. The garment whispered against the wooden floor as she moved, exuding the faint scent of *pikake* and something distinctly more expensive—the French perfume I'd given her for Christmas this last year.

"Wow, Mom, you're looking fancy." Keone enveloped Ilima in a hug that lifted her sandal-shod feet slightly off the ground. "We weren't expecting you."

"I have news that couldn't wait, and neither of you would answer your phone." The gentle rebuke carried exasperation.

I reflexively checked my phone and winced seeing three missed calls. "Sorry, Auntie. We were just discussing—"

"No worries. I know you're both busy." She turned to me, arms outstretched. "Come here, Kat." I stepped into her embrace, breathing in her scent as she hugged me. Ilima's hugs were legendary—somehow both gentle and fierce, like she was imparting strength directly into your soul. When she pulled back, she took my wrist in her hand, examining the gold bracelet that had once been hers. She admired the arc of gold with raised black enameled letters, her thumb brushing over the intricate Hawaiian pattern spelling out *Kuuipo* (sweetheart.) "Beautiful," she said softly, "Just as when Keone's father gave it to me as an engagement gift. It looks good on you."

"Thanks, Auntie Ilima. It means a lot to me." The bracelet had been passed to me last Christmas by Keone on her behalf. It wasn't just jewelry; it was acceptance into a family I'd grown to love deeply.

"So what's this news that brings you all the way out to our humble headquarters?" Keone asked, as he pulled our least rickety chair out for his mother and handed her a glass of iced tea he'd poured. "We're trying to understand what happened to Pearl."

"As am I," Ilima replied, taking a refreshing sip. "Particularly since Pearl was to play a significant role in my announcement next week." Her eyes widened with excitement. "A role I was hoping you two might share in as well."

"Announcement?" I echoed. A breeze through the open window on the back wall stirred the humid air.

"I've decided to run for mayor of Hana and Ohia in the upcoming special election." Ilima straightened, the movement causing her *lei po'o* to shed a single purple petal that drifted to the floor like a tiny royal proclamation. Outside, a mynah bird called raucously, as if announcing the news to all of Ohia.

"Mayor?" Keone's surprise was evident, but his expression

quickly transformed into a proud grin. "Mom, that's incredible. You'll rock that office!"

"It's about time someone with actual integrity took on the role," I added sincerely. "Mayor Santos doesn't have the best reputation after that last public budget meeting."

"I decided recently," Ilima explained, her gold bracelets jingling as she gestured. "After Mayor Santos's financial improprieties came to light, several community leaders approached me. At first, I said no—you know how I value privacy. But then Pearl convinced me."

"And Pearl was going to help with the campaign?" I asked, thinking of the mysterious note about "the garden" and Pua's comment about an unsigned development contract.

"Pearl was to be my campaign chairwoman," Ilima confirmed, her mouth turning down with concern. "That woman has more energy at seventy-eight than most people have at thirty. She was passionate about developing our platform around balanced growth, with cultural preservation at its heart."

Keone and I exchanged a silent glance, communication born of months working side by side: this was a piece of the puzzle we hadn't known.

"The Heritage Tea Garden project," I said slowly. "Was that part of your campaign platform?"

"Yes, and Pearl's brainchild entirely," Ilima nodded, her eyes brightening with enthusiasm. "You have seen her plans, Kat—a beautiful fusion of traditional Japanese gardens with native Hawaiian plants. A place for education, meditation, and community gatherings. She wanted it to be her legacy to Ohia."

"Unlike the New Ohia development disaster," Keone added, referencing the corrupt land deal that had nearly destroyed our town, before being exposed.

"Exactly." Ilima's expression clouded momentarily. "What many people don't realize is that Mayor Santos was quietly supportive of that development, despite his public statements to the contrary. He stood to benefit considerably from certain . . . arrangements."

"Are you saying he was corrupt too?" I asked, surprised. "Working with the Changs?"

"Not openly," Ilima clarified, leaning forward confidentially, her voice dropping. "But willing to look the other way for the right incentives. Pearl had evidence of his duplicity—emails and meeting notes from when she served on the planning commission."

I felt a chill despite the warm afternoon air and rubbed my arms. "Evidence she was planning to make public as part of your campaign announcement?"

"Next Tuesday," Ilima confirmed. "We were going to hold a press conference at her house, the proposed Tea Garden site. The location itself is magical at sunset—the perfect backdrop for our vision of Ohia's future." Her expression grew wistful. "Pearl was so excited about it. We were going to share all this at the tea party, but then . . . you know what happened."

"Mom, did anyone else know about this evidence?" Keone asked.

"Only our core campaign team—Pearl, Councilman Akana, and me." She paused, her intelligent eyes connecting the dots. The purple orchids trembled around her face. "Oh. You think—you think Pearl's collapse might be connected to our announcement?"

"We don't know," I admitted. "But it's a concerning coincidence."

Ilima set down her iced tea glass with purpose, her expression transforming to determined leader in an instant. It was the same look I'd seen Keone wear when facing a challenge—that Kaihale resolve that made you believe anything was possible. "I need to see those documents. Pearl kept them in a sandalwood box in her home office." She turned to Keone. "She gave me a spare key to her house years ago. We should go there immediately and grab that box."

"Wait," I said, remembering Opal's words about the carved box with the crane design. "A sandalwood box with a crane carved on it?"

Ilima looked surprised. "Yes. How did you know?"

"Opal mentioned seeing Pearl put something in it before the tea party." I exchanged another side-eye with Keone. "She said Pearl locked it with a key she wore around her neck."

"Yes. She always kept that key with her," Ilima confirmed. "If someone hurt Pearl because of these documents . . ."

"Then we'll find out who," Keone finished firmly, standing. He offered his hand to his mother. "K & K Investigations is on the case —with special consultant Ilima Kaihale."

Ilima accepted his help with a grateful smile, rising to her feet. "I've always wanted to be a detective. Your father used to say I missed my calling because I could extract a confession from a stone."

"And you still can," Keone laughed, dropping a kiss on top of her head, careful not to disturb the *lei poʻo*. "Let me grab my keys. We'll take my truck."

As we headed out, I cast one last glance at the file drawer containing the mysterious envelope. *The crane will fly once more. The garden reveals all.*

What could it possibly mean?

Ilima paused at the door, turning back to take in our modest investigation headquarters with genuine affection. "You two have built something special here," she said. "Not just this business, but your partnership. It reminds me of your father and me, Keone." Her smile was bright despite the worry in her eyes. "He would be so proud of you both."

I touched the gold bracelet on my wrist, drawing strength from its connection to this remarkable woman and her son.

But as we descended the porch onto the beach rock and out into the golden afternoon light beside our cars, I couldn't shake an ominous feeling.

I rolled my shoulders back determinedly. With Ilima's regal presence, Keone's steady strength, and my Secret Service skills, we'd deal with whatever awaited us at Pearl's house as best we could.

Even so, I kind of wished Tiki was coming too—but when I peeked under the porch, she was nowhere to be found.

4

THE DRIVE to Pearl's beach house took us along the winding coastal road, a journey I'd made just yesterday for what was supposed to be a simple tea party. Late afternoon sun cast long shadows across the pavement as Keone navigated the turns with practiced ease. How different everything looked now, though the same turquoise waves still crashed against black lava rocks and the same rainbow-colored bougainvillea spilled over lichen covered stone garden walls.

Ilima sat in the front passenger seat, her *muumuu* arranged elegantly. She'd been quiet for most of the drive, her fingers absently touching the orchids in her *lei po'o* or pleating the fabric of her dress as she gazed out the window. I could almost see the campaign speeches and community plans forming behind her thoughtful eyes.

Pearl's home came into view—a charming single-story plantation style house perched on a bluff overlooking the Pacific. The plantings and acreage around it that were to become the Heritage Tea Garden looked rather ordinary now, but I had glimpsed what was intended for them.

Yesterday, the property had seemed welcoming and peaceful. Today, the shadows slanted long and hinted at secrets.

As we pulled into the crushed coral driveway, I noticed a blue Honda Civic parked near the back steps. "That's Kawika's car," I said, recognizing the faded surf shop sticker on the bumper.

"Good," Ilima nodded. "I was hoping he'd be here."

We got out of the pickup, the warm air heavy with the scent of plumeria from the trees that lined Pearl's walkway. Their fallen blossoms created a fragrant carpet beneath our feet as we approached the small back porch. Before we reached the steps, the door opened and Kawika stepped out. Today he wore pale blue scrubs and his long black hair was tied in a neat ponytail, suggesting he'd come straight from his other job, which Pearl had told me was as a nurse at the Hana Health Clinic.

His grim expression brightened at the sight of us. "Auntie Ilima!" he called, hurrying down the steps to embrace Keone's mother with obvious affection.

"Kawika. My boy." Ilima cupped his face in her hands the way only Hawaiian aunties can, studying him with concern. "You look exhausted."

He shrugged broad shoulders, the gesture conveying both acknowledgment and dismissal of her worry. "Been a long day." His eyes moved to Keone. "Good to see you, cuz. And Kat, good to see you again."

I blinked in surprise. "Cuz? Like—really a cousin or just social cousin? Because everyone seems related on this side of the island."

Keone slanted me a smile. "Did I never mention that Kawika is my father's sister's son's son. First cousin once removed."

"Which makes him my grandnephew by marriage," Ilima added, patting Kawika's shoulder fondly. "Though removed enough that I don't feel quite as ancient as that makes me sound."

"Huh. I don't know how you all keep track of that," I said, feeling a little pang. "Aunt Fae is my only living relative that I'm aware of."

"Well, I am not a Kaihale—my last name is Pali," Kawika said.

"But in Hawaii, if we had to explain how every cousin was related before getting down to business, we'd never get anything done."

That drew a chuckle from all of us.

"How is Pearl?" I asked, unable to contain my concern any longer. "Any change since this morning?"

"Ms. Pearl's stable but still unconscious. They're talking about bringing her back to Maui, where her regular medical team can work with her." Kawika's smile faded. He gestured toward the house. "Let's go inside. We can talk more comfortably there."

The interior of Pearl's home was immaculate and tastefully decorated with a blend of Japanese and Hawaiian influences. Delicate rice paper screens divided the open living area, creating intimate spaces filled with treasures from Pearl's long life: antique Japanese woodblock prints, koa wood carvings, and photographs spanning decades of Hawaii's history.

We settled in the sitting area near large windows that framed the ocean view. The late afternoon sun streamed in, illuminating dancing dust motes in the air. Everything looked the same as it had yesterday—except for the tea service, which had been cleared away.

"The neurologists are actually keeping her sedated right now," Kawika explained, sitting on the edge of an armchair, his posture suggesting he might need to rush away at any moment. "They believe it's best for her brain to rest while they monitor the swelling."

"Swelling?" Ilima asked sharply. "What caused that?"

Kawika hesitated as if choosing his words carefully. "The initial diagnosis was a stroke, but some of her symptoms didn't quite fit that profile." He lowered his voice, though we were alone in the house. "After the toxicology screen came back, they found elevated levels of certain compounds consistent with a plant-based toxin."

"Oh no," Ilima whispered, her hand flying to her mouth. The orchids in her *lei po'o* trembled. "So it wasn't natural."

"Between us—yes, the medical team is treating this as a poisoning case. MPD has been notified," Kawika said. "But please, don't tell anyone."

"Of course we won't." My bracelet suddenly felt hot against my skin as I rubbed it back and forth. "I thought something was off yesterday, so I took samples of the tea. Keone delivered them to Detective Texeira at the MPD in Kahului. She said she would test them at their lab."

Kawika nodded. "Good initiative, Kat. That could help the doctors identify exactly what we're dealing with." His gaze moved to Keone. "Your girlfriend has good instincts, cousin. If she hadn't thought to preserve that evidence . . ."

"She's saved lives before," Mr. K said, his hand finding mine to give it a warm and reassuring squeeze. "And she'll help save Pearl's too."

"We came for a reason, Kawika." Ilima rose from her seat with purpose, adjusting her *muumuu* to fall into its usual graceful lines. "We need to find the sandalwood box where Pearl kept important documents."

Kawika's brows drew together. "What kind of documents?"

"Possible evidence of corruption," Keone said. "Related to Mom's upcoming mayoral campaign and Pearl's Heritage Tea Garden project."

"Wow. I had no idea something like that was going on, let alone that she was gathering evidence," Kawika said, frowning. "But I did know you two had a big announcement to make. She was so excited about your campaign, Auntie Ilima." He stood. "Her home office is this way."

Kawika led us down a short hallway lined with more photographs—Pearl with various dignitaries through the decades, Pearl receiving community service awards, Pearl standing proudly before her school when she was still teaching. Through it all, she'd never let her spinal injury keep her down.

The final photo showed a much younger Pearl, dressed in traditional costume, beside a handsome Japanese man, also in vintage cultural fashion. He had to be her husband, who had died decades ago.

The office was a small but well-organized space, dominated by a beautiful koa wood desk positioned to face a window overlooking the garden. Bookshelves lined one wall, filled with volumes on Hawaiian history, Japanese culture, and botanical references.

"The box should be in her desk drawer," Ilima said, moving toward the desk with purpose. "Pearl showed me where she kept it."

Kawika hung back in the doorway, his expression troubled. "I should mention—someone was in here looking for something."

We all froze and stared at him. "What do you mean?" Mr. K asked.

"When I came by this morning on my way to work to water the plants, the office was . . . not like this." Kawika gestured to the perfectly organized space. "It wasn't ransacked or anything obvious, but things had been moved. Books rearranged, desk drawers not quite closed. Someone went through her things very carefully, trying not to show they'd been here. I couldn't find any signs of forced entry, so I tidied up, thinking someone from the tea party must have poked around in here yesterday."

Ilima pulled open the center drawer of the desk. Her sharp intake of breath told us everything we needed to know before she spoke. "The box is gone."

The four of us stood in silence as the implications sank in.

Someone had poisoned Pearl and stolen the evidence she planned to reveal.

And whoever it was had been meticulous enough to get in and search her home without leaving obvious signs of disturbance.

"We need to search the house," Ilima declared, her regal bearing vibrating with energy and indignation. "Whoever took the box might have taken something else, or Pearl might have hidden copies of the documents elsewhere."

Kawika shifted uncomfortably, moving to stand in the doorway. "I'm sorry, Auntie Ilima, but I can't allow that."

Ilima blinked in surprise. "What?"

"Pearl named me power of attorney, executor of her estate, and medical power of attorney," Kawika explained, his tone gentle but firm. "I'm legally responsible for her property and privacy. Without her conscious permission or a court order, I can't authorize a search of her home."

"But Kawika, sweetheart," Ilima's voice held an edge of disbelief, "we're family. We're trying to help Pearl."

"I know," he said. "And I appreciate that. But Pearl values her privacy above all else." He gestured to the now empty drawer. "The fact that someone has already violated that makes me even more determined to protect what remains. I'm going to move into the spare bedroom here until she returns. Maybe after she's home too, to keep an eye on her safety."

"Good of you, Kawika. She might also need round-the-clock care." Keone placed a restraining hand on his mother's arm. "He's right, Mom. Legally speaking, Kawika has to protect Pearl's interests."

"This *is* about Pearl's interests!" Ilima protested, the orchids in her *lei po'o* shedding petals with her agitation. "Someone poisoned her, Kawika. Someone tried to kill her."

"And the police are investigating," Kawika replied calmly. "If Detective Texeira wants to search the house, she can. I'll cooperate fully with any official investigation." His eyes softened. "Please understand, Auntie. I made a promise to Pearl to watch over her home."

Conflicting emotions play across Ilima's face—concern for her friend, frustration at the obstacle, and pride in her nephew's integrity all battled for dominance.

"Well," Ilima said, drawing herself up to her full height, "I suppose Pearl would appreciate your dedication to your responsibilities." The words were gracious, but her tone suggested she was far from pleased.

"*Mahalo* for understanding," Kawika said diplomatically.

"We should get going," Mr. K said, sensing the tension. "Kawika needs to tie up loose ends to stay here, and we have other avenues to explore."

Ilima gave a nod, her *muumuu* swishing as she turned toward the door. "Of course. Keep us informed of any changes in Pearl's condition, Kawika."

"I will, Auntie. Every update, I promise."

We followed Ilima back through the house. Her shoulders were stiffer than when we'd arrived, and her normally flowing stride had taken on a determined cadence that spoke volumes about her mood.

When we reached the porch, Kawika touched my arm lightly, holding me back as Keone escorted his mother to his truck.

"Kat," he said quietly, "I truly am sorry. But Pearl has secrets beyond what you know. She would want them protected."

"I understand," I said, surprising myself by meaning it. "But if those secrets got her poisoned—"

"Then the truth needs to come out," he agreed. "Just . . . through the proper channels."

I nodded, watching as Keone handed Ilima up. She got into the truck with offended dignity, her back straight and her chin high.

"Take care of Pearl for us," I said, giving Kawika's arm a pat before joining the others.

As we pulled away from Pearl's peaceful beach house, I glanced back to see Kawika standing on the porch, his tall figure silhouetted against the golden afternoon light. He raised a hand in farewell, looking very alone with the weight of his responsibilities.

In the front seat, Ilima adjusted her *lei po'o* with precise movements. "Well," she announced to no one in particular, "it seems

Pearl trusted her affairs to the right person. Loyal to a fault, that boy."

Despite her huffed tone, I caught the flash of respect in her eyes. Family was complicated, especially Hawaiian family. But at the end of the day, integrity mattered more than convenience to future mayor Ilima Kaihale.

And somehow, that made me love her even more.

5

THE DRIVE back to our office from Pearl's house was tense. Ilima sat in the passenger seat with the rigid posture of a queen who'd had a royal decree ignored, while Keone kept shooting me glances in the rearview mirror as if to check I was okay—which I was, even if worried by this escalation of events.

Afternoon light had faded to the soft lavender of evening by the time we pulled up to K & K's little shack.

"Well," Ilima said, breaking the silence as her son cut the engine, "that was a waste of time."

"We learned a lot, actually," Mr. K said. "We confirmed the box is missing, which means someone else knows about the documents. That's big."

"And we know Pearl was poisoned," I added as we exited the vehicle. "That's significant."

"What would be significant is having actual evidence in our hands," Ilima huffed. "I still can't believe Kawika refused to let us search the house. His own family!"

"He was doing his job," Keone said. "You'd be proud of him if it were anyone else's privacy he was protecting."

Ilima's expression softened. "You're right, of course. Integrity is a

Kaihale family trait." She sighed dramatically. "Even when it's inconvenient."

As we reached the porch steps, my phone buzzed with an incoming text. It was from my Aunt Fae: *"Maile is here visiting. She's asking when you'll be home for dinner. Also, Tiki knocked over my fern AGAIN and is giving me the evil eye from atop the refrigerator. Rescue me from this feline overlord?"*

Maile was a foster child I'd helped find a home for with Rita, one of our Red Hats. We served as backup aunties when Rita needed a night off. I showed the message to Keone, who grinned. "Feline overlord. That's about right."

"She's probably feeding Tiki fancy tuna from the can while composing dramatic texts," I said. I quickly typed back that I'd be late, to please have dinner with Maile without me, and not to worry about the cat's demands.

When we entered the shack, Keone flipped on the lights and headed straight for the coffee maker. "I think we need caffeine for this strategy session."

"Make it strong," Ilima instructed, settling onto her chair with the same elegance she'd display on a throne. "We have much to discuss."

I moved toward the file drawer where I'd hidden the mysterious envelope, eager to show it to Ilima. "Before we get started, there's something you should see."

My words dried up as I pulled open the drawer. Where the cream-colored envelope had been carefully placed, there was nothing but a stack of file folders and a forgotten granola bar wrapper.

"It's gone," I whispered, my stomach clenching; I'd eaten that beef stew too long ago. "The note is gone."

Keone abandoned the coffee preparations and joined me. "Are you sure this is the right drawer?"

"Positive." I rifled through the folders, thinking it might have slipped between them. *Nothing.* "Someone's been here while we were gone."

"What note?" Ilima asked, leaning forward.

As Keone explained about the mysterious message addressed to "The Keeper of Secrets," I examined the lock on the file cabinet drawer. No signs of forced entry.

"The shack was secure when we arrived, wasn't it?" I asked, trying to remember.

Keone nodded, his mouth tightening. "I unlocked it myself."

"Then whoever took it either has a key or nefarious skills," I concluded.

"We should check to see if anything else is missing," Keone said, moving toward our case file drawer.

A quick inventory revealed that nothing else had been disturbed—not our computer, not our case files, not even the petty cash we kept in a shortbread cookie tin labeled "Bail Money" (Keone's idea of detective humor).

"They knew exactly what they came for," I said, sinking into my chair. "The question is, how did they know it was here?"

"We have a leak," Ilima declared. "Someone is tracking your movements."

Before we could follow this disturbing thought, my phone rang. The screen displayed "Detective Texeira," and I quickly answered, putting it on speaker.

"Lei, you're on speaker with me, Keone, and Ilima Kaihale," I said by way of greeting.

"Good." Lei's voice was crisp and professional. "We got the results back on your tea samples, Kat. Preliminary testing confirms high concentrations of oleander toxin. Someone definitely poisoned that tea."

"Then Pearl was deliberately targeted," I said.

"Looks that way. The concentration was high enough to be fatal if she'd consumed more."

I glanced around; Keone's jaw had gone rigid and so had Ilima's. Their family resemblance was remarkable in that moment.

Lei continued, "I've opened an official attempted murder investigation. I'll need statements from everyone at that tea party."

"Of course," I agreed. "I can get you contact information for all the Red Hats who were there."

"Already have it from Pearl's phone records, which we got a warrant for along with her house and grounds. I've got appointments with Edith Pepperwhite and Clara tomorrow morning. Josie's in Honolulu visiting her daughter but flying back tonight."

I smiled despite the seriousness of the situation. Detective Lei Texeira was fast-moving and thorough. "What about Rita?" I asked, remembering the newest member of the Red Hats. "She was sitting next to Pearl and seemed really shaken by what happened."

"On my list for tomorrow afternoon," Lei confirmed.

"We have some updates for you," I said. "Ilima, can you fill Sergeant Texeira in on your run for mayor and the documents Pearl was collecting?"

Ilima did so, concluding with our aborted trip to Pearl's house and Kawika's denial of our attempt to search for the missing box.

"Well, now that we know for certain that this was attempted murder." Ilima smoothed her *muumuu* with a determined gesture. "It's time I tell you exactly what Pearl discovered about Mayor Santos, and why someone might want to kill her over it."

Keone jerked as he poured coffee, splashing the dark roast over the counter in surprise. "We're all ears, Mom."

"Me too," Lei said, her voice tinny in the phone's speaker. "Sounds like you've been holding out on us, Ilima."

I grabbed a wad of paper towels and dabbed at the puddle as Keone finished pouring three cups, adding a splash of coconut milk to each.

Ilima accepted her cup gratefully. "The Heritage Tea Garden project wasn't just about creating a beautiful space," she pronounced. "It was about reclaiming a stolen legacy."

For the next twenty minutes, she outlined a complex history I'd never imagined. The proposed garden site adjacent to Pearl's home, a large oceanfront parcel, had once belonged to Pearl's family before they were sent to internment camps during World War II. While they were detained, their property—like that of many Japanese-American families—was seized and later sold for a fraction of its value.

"Mayor Santos's grandfather was on the commission that handled these seized properties," Ilima said. "Pearl discovered records showing he personally acquired several parcels at absurdly low prices, including her family's land. That same land eventually became part of the Santos family real estate portfolio."

"That means the current mayor inherited Pearl's stolen property," Keone said, connecting the dots.

"Precisely. And when Pearl approached him privately about returning the parcel for the Heritage Garden—as a form of historical reconciliation—he was initially supportive. Until she mentioned making the full historical record public as part of the garden's educational mission."

"Let me guess," I said dryly. "His support suddenly evaporated."

"Like morning dew," Ilima said. "He claimed budgetary concerns, zoning issues, all manner of bureaucratic obstacles. Meanwhile, Pearl discovered he was in talks with New Ohia Development to build luxury condos on the site."

"The same developer behind the New Ohia state park project we stopped?" The hair rose on the back of my neck, remembering the corrupt scheme that had nearly destroyed our village.

"Same players," Ilima nodded. "Pearl had emails, meeting notes, even a draft contract that Santos had initialed. All proof that while publicly claiming to support cultural preservation, he was privately selling out to developers."

Keone whistled. "That could tank his political career if it became public."

"And your campaign announcement next week would have been the perfect stage to reveal it all," I added.

"With evidence in that sandalwood box," Ilima finished, a note of frustration returning to her voice. "Evidence that's now missing."

"Speaking of. It's a very good thing you didn't search Pearl's house and corrupt the chain of evidence collection," Lei said. "I need you folks to stay within the lines and let me do my job—especially if we're dealing with someone well-connected politically."

We sat in thoughtful silence, the gravity of the situation settling around us. This wasn't just about local politics or a garden project —it was about historical injustice, corruption, and an attempted murder plot to keep it all buried.

"It appears there's a strong motive for someone to stop that info getting out, and your campaign, possibly, Ilima," Lei summarized. "I'll try to fit a search of Pearl's house into the next few days—but it's such a long drive out there. I'll need to fill my day top to bottom to make the commute worthwhile." The road to Hana and Ohia was a famous minimum of two hours consisting of one-lane ways, antique bridges, stunning views, waterfalls—and many hairpin turns. "I'll keep you posted, and meanwhile—be careful, all of you." She ended the call.

"All right, team. What's our next move?" I asked, looking from Keone to his mother.

"We need to find out who took that note," Keone said firmly. "It's our only concrete lead at the moment."

"Well I for one am glad we didn't share that little tidbit with Lei," I said. "I don't want to get dinged for tampering with the mail."

"Meanwhile, we need to investigate Mayor Santos more thoroughly," Ilima said. "Follow the money trail back to these developers. I can use that in my campaign once I have something solid."

My phone buzzed yet again. This time it was Edith Pepperwhite, the Red Hats' most outspoken member: *Kat, Lei Texeira just called about Pearl's POISONING! Was it the tea? Call me IMMEDIATELY!*

I showed the message to Keone, who raised an eyebrow. "The Red Hat intelligence network is activating. Between Edith, Josie, Clara, and Rita, they probably know more town gossip than the NSA."

"Don't forget Opal," I added. "Her rune reading was spot-on about the danger."

"That reminds me," Ilima said, reaching into her large handbag. "I brought something that might help." She pulled out a sleek laptop. "Pearl gave me copies of some of the preliminary historical research on the garden project. Not the evidence against Santos— she kept that secure—but background on the extended site itself. It might give us some direction."

As Ilima opened the laptop, Keone turned to me with a grin. "So much for our quiet life running a small-town post office and occasionally solving minor mysteries."

"Hey, at least Tiki isn't here giving us stink eye for getting involved," I quipped.

"No, but my mother is," he whispered, gesturing to Ilima, who was now typing with fierce concentration, her *lei po'o* bobbing with each keystroke.

"I heard that," she said without looking up. "And for the record, I'm extremely proud of you both for helping Pearl." She paused, fixing us with a warm but determined gaze. "Now, shall we catch ourselves a poisoner and corrupt mayor, or would you prefer to continue whispering about me as if I'm not three feet away?"

"Yes, ma'am," we replied in unison.

I took out my phone. "And I need food if we're going to be here any longer. I'll call Opal and Artie and see if they've got any left-overs we can heat up."

With that, we gathered around Ilima's laptop, beginning a deep dive into land records, historical documents, and the tangled web of Maui politics.

Outside, the evening deepened into night, crickets and frogs began their chorus, and somewhere across town, a cat named Tiki was plotting from atop a refrigerator.

6

WE SPENT an hour or two poring over historical websites with Ilima until her orchids had wilted and so had her energy. "I'm going home to bed," she announced. "I need my beauty sleep."

After she departed, Mr. K gestured toward his laptop. "I didn't want to get into this with Mom here, but a while back I set up a hidden security camera on the porch. Just had a feeling we might get a visitor now and again. It's motion-activated."

My pulse quickened as I slid into the chair beside him. "And did we?"

"See for yourself." Keone pulled up the footage from when we left the shack with Ilima, and I leaned in to watch. A familiar figure approached the shack from the direction of the post office, looking cautiously around before climbing the steps.

"Is that—" I began.

"Pua Chang," Keone confirmed. "Your trusty postal assistant."

On-screen, Pua reached into her pocket and withdrew what looked like lock picking tools. With impressive efficiency, she unlocked our door, slipped inside, and closed it behind her.

"How long was she in there?" I asked, dismayed that our investigation headquarters had been compromised.

"Four minutes and twenty seconds," Keone said, fast-forwarding to show Pua exiting, carefully relocking the door behind her, and hurrying back toward the post office. "Just enough time to find what she was looking for."

"The mystery note," I realized. "It wasn't in my desk drawer at the post office, so she tried here."

"And found it," Keone confirmed grimly.

I flopped back in my chair, feeling violated on multiple levels. "Pua and I have come through so many challenges. I trusted her. Why would she do this?"

"You know her better than I do."

I shook my head. "I thought I did." Suddenly, I was just exhausted. "I need to go home and get some sleep, especially if I'm going to confront Pua tomorrow."

Keone got up, pulled me to my feet. Gave me a hug and a kiss on my forehead; he seemed to know when to press in, and when to hold me lightly. "Yup. Tomorrow is another day, and you can tackle Pua when you get to work. You got this, Trouble."

I loved Mr. K's confidence in me.

I loved *him,* and admitting it was getting easier.

I ENTERED OUR SILENT, darkened house in New Ohia State Park. Aunt Fae and I lived in one of the former model homes of the defunct development, trading caretaker duties for rent. Misty, Tiki's grown kitten, asleep in her bed by the couch, lifted her head to greet me with a gentle mew as Tiki appeared silently at my feet, fixing me with her imperious, yellow-eyed stare.

Aunt Fae and Maile had already gone to bed; Auntie had left a plate of homemade cookies out for me on the counter with a drawing Maile had done of the three of us, Tiki, and Misty in front of the house.

I put the drawing on the fridge with a magnet; it was too cute.

"Yes, I know I'm late," I told my cat, bending down to scratch behind her remaining ear. "I heard you've been terrorizing the household."

Tiki blinked slowly, neither confirming nor denying the allegation. She flicked her kinked tail as she padded over to her full bowl of kibble and deigned to nibble at the offering, now that I was home.

I drank a cold glass of milk while standing at the counter, scrolling through the dozen messages from the Red Hats that had accumulated on my phone.

Edith Pepperwhite had texted three more times with increasingly CAPITALIZED demands for information.

Josie had sent a selfie from the Honolulu airport with the caption *"Flying home to solve a CRIME!"*

Clara, the quietest of the group, had simply written, *"Thinking of Pearl. Let me know if I can help."*

Even Rita had checked in. Rita's text included a photo of Maile playing with a litter of newly rescued kittens with the caption: *"Your honorary niece has been a huge help with the new rescues. Thanks for letting her stay over. My monthly night of peace and quiet is the only thing keeping me sane with seven cats in the house and all the others in the cathouse outside! Please let me know any news about Pearl."*

I smiled at the image of Maile and the newborn kittens and saved it to my camera roll. Rita had adopted Maile last year after fostering her for months. The monthly sleepover with Maile had started as a way to give Rita—a dedicated but sometimes overwhelmed cat rescuer—a breather.

Maile's visits filled our house with fun and laughter and had evolved into something we all looked forward to.

After responding to the Red Hats with a brief update that there was no change in Pearl's condition, I dragged myself to bed, Tiki following to claim her designated spot by my feet.

I really did need to recharge my batteries if my first chore of my next workday was confronting Pua Chang about breaking into our office.

I DIDN'T SLEEP WELL and got up early, deciding to work off the angst with a swim at the beach before work. Tiki took it upon herself to accompany me; I swear that cat was more canine than feline sometimes. Auntie and Maile were still asleep when I filled a travel mug with yesterday's microwaved coffee, donned my bikini, and stuffed a backpack with my work clothes and shoes.

Morning was a promise of rose gold on the horizon, tinting the clouds the color of angels' wings, as Tiki and I walked down the smooth blacktop road of New Ohia State Park. We soon passed my friend Elle's house. She was home, judging by her little car in the open garage, but the lights were still out in her home. She worked hard as an event planner for the Hotel Hana; they must have had a big shindig last night for her to sleep past her usual morning jogging time.

The beach was cool and the ocean dark blue until the first rays of daylight broke over the horizon and teased aqua and turquoise highlights out of the tiny waves lapping on the shore. A green sea turtle had pulled itself up onto the sand, just out of reach of the tide line. I was careful to pass it with at least ten feet to spare, the guideline for allowing these creatures their personal space.

I spread my towel on the cool sand, and Tiki promptly sat down on it. "Okay, lady. Hold down the fort while I get my laps in." She licked her paw, giving me a side-eye.

I snapped on a pair of goggles and got a running start to dive into the ocean; early in the morning it was best to get the shock of the cold water over with quickly. Not that it was actually cold; this was Hawaii after all, and I had grown up in Maine and done the occasional Polar Bear Swim near our coastal village.

Once I was moving through the water, all the stress I'd accumulated seemed to wash away. My arms and legs churned powerfully, and I burned off the angst I'd been carrying around since Pearl collapsed.

Swimming gave me time to process my feelings.

Beyond the sense of betrayal, I was genuinely confused by Pua's break-in. She had always been nosy, but this went beyond harmless curiosity. Could she have been involved in a plot that had culminated in Pearl's poisoning?

There was no way to tell except to grab that bull by her perfectly manicured horns.

I ARRIVED at the back door of the post office just as Pua was unlocking it. My co-worker started visibly at the sight of me approaching from the nearby shack, my face dead serious and my long brown hair leaving dark wet streaks on the shoulders of my navy polo shirt, attesting to a hasty no-frills shower.

"Kat! You're early." Her voice was a touch too bright. "I was just opening up."

"We need to talk, Pua," I said firmly. "Inside, please."

Pua's smile faltered, but she pushed the door open and led me into the darkened space inside. The familiar smell of paper, ink, and the faint mustiness of old buildings greeted us as she flipped on the fluorescent lights.

"What's this about?" she asked, hanging her purse on a hook and shrugging out of a pastel cardigan. Today she wore a bright yellow blouse with tiny pineapples printed on it—an incongruous wardrobe choice for a criminal mastermind.

"You tell me," I said, my voice calm but Secret Service Agent tough. "Starting with why you broke into our office yesterday."

Pua's back was to me as she stood frozen in front of the dangling purse and cardigan. "You saw me, then."

"We have it on camera, actually," I confirmed. "That's breaking and entering, plus mail theft—serious offenses."

She turned slowly to face me, her expression a complicated mix of defiance and embarrassment. Her dark eyes flashed and her small mouth tightened. "I didn't steal anything. I borrowed that note."

"With lock picks?" I asked incredulously.

A flicker of pride crossed her face. "My grandfather was handy. He taught me when I was ten." She sighed. "I know how this looks, but I can explain."

"I'm listening," I said, folding my arms across my chest.

Pua reached into her pocket and pulled out the cream-colored envelope, placing it on the nearby counter. "I wanted to know what was inside. After Pearl's collapse and all the whispers around town . . . then this mysterious envelope arrives . . . I just needed to know what was going on."

"So you went into my office, and when you realized I'd moved the envelope, you broke into the shack and took it?" The hurt in my voice was evident even to me.

"I was going to put it back!" She looked genuinely distressed. "I just wanted to read it. I was worried about Pearl too, you know."

"That means you read it?" I asked, softening slightly at her obvious distress.

Pua nodded, rolling her lips in with embarrassment. "I steamed it open. Very carefully."

Keone and I had done exactly the same thing. I was hardly a saint in the situation, but I wasn't going to tell her that at the moment.

"And what did you make of the contents?" I asked.

"'*The time has come. The garden reveals all. The crane will fly once more,*'" Pua recited. "Cryptic nonsense. But I think it has something to do with Pearl's Heritage Tea Garden plans."

"How do you know about that?" I asked.

Pua rolled her eyes. "Everyone in Ohia knows about it. Pearl talked about it all the time. It's her passion project."

"Well, I didn't know about it until the tea party," I frowned. If the project was such common knowledge, then the circle of potential suspects who knew about Pearl's plans expanded considerably. "Did Pearl ever mention anything specific about the garden's significance? Any historical connections?"

Something flickered in Pua's eyes. "She did act strangely at bridge club last week. We were partnered together, and between hands, she kept muttering about 'making things right after all these years.' When I asked what she meant, she said something about stolen legacies and how the truth always finds its way."

"Did she say anything more?" I pressed.

"No, but she mentioned a name—Santos. Said the Mayor's family had built their fortune on other people's misfortunes." Pua paused. "I thought she was just being dramatic. Pearl can be that way."

"I'm aware." I picked up the envelope, confirming it was indeed the same one we'd examined. "Pua, this was wrong on multiple levels. You violated federal mail regulations, broke into private property, and tampered with potential evidence in what's now an attempted murder investigation." I was a hypocrite since I'd taken the envelope and steamed it open too; but I had to stop Pua's snooping.

Pua's eyes widened. "Pearl really was poisoned?"

"Yes, the police have confirmed it was oleander poisoning in the tea." I might as well tell her; or she'd find out some other way.

Pua sank onto a nearby stool, her poise deserting her. "I had no idea it was that serious. I thought maybe she had a stroke or something." She looked up at me, genuine remorse in her eyes. "I'm sorry, Kat. I swear I wasn't trying to interfere with an investigation for any other reason but—I'm nosy and obsessed."

I studied her face. My instincts told me Pua wasn't involved in the poisoning. Just cursed with an excess of curiosity and a troubling disregard for locks.

Kind of like me.

Pua went on. "I'll do anything to make it right. I can help with your investigation. I know things about people in this town—who's connected to whom, who has grudges, who has secrets."

I raised an eyebrow. "The coconut wireless gossip network could be useful. But this can never happen again, Pua. I mean it."

"I promise, no more lock picking. Unless you need me to," she added with a hopeful glint in her eye.

As if on cue, my phone chimed with an incoming text.

I glanced down, expecting another message from the Red Hats or perhaps Aunt Fae reporting on Tiki's latest household crime.

Instead, the screen displayed a message from an unknown number: *"Stop digging or join Pearl."*

"What is it?" Pua asked, noticing my reaction.

"A threat," I replied, forwarding the message to Keone and Lei. "Someone doesn't like that I'm looking into things."

The post office would be opening in a few minutes, and customers would soon be lining up for their morning mail; in fact, Chad pulled up in the mail truck at the back door with a noisy crunch of gravel and squeak of brakes. Even so, the day's postal duties seemed trivial compared to the warning glowing on my phone screen.

"Pua, can you handle opening by yourself?" I asked. "As soon as we unload the truck, I need to follow up on this."

She nodded enthusiastically, eager to make amends. "Of course. I'll hold down the fort. And Kat? I really am sorry about the envelope. And the invasion of privacy." She winced at her own admission.

"Just don't do it again," I warned. "And if anyone asks about Pearl or the Heritage Garden project, let me know immediately. Don't pass on the news about the attempt on Pearl's life."

"Will do. Oh! That reminds me," she called as we headed for

the back door. "Edith Pepperwhite called me this morning asking if you'd gotten her texts. Said it's URGENT—" Pua mimicked Edith's distinctive emphasis, "—that you meet her at her law office. Something about Pearl's paperwork for the garden project."

"Edith is handling the legal side of Pearl's project?" I asked. I sort of remembered that from the tea party, but had forgotten in all the subsequent drama.

"Apparently so," Pua confirmed. "And you know Edith—if she says it's urgent, she'll probably send a search party if you don't show up."

As I left the post office after unloading the mail truck with Chad and Pua, my phone buzzed with another text. This time it was from Maile:

"Hi Auntie Kat! Aunt Fae says to tell you you're out of cat food AGAIN and can you pick some up? And to remind you it's your turn to cook dinner next month when I stay over. PLEASE, not tuna casserole again. Tiki ate most of it anyway. Love you and miss you! PS: Opal came by this morning and said to tell you 'the stars are aligning but beware the serpent.' Whatever, lol."

Maile was clearly loving having her own phone, a recent development. Despite the threat still weighing on my mind, I smiled at the message. Between Aunt Fae's culinary experiments, Maile's preteen directness, Tiki's perpetual appetite, and Opal's cosmic warnings, my extended 'ohana was a chaotic source of love in the midst of this growing mystery.

I texted Maile a quick reply and then alerted Edith that I was on my way to see her, and no more alarm bells needed to be rung that we were overdue to meet.

As I drove toward Edith's law office, I couldn't shake the chill from that anonymous text. Someone was watching, tracking our investigation closely enough to know we were "digging" into Pearl's poisoning. And they were bold enough—or desperate enough—to issue direct threats.

I checked my phone once more before putting it away—Lei had not responded. I had to trust that my more than competent detective friend was doing her part.

The Heritage Tea Garden project clearly threatened someone's interests more deeply than we'd realized. The question was: how far would they go to protect those interests?

7

EDITH PEPPERWHITE'S law office occupied the second floor of a restored Victorian building on Hana's main street. A brass plaque beside the door proclaimed "Pepperwhite Legal Services: Family Law, Estate Planning, and Historical Property Rights" in bold, elegant script that somehow managed to convey Edith's forceful personality.

I turned the knob of the office door. A bell chimed somewhere inside as I stepped over the threshold. "THERE you are!" Edith exclaimed, the volume making the framed law degrees on the wall vibrate. "I've been going bananas worrying!"

Edith Pepperwhite, five-foot-no inches of pure legal determination and personality—swooped out of the back. She wore a lavender *muumuu*, with a red hat adorned with what appeared to be artificial fruit. The effect was somewhere between eccentric grandmother lawn gnome and tropical Carmen Miranda. She grabbed me in a hug like a purple-clad hawk landing on a pigeon.

"It's only ten a.m., Edith," I pointed out, disentangling myself. Edith was someone whose hugs I still occasionally found claustrophobic, a throwback to the touchphobia I'd worked hard to overcome. "I came as soon as I could."

"Well, you're here now, that's what matters." She led me into her office, towing me by the hand with surprising strength for someone her size. "Terrible business with Pearl. TERRIBLE. And now the police asking questions about poison of all things!"

"Detective Texeira interviewed you already?" I asked, settling into one of the leather chairs across from Edith's imposing desk.

"First thing this morning!" Edith confirmed, bustling around to sit behind her desk. "We did a Zoom. But—as if I would know anything about plant toxins!" She shook her head, refocusing. "That's neither here nor there. I called you about Pearl's papers."

"For the Heritage Tea Garden project?"

"Exactly!" Edith pulled a thick folder from a neat stack on her desk. "Pearl asked me to handle all the legal aspects. Historical site designation, educational trust setup, the works." She lowered her voice dramatically. "What she didn't tell me initially was how politically explosive this project would be!"

"Because of Mayor Santos?" I asked.

Edith's eyes widened. "You know about that connection?"

"Ilima filled us in on some of it," I said. "Something about land seizure during the internment period?"

"Land seizure is right," Edith said, her voice dropping as she leaned forward conspiratorially. "And therein lies the scandal." She flipped open the folder, revealing yellowed documents protected in plastic sleeves. "I've been researching what happened. The paper trail is quite . . . illuminating."

She pulled out a document and handed it to me. It was a property deed dated 1939, with the name "Yamamoto" clearly visible.

"Pearl's family owned the entire plot of land since the 1920s," Edith explained. "Prime oceanfront property consisting of what's now Pearl's current house and the adjacent five acres she wants for the garden. But here's where it gets interesting."

She pulled out another document—this one a bill of sale dated April 1942.

"After Pearl Harbor, Japanese-Americans were given just days to settle their affairs before being sent to camps. Felix Santos—our current mayor's grandfather—was on the local property commission that facilitated these transfers."

"Let me guess," I said. "He tried to acquire the Yamamoto property?"

"EXACTLY!" Edith's volume returned. "This document purports to be a bill of sale for the entire Yamamoto estate, transferring it to the Santos family for one-tenth of its value. Felix Santos even had the gall to have it notarized."

"But it didn't go through?" I asked, studying the paper, which had "DISPUTED" stamped across it in faded red ink.

"That's the miracle," Edith said, her blue eyes gleaming. "Pearl's grandfather was remarkably foresighted. Before the war, he had established a trust with a Honolulu law firm, with specific provisions that no sale of the property during wartime could be valid without the firm's approval."

"Smart man."

"Brilliant, actually," Edith said. "When Felix Santos tried to register the deed, the law firm challenged it. The matter was tied up in legal limbo until after the war, when the Yamamotos fought to reclaim their property."

"So they won?"

"Eventually, yes. But they only got the house and its immediate grounds. And not without consequences." Edith pulled out a newspaper clipping from 1947. The headline read: "Japanese Family Reclaims Disputed Property After Legal Battle."

"Felix Santos was publicly humiliated," Edith explained. "He had already started developing plans for the property, assuming it would be his. The scandal nearly ruined him."

"But the Santos family recovered," I said. "They're one of the wealthiest families on the island now."

"Yes, but they never forgot that defeat, and they haven't been able to develop the five-acre parcel they kept from the Yamamotos," Edith said. "And here's another aspect: the entire

Yamamoto property became a military processing center during the war."

"Processing center?" I frowned. "You mean like a detention facility?"

"A temporary one for this side of the island," Edith said. "Before Japanese-Americans were sent to the main internment camps on the mainland, they were processed at local facilities."

"So Pearl's family was processed for internment on their own land?" I asked, the bitter irony not lost on me.

"And Felix Santos was appointed as the civilian liaison to that processing center," Edith said. "He had authority there, despite not being able to claim the land fully."

"And now, eighty years later, Pearl wants to turn that land into a memorial garden," I said, tapping my chin thoughtfully. "Which will publicly expose the Santos family's land grab and whatever else went on. Maybe that's why someone tried to kill Pearl before the Garden could go public."

Edith raised a hand to her mouth, her eyes widening. "It's so drastic. You really think that's why? Because of this historical project?"

"It's a strong possibility," I said. "Especially with Mayor Santos facing a tough reelection campaign against Ilima Kaihale. This kind of historical scandal could end his career."

"And destroy his family's reputation. The Santos name is everywhere on this side of the island."

"Is there anything else in these documents that might help us understand what Pearl discovered?" I asked.

Edith pulled out a small slip of paper. "Pearl left this with me last week. Said if anything happened to her, I should give it to you." She handed me what looked like an old receipt. On the back, in Pearl's neat handwriting, were the words: *Under the plumeria, where the crane once stood . . . the truth is buried but not forgotten.*"

"Interesting," I said, thinking of the mysterious message in the note we'd steamed open.

"Pearl has a flair for the dramatic," Edith said with affection. "But I think she could be referring to the old plumeria tree at the edge of her property, butting up against the disputed five-acre parcel. It's been there since before the war, she said."

I tucked the note carefully into my backpack. "I could check the Hana History Museum before visiting the site. They might have photographs or records from the processing center era."

"Excellent!" Edith boomed, making me jump. "I've been meaning to dig deeper there myself. Talk to Leilani—she's been helping Pearl with the historical research for the garden project."

"Auntie Leilani?" I asked. "Rita's cat-feeding volunteer? I know her."

"One and the same!" Edith adjusted her fruit-laden hat. "Just don't get her started on the sugar plantation era unless you have hours to spare."

With that, I thanked Edith and headed for the Hana History Museum, housed in a plantation era building near the center of town.

I hadn't had breakfast and the day had been busy; my belly complained loudly of neglect. Keone had flights today, but I had time to swing by Ilima's house and beg for some food—and catch the third party in our little investigative team up on recent events.

"With my luck she'll want to come along," I muttered. "But I bet Leilani will roll out the red carpet for Ilima and make my job easier at the museum."

People tended to do that for Ilima, and that could be to our advantage.

THE HANA HISTORY Museum occupied a vintage building that was a part of a small village complex. Though small by mainland standards, it housed an impressive collection of artifacts, photographs, and documents chronicling the area's rich multicultural history.

I pushed open the museum's door, and the old-fashioned bell over the portal tinkled as Ilima Kaihale and I entered the cool interior with its creaky wooden floors. I spotted Leilani crouched behind a display case, carefully arranging what looked like antique fishing implements inside the glass rectangle. Her silver-streaked dark hair was pulled back in a loose bun, and she wore a simple blue *muumuu* with a subtle floral pattern.

"*Aloha* Leilani," Ilima called.

Leilani straightened and turned, her face lighting up with recognition. "Ilima Kaihale! And Kat the postmaster!" She came around the display case to greet us, offering hugs that smelled of plumeria and the faint hint of catnip—evidence of her volunteer work at Rita's shelter. "What brings you two to my little museum?"

"First—where's Poi Dog?" I asked, glancing past her into the rooms beyond for her aged hound, whose clicking toenails had accompanied Leilani's every move during the case we'd investigated at Christmas.

A shadow fell across Leilani's face; her smile disappeared. "Poi Dog has crossed the rainbow bridge."

"Oh no!" Ilima exclaimed. "He was a fixture here! I'm so sorry, Leilani."

"As am I," I said. "He was such a sweet old boy."

"Poi Dog had a good long life. Rita has promised me a kitten to keep me company, but there are so many cuties at her shelter I haven't been able to make up my mind and choose one yet." Leilani rolled her shoulders and put the smile back on her face. "So. To my original question. What brings you two by? You're both so busy, I'm sure it's something important."

"We're looking into what happened to Pearl," I said. "And we need to learn more about the Japanese processing center that was on her property during World War II."

After asking after Pearl's health, Leilani frowned. "I heard about that processing center. And Pearl's Heritage Garden project, of course." She nodded. "Pearl has spent time researching that history here—gathering documents and making copies. Come, I have a special collection she's been working with. You can take a look at it."

She led us through the museum's main gallery, past displays of ancient Hawaiian fishing tools, plantation era photographs, and modern cultural revival artifacts. At the back of the building was a small research room lined with archival boxes and leatherbound volumes.

"This is our special collections area," Auntie Leilani explained, using a key from the ring at her waist to unlock a cabinet. "Pearl donated many of her family's papers to us over the years, but recently she's been particularly interested in the wartime period."

She pulled out a large archival box labeled "Yamamoto Collection – WWII" and placed it on the reading table. "These materials are quite fragile. Some haven't been fully cataloged yet."

"Thank you for sharing them with us," I said sincerely.

Auntie Leilani smiled, the crinkles around her eyes deepening. "Pearl would want you to see the papers." She paused, her expression growing serious. "Is it true, what the rumors say? Was she poisoned?"

"I really can't discuss it, I'm sorry," I said quietly.

"I'll take that as a yes." Auntie Leilani crossed herself, a gesture that reflected the islands' complex religious heritage. "Such wickedness. Pearl is a treasure to this community—to this island."

"We think it might be connected to her Heritage Garden project," Ilima said. "And possibly to the Santos family."

I darted a glance at her; we hadn't decided to share that much with Leilani.

Leilani nodded, though, taking this disclosure in stride. "That wouldn't surprise me. There are dark chapters in Hana's history that some powerful families would prefer to keep buried." She gestured to the box. "These might help you understand why."

She pulled a pair of white cotton gloves from a cardboard dispenser and donned them. With practiced hands, she began to carefully remove items from the archival box: a leather photo album, bundles of letters tied with faded ribbon, official-looking documents in protective sleeves, and several manila folders containing newspaper clippings.

"This album contains photographs from the processing center," she explained, opening it to reveal black and white images that made my heart ache with their stark documentation of suffering.

Families stood with small suitcases, identification tags pinned to their clothing. Military police with rifles stood guard beside a large wooden building with a sign reading "Processing Center #3."

"That building stood where Pearl's garden shed is now," Auntie Leilani said, pointing to the photograph. "They processed over three hundred local Japanese-Americans through that facility in 1942."

"Including Pearl's family?" Ilima asked.

Auntie Leilani nodded solemnly, flipping to another page. "Here."

The photograph showed a young Japanese couple with three small children. The woman held an infant, while two young girls—perhaps five and seven—stood stoically beside their father. A hand-written caption below read: "Yamamoto family, April 1942."

"Pearl is the baby," she said softly. "She was just six months old when they were sent to a camp on the continent. Her older sisters both died of influenza there. Her parents returned to Maui after the war with only Pearl surviving."

My throat tightened at the casual documentation of such profound loss. "And they had to fight to keep their home and lost the bigger portion of land."

"The legal battle took nearly two years," Leilani confirmed, pulling out a folder of legal documents. "During that time, Felix Santos acted as civilian administrator for the processing center property. When the Yamamotos finally won their case and returned, they found their gardens destroyed and their home ransacked."

Ilima's expression darkened. "And no compensation, I'm guessing."

"None," Auntie Leilani agreed. "But here's an interesting twist— Felix Santos was dismissed from his position on the property commission shortly after the Yamamotos won their case. Rumor was that certain improprieties came to light."

"What kind of improprieties?" I asked.

Auntie Leilani's voice dropped, though we were alone in the room. "The official records are vague. But there were suggestions of theft, abuse of power, maybe worse." She pulled out a folder marked "Oral Histories" and selected a transcript. "This is from an interview I conducted with Mrs. Tanaka in 1998, shortly before she passed. She was processed through Center #3 and spoke about valuables being confiscated, never to be returned. About beatings for minor rule infractions."

She hesitated, then added, "There was even mention of a death —a man who protested the treatment of his elderly mother. Mrs. Tanaka wouldn't name names but said 'the man in charge' was responsible."

"Felix Santos," Ilima said grimly.

"That was the implication," Auntie Leilani nodded. "Pearl believes her father had evidence of Santos's misconduct—something so damaging that the Santos family has been trying to suppress it for generations."

I turned more pages in the photo album, studying images of the processing center grounds. One showed a stone garden with a wooden crane sculpture at its center. "Is this—"

"The original Japanese garden on the property," Auntie Leilani confirmed. "Pearl's father was a master gardener who created a traditional meditation garden before the war. The crane statue was carved by her grandfather."

"'*The crane will fly once more*,'" I murmured, remembering the note.

"Exactly," Auntie Leilani smiled. "Pearl wants to recreate her father's garden as part of the Heritage site. The original crane statue disappeared during the war, but she commissioned a replica based on these photographs."

We spent another hour poring over the historical documents, learning that after the war, the processing center buildings were dismantled, and the Yamamoto family slowly rebuilt their lives on their reclaimed property.

"Pearl inherited the house in the 1980s when her parents passed away; she still wants the five acres next to it for the Heritage Garden. She considers it hallowed ground. The Heritage Garden would be her way of honoring those who suffered there while reclaiming the beauty her grandfather originally created."

"And Mayor Santos has been fighting the project through zoning regulations and permit denials," I noted. "Not to mention refusing to release the property back to Pearl."

Auntie Leilani's eyes flashed with rarely seen anger. "Politics and pride. The Santos family has spent generations crafting their image as Hana's benefactors. Pearl's garden would reveal the ugly truth beneath that facade." She carefully closed the photo album. "Two nights ago, Pearl called me, very excited. Said she'd found 'the final piece' and that justice would finally be served."

"Maybe that's what was in the sandalwood box," Ilima said, touching her intricate shell necklace.

Leilani looked surprised. "You know about the crane box?"

"We know it's missing," I explained. "And that it might contain evidence about what happened at the processing center."

Leilani frowned. "Bad news that it's gone. Pearl believed her father's journal from that period survived. Something he hid for safekeeping." She set aside some documents. "I'll make copies of what might be helpful to your case." After she gave me the copied papers, she repacked the archival materials. "If someone poisoned Pearl to prevent that evidence from coming to light . . ."

"Then they might go after anyone else who knows about it," I said.

Auntie Leilani met my gaze steadily. "I've lived a long life. I'm not afraid of threats. But Pearl—" Her voice caught slightly. "Pearl deserves to see her garden of truth and reconciliation become reality."

"We'll find who did this," I promised, helping her replace the last of the documents.

"I know you will." She patted my arm, her palm warm and slightly calloused from years of museum and other work. "When you visit her property, talk to old Mr. Takahashi if he's there. He was processed through Center #3 as a child. He helps Pearl with the garden now—a healing circle, as she calls it."

"Mahalo for all the help," Ilima said, standing to smooth her *muumuu*.

"One more thing," Leilani said, reaching into her pocket. "This fell out of one of Pearl's folders the last time she was here. I've been meaning to return it to her." She handed me a small black and white photograph, creased and worn with age. It showed the wooden crane statue, but upon closer inspection, I noticed something else—a small compartment visible in its base.

"The crane was a hiding place," I said.

Leilani nodded. "In Japanese tradition, the crane represents longevity and good fortune. In Pearl's family, it seems it also protected their legacy. Perhaps that's where her father's journal was kept."

As we left the museum, my phone chimed with a text from Rita: *"Maile wants to know if you're coming to the shelter later? We have SEVEN new kittens! PS: Tell Auntie Leilani we need more volunteer hours this week, and we'd love her to take a couple of these rascals home!"*

Despite the gravity of what we'd just learned, I smiled at the message and passed it on to Leilani. It was good to see her smile, too. "I guess I'll have to make up my mind which kitten to take."

"Or two or three," I said. Ilima and Leilani chuckled.

Even amid historical injustice and attempted murder, life in

Ohia continued its small-town rhythm of kittens needing homes and friends gently pressuring each other into volunteer work.

"Ready to visit the garden site?" Ilima asked as we climbed into Sharkey and I fired up the SUV.

"Later, after work. I can't leave Pua alone any longer," I said, tucking the photograph Leilani had given me safely into my bag. "I'll run you home. But as soon as we can, we should go see what might be buried under that plumeria tree on the grounds."

8

THE AFTERNOON CROWD at the post office had finally left, leaving me with just enough time to sort the last of the day's mail before closing. I'd been distracted all afternoon, my mind repeatedly drifting back to what I'd learned at Edith's office and the historical photographs from the Hana History Museum.

Pua had noticed my preoccupation, offering to handle the counter while I retreated to the back room to "sort packages," which really meant texting Keone about our next investigative steps and examining the photo Leilani had given me, as if it would yield any new information.

As I locked the front doors at precisely four p.m., flipping the Post Office's sign to "CLOSED," I spotted Keone's Toyota pulling into the parking lot. He'd changed into board shorts and had a rash guard and a towel slung over his shoulder.

"Perfect timing," I called as he approached. "Let me grab my things."

Ten minutes later, we crossed the street to the small public beach that fronted the post office. It was a local spot, rarely visited by tourists who preferred the more famous stretches of sand along the coast. Late afternoon sun cast a sparkle across the water, and the heat of the day had passed.

"You're a genius," I said, dropping my swim bag on the sand. "This was such a good idea. I need to get into the water. I've been obsessing all day about historical injustice and poisoned tea."

Keone grinned, already pulling his rash guard on over his head. "Nothing clears the mind like saltwater. Since we're heading to check out Pearl's plumeria tree after this, I want to be sharp."

"Your mom will be bummed not to be coming with us," I said.

"I let her know already, and she understood. Mom can't get in on every adventure, and she's a busy lady. Meanwhile, I need some alone time with my girl." He leaned over to give me a peck on the cheek.

The water was perfect—cool enough to be refreshing but warm enough to feel good. We swam parallel to the shore, strong strokes carrying us through the gentle swells side by side. The tension of the day washed away more and more with each pull through the crystalline water.

"What did you think about what Leilani told us about the processing center?" I asked during a brief rest, treading water as a small fishing boat puttered past in the distance.

"Enough to make me understand why someone might resort to murder to keep this whole thing quiet," Keone replied, droplets glistening in his dark hair. "The Santos family has a lot to lose if Pearl's evidence comes to light, including that piece of land they illegally obtained."

By the time we got out and showered at the shack, toweling off as the sun began its descent toward the horizon, we had a clear plan for our visit to Pearl's property. "I want to see that garden site before we lose the light," I told Keone. "Let's move."

He tweaked my wet hair as I got into his truck on the passenger side. "Have I mentioned that you're the perfect woman? Five minutes of shower time and no primping, and you look gorgeous."

"Ha," I said, and punched him on the arm—but my cheeks warmed at the compliment.

The drive to Pearl's beach house took us along the coastal road, past groves of palms and patches of wild ginger whose spicy-sweet scent wafted through the open windows. The late afternoon light had shifted to that magical golden hour that photographers chase, casting everything in a honey glow that softened edges and deepened colors.

"I've been thinking about those blueprints Pearl showed us at the tea party," I said as we rounded a curve that revealed the ocean, stretching to the deep blue horizon. "Pearl's garden plans are really something special—a perfect blend of Japanese tradition and Hawaiian plants."

"Mom's been talking about it for months," Keone replied. "She said Pearl consulted with landscape architects from Kyoto and native plant specialists from the University of Hawaii."

"It's more than just a garden," I said. "It's reconciliation. Reclaiming something that was nearly destroyed. Giving it to the public."

"Which makes it all the more important that we find out who tried to stop it from going forward. Hmm. No sign of Kawika's car," Keone observed as we pulled into the crushed coral driveway, the tires crunching beneath us.

"He's probably at the hospital with Pearl," I said, recalling his protective manner during our last visit. "He said they were moving her back here to Maui."

Pearl's house looked different in the late afternoon sunlight than it had during our tense visit with Ilima. White paint gleamed warmly against the blue trim, and fallen plumeria blossoms carpeted the walkway in a fragrant mosaic. Every time I saw the place, I could appreciate more what a peaceful sanctuary she had created—the way the house nestled perfectly against the sloping landscape, how the lanai wrapped around two sides to maximize the ocean view, the sound of the subtle wind chimes that tinkled softly in the salt-laden breeze.

The air was thick with the heady perfume of the fallen blossoms as we stepped out of the truck. A pair of mynahs squabbled noisily in a nearby monkeypod tree, their glossy black feathers catching the sunlight. The distant crash of waves against the shore below provided a soothing backdrop, a constant reminder of the ocean's proximity.

We walked around to the back of the house, where the land sloped gently toward the sea in a series of natural terraces. A large area had been cleared of underbrush and marked with colorful flags on thin metal stakes—blue, red, and white ribbons fluttering in the gentle breeze.

The garden design was ingenious in how it worked with the natural contours of the land. Standing there, I could mentally overlay the blueprints onto the physical space: here would be the meditation pavilion, positioned to catch both sunrise and sunset, its wooden platform elevated just enough to provide an unobstructed view of the ocean. There, a series of stone pathways would meander through beds of native Hawaiian plants mixed with traditional Japanese garden elements—*ti* plants alongside carefully pruned black pine, birds of paradise complementing ornamental bamboo.

Near what would become the center of the garden, a stone arrangement marked the future location of a koi pond, designed to capture the reflection of the moon on clear nights. A dry riverbed of smooth lava stones indicated where seasonal rainfall would be channeled through the garden, bringing life and movement during the winter months.

I could almost see the finished garden in my mind's eye: lava rock formations arranged to represent mountains, a small stream fed by captured rainwater, strategic openings in the foliage to frame the perfect view of the Pacific stretching to the horizon. The garden would tell a story—of loss and reclamation, of cultures intersecting, of healing after trauma.

At the far edge of the lawn, butted up against an old wooden fence that must mark the disputed five acres of land, stood a massive plumeria tree. Its gnarled trunk and spreading branches suggesting age; the bark was mottled gray and brown, twisted and furrowed like the skin of an ancient being. Its canopy spread at least thirty feet across, creating a dappled shade beneath, while cream and yellow five-petaled blossoms released their sweet fragrance into the warm air.

"That must be the tree Edith mentioned," I said, heading toward it, my rubber slippers sinking into the grass.

As we approached, an elderly Japanese man kneeling beside some plantings looked up. His weathered hands moved with practiced knowledge as he carefully positioned small ferns along what would eventually become a pathway. He wore faded blue work pants and a short-sleeved shirt that had once been white but was now stained with the ruddy red earth. A wide straw hat shielded his face. He straightened slowly, leaning on his garden rake for support to stand upright.

"You friends of Pearl-san?" he called out, his voice surprisingly strong for someone who appeared to be in his eighties or nineties.

"Yes," Keone replied as we walked over and neared the tree. "I'm Keone Kaihale, and this is Kat Smith. We're helping look into what happened to Pearl."

The old man nodded solemnly, removing his hat to reveal a fringe of white hair. "Bad business, very bad. I am Takahashi. I help with garden twice a week." He gestured to the cleared area with a hand that gestured with purpose. "Pearl-san's dream, this garden. Very important place."

"You know about the history here?" I asked, noticing how his deep-set eyes seemed to look both at us and through us to some distant memory.

The lines deepened around Takahashi's mouth. "I know. I was

here since 1942." He pointed to the large plumeria tree, its trunk as wide as Keone's broad shoulders. "That tree, same tree from back then. We waited under it, my family, before they took us away."

"You were processed through this center?" I asked.

He nodded, his expression momentarily distant. "I will never forget." He looked around, as if seeing ghosts among the tropical foliage. "Yamamoto-san's garden began there," he pointed to an area near the tree where butterfly-shaped markers fluttered in yellow and orange. "Beautiful garden with stone paths and crane statue. All destroyed when they built processing center."

The air seemed heavier now, the cheerful birdsong at odds with the painful history beneath our feet. I could almost hear the echoes of that time—frightened whispers, shouted orders, the crunch of military boots on gravel paths where meditation spaces had once been.

"Did you know Pearl's father?" Keone asked, his voice gentle against the backdrop of rustling palm fronds.

"Yamamoto-san was a friend, yes." Takahashi's face softened with the memory, the creases around his eyes crinkling. "After the war, when we came back, I helped rebuild." A hint of anger flashed in the old man's eyes, sharp and sudden like the darting of a tropical fish, as he pointed to the overgrown adjoining lot. "The Santoses stole this land. Felix was a bad man; did things when he ran the processing center."

"What kind of things?" I asked, swiping damp hair back with my arm. The cooling humidity made me shiver.

Takahashi glanced around, the sound of wind through the distant chimes seeming to make him cautious. He leaned closer. "Took valuables from families. Jewelry, watches, family treasures. Say 'for safekeeping,' but never returned anything. Some people protested, they got beaten." His voice dropped to a whisper that seemed to sink into the earth itself. "One man wen' die."

Keone and I exchanged glances, the weight of his words settling between us like the stillness before a storm. This went beyond a disputed land grab and confirmed what Leilani had told me was included in the oral memories she had recorded at the museum.

"And now, Pearl wants to create a memorial that would expose this history," I said.

Takahashi nodded, his calloused fingers tightening on the rake handle. The wood was smooth from years of use, the grain polished by his hands. "Someone does not want old stories told. Someone dug here, two nights ago."

That caught our attention. "Dug where?" Keone asked.

The old gardener led us to the plumeria tree, its broad canopy creating a cathedral-like space beneath. The ground was cooler, shaded from the sun, and the air seemed to hold the scents of decades—blossoms, earth, secrets. He pointed to an area where the soil appeared recently disturbed, the soil looser and not yet settled like the surrounding ground. "Here. Where the crane statue used to stand. I found it like this when I come yesterday morning. I told Kawika-san, but he say leave it, the police will handle."

Keone and I exchanged glances as the dappled sunlight through the leaves played across our faces. "Did the police come?" I asked.

Takahashi shook his head. "Nobody come yet."

I knelt by the disturbed area. The rich red soil clung to my fingers as I examined it more closely. "Yes, someone dug here recently. The soil's still loose."

Keone joined me. He pushed some of the dirt aside with his hand. "Either they found something or they didn't."

As he shifted more soil, something metallic glinted in the sunlight that broke through the branches—a brief flash like a fish's scales underwater. Keone carefully extracted a small metal tag attached to a broken chain, crusted with dirt and tarnished by years underground.

"Military ID," he said, his thumb wiping away the soil to reveal engraved numbers and a name. The metal was cool despite the warmth of the day, as if it held the chill of its buried years. "Santos, F."

"Felix Santos," I said. "The mayor's grandfather."

"What would his military ID be doing buried under Pearl's family tree?" Keone wondered, turning the tag so it caught the light filtering through the leaves above.

Takahashi had been watching us. "Yamamoto-san say once he have proof of Santos crimes. Maybe bury it for safekeeping."

"Or as insurance," I suggested, brushing soil from my knees as I stood. The scent of plumeria was stronger now, almost dizzying in its sweetness.

"I think Yamamoto-san hide more than ID tag," Takahashi said, his shadow stretching long as the sun began its descent. "Pearl-san find old journal last month. Very excited. Say now she have proof of everything."

"A journal?" Keone asked sharply, the tag still held in his palm. "Did she keep it in a sandalwood box with a crane carved on the lid?"

The old man's eyes widened slightly. "Crane box, yes. Pearl-san showed me once. Inside is proof of old crimes. Not just attempted land theft."

"Did she say what kind of proof?" I asked.

"This tree remembers everything." Takahashi shook his head, the movement deliberate. He tipped his head to gaze up at the ancient plumeria, its branches heavy with fragrant flowers that seemed to float against the deepening violet sky. "Too bad it can't tell us what it knows."

The leaves swooshed overhead, as if in agreement. I felt a strange prickling at the back of my neck. "Wouldn't that be interesting," I said, and a plumeria pinwheeled down to land on my shoulder, as if the tree understood.

9

My phone buzzed with a text, the electronic chime startlingly modern in the setting of Pearl's sunset-lit garden. It was Lei: *"Let's catch up soon. Toxicology report shows oleander wasn't only toxin in tea."*

I showed the message to Keone, whose expression darkened as his brows drew down. "We need to tell her about this ID tag we found and the disturbed soil."

"I think we have the motive for Pearl's poisoning," I said. "Whatever evidence she found, it goes beyond covering up land theft..."

"And the current mayor, Felix Santos's grandson, has every reason to keep the past buried," Keone said. The tag and its chain clinked softly as he tucked them into his pocket.

We thanked Takahashi for his help and promised to return soon. As we walked back to Keone's vehicle, our feet leaving temporary impressions in the soft grass, the old gardener called after us, his voice carrying on the still evening air.

"Be careful! Old secrets have sharp teeth!"

A shiver zipped up my back at his words, canceled out by my stomach growling audibly as we got into the truck.

"I guess crime solving works up an appetite," Keone teased, starting the engine.

"I haven't eaten since your mom made me a kalua pork sand-wich earlier in the day," I admitted. "Any chance we could grab dinner?"

Keone glanced at his watch. "Braddah Hutts food truck should still be open in Hana. Perfect for a quick dinner before—" he paused, a gleam in his eyes, "before we visit the history museum again, this time without a chaperone."

"The museum closes at 5:00," I pointed out.

"True," he agreed, pulling onto the main road. "But I bet we could learn a lot more from those archives about Pearl's father and Felix Santos. This military ID tag is just the beginning."

I considered, watching the tropical landscape blur past the window. "I'm sure Auntie Leilani would open up for us if we called her."

"Yes," Keone said, "but she's eating with Rita and Maile tonight. Something about a fundraiser for the cat shelter."

"How do you know that?"

"Maile told me when I dropped off a big bag of cat food from Kahului on my way to meet you." Keone often found ways to smuggle groceries and other supplies onto his flights to Hana, saving seniors and low-income friends the lengthy, gas-consuming trip. "Apparently, it's a monthly planning session for their next adoption event."

Rita and her dedication to homeless cats, with Leilani and Maile as her steadfast supporters, were a powerful trio. "So. The museum is closed; Leilani is busy . . . are you suggesting what I think you're suggesting?"

Keone kept his eyes on the road, but the corner of his mouth quirked up. "I'm not suggesting anything. I'm just stating facts."

"Uh-huh," I said. "And what about the breaking and entering laws?"

"Technically, it would be entering without breaking if someone happened to have certain skills," he replied. "We're just research-ing. Nothing will be taken or damaged. Hypothetically speaking."

"And here I thought Pua was nosy." I laughed, shaking my head. "Let's get food first. I make better bad decisions when I'm not starving."

BRADDAH HUTTS FOOD truck was parked in its usual spot just outside of town. A line of locals and a few adventurous tourists were already queued up for his famous *poke* bowls and plate lunches. The scent of grilled fish, roast pork, and sweet-spicy sauce made my mouth water as we joined the line.

"Keone! Kat!" a booming voice called out. Braddah Hutts' manager waved from the service window. "Come, come! I make you a special plate!"

"Does everyone in town give you preferential treatment?" I whispered to Keone as we moved to the front of the line, ignoring good-natured grumbles from those waiting.

"Only the ones who owe me for carrying supplies or fixing their engines," Keone replied with a wink.

The manager presented us with two enormous plates of fresh ahi *poke* and rice, with a side of mac salad and his secret recipe grilled vegetables.

"On the house," he insisted when Keone tried to pay. "I hear you looking into what happen to Pearl. She good lady, deserve justice."

"Thanks, man," Keone said, accepting the plates. "You hear anything around town about who might have had it in for her?"

The big man leaned forward conspiratorially, his voice dropping to what he probably thought was a whisper but was really normal speaking volume. "Mayor Santos is looking nervous these days. His boy too—the one working for the planning department. They been having big arguments."

"The mayor's son is on the planning commission?" I clarified, accepting a pair of chopsticks.

"Yeah. David Santos. He's in charge of permits for historical buildings, among other t'ings. Pearl been fighting with him about her garden project." We thanked him for the information and the food, then found a picnic table overlooking the view.

The *poke* was perfect—fresh ahi tuna marinated in soy, sesame oil, and *limu* seaweed, topped with crisp onions and avocado. Before my move to Maui, I'd never have imagined enjoying such a dish, but I'd come to love it.

We ate in appreciative silence for a few minutes, watching the sunset dimming in the distance. "So, David Santos," I said finally, setting down my chopsticks. "Hmm. The mayor's son runs the department that's been blocking Pearl's permits."

"And if Pearl had evidence that his grandfather was involved in crimes at the processing center . . ." Keone let the implication hang in the air between us.

"It's a solid motive," I agreed. "But we need more than circumstantial evidence and old rumors to tie them to this."

"Which is why we need to get more information." Keone collected our empty paper luau plates and disposed of them in a nearby bin. "So, what's your decision, Postmaster Smith? Are we going to be law-abiding citizens who wait until tomorrow, or . . ."

I sighed, already knowing what I was going to do. "Let's drive by the museum and assess the situation."

THE HANA HISTORY Museum was dark and silent as we pulled into the small parking lot beside it. The restored storefront looked almost imposing in the deepening twilight, its white exterior ghostly against the darkening sky.

"No lights, no cars," Keone observed. "Definitely closed."

I pulled out my phone and tried Leilani's number, but as expected, it went straight to voicemail. "She's probably in the middle of dinner with Rita."

We sat in silence for a moment, the truck's engine ticking as it cooled.

"We could come back tomorrow," Keone suggested, though his tone made it clear he wasn't enthusiastic about that option.

I drummed my fingers on the dashboard, weighing the moral implications against the urgency of our investigation. Pearl was still unconscious in the hospital. Someone had tried to kill her. And the answers to why might be sitting in those archives, just waiting to be discovered. We had to help Lei put together the background of her case.

"Leilani would let us in if she were around," I finally said. "And we won't disturb or disrespect anything. Do you have a flashlight?"

"In the glove compartment."

I reached in and retrieved a small but powerful tactical light, then fished in my purse for the leather case I'd started carrying months ago. Lock picking was a useful skill for a postal employee who occasionally dealt with stuck mailboxes as well as her own private investigator business.

"You know," Keone said, watching me unzip the case to reveal the slim metal tools inside, "you were pretty hard on Pua for doing exactly what you're about to do."

"That's different," I protested. "She was satisfying her curiosity. We're investigating an attempted murder."

"Uh-huh," he said with a twinkle.

Mr. K's twinkle was one of my favorite things, but I was getting grumpy with my conscience acting up. "Are you going to help or just give me bad ideas and then provide commentary?"

"Both. I'm a multitasker."

The museum's back door was solid but old, its lock a simple deadbolt that presented little challenge. The lock clicked open with satisfying ease, and I turned the handle, edgy with the knowledge that we were definitely breaking a few laws.

"We're in," I whispered. "Now we just need to find the archives without turning on any lights that might be visible from outside."

The museum was eerily quiet, the displays creating shadowy silhouettes in the dim light filtering through the windows. We tiptoed through the main gallery, our footsteps muffled on *lauhala* mats covering the wooden floors.

The research room was at the back of the building, and we made our way there by the beam of Keone's flashlight. I made sure the blackout blinds were down, before turning on a light.

"Leilani showed us the Yamamoto Collection earlier," I said, scanning the cabinet labels. "Now we need to look for anything related to Felix Santos and the processing center."

We found the cabinet marked "Internment Records – Maui County" and donned white gloves from the nearby box. We began carefully sifting through the files.

Time seemed to stretch as we worked methodically through decades-old documents, the only sounds our breathing and the occasional crackle of paper.

"Look at this," Keone said after about twenty minutes. He'd found a folder labeled "Processing Center Staff – 1942-1943" and was examining a typewritten roster. "Felix Santos is listed as 'Civilian Liaison – Security Division.'"

"And here's something interesting," I said, poring over a different file. "Pearl's father, Takeo Yamamoto, is listed as a translator for military intelligence."

"A translator?" Keone moved to look over my shoulder. "That's not something they would typically advertise about Japanese-Americans during internment."

"No, it's not," I agreed, reading further. "According to this, he was recruited because of his fluency in several Japanese dialects. He worked with military intelligence to translate intercepted communications."

"He was helping the American war effort while his family was being detained on their own property," Keone said, the irony evident in his voice. "Ouch."

"And look who was assigned as his military police escort," I said, pointing to a notation on the document. "Corporal Felix Santos."

"They knew each other," Keone said slowly. "And not just as administrator and detainee."

"The plot thickens," I murmured, carefully photographing the document with my phone.

We continued searching, and in a folder marked "Personal Correspondences – Restricted," I found a letter that made my pulse quicken. It was from a military commander to his superior, dated September 1942:

"Regarding the incident at Processing Center #3 on August 12, I have concluded my investigation. While the death of detainee Hiroshi Tanaka was ruled accidental by the medical examiner, I find Civilian Liaison Santos's account of events inconsistent with witness testimony. Translator Yamamoto's statement is particularly concerning, as he alleges Santos confiscated valuable items from multiple detainees, including Tanaka, who protested the seizure of a family heirloom before his 'fatal fall.' I recommend Santos be reassigned pending further investigation."

"This is it," I breathed. "This had to be what Pearl found. Evidence that Felix Santos was involved in the death of a detainee. And, that her father witnessed it."

"There's more," Keone said, pulling out another folder labeled "Post-War Property Claims." Inside was a detailed record of items reported missing by Japanese-American families after internment —jewelry, art, ceremonial items, family heirlooms—along with a handwritten note from Takeo Yamamoto listing items he had personally witnessed being confiscated by Felix Santos.

"He was stealing from people who had already lost everything." A surge of anger on behalf of those long-ago victims lit up my nervous system.

"And at least one person died trying to stop him," Keone added grimly.

As we continued searching, another document caught my eye— a letter from Pearl's father to a lawyer in Honolulu, dated 1946:

"I have secured certain evidence regarding F.S.'s activities at the Center, including his military identification which he lost during an altercation with H.T. Should he continue to pursue his fraudulent claim to our property, I am prepared to reveal everything I know about the events of August 12, 1942."

"The ID tag," Keone said. "Takeo Yamamoto kept it as insurance against Santos."

"And buried it under the plumeria tree where the crane statue once stood," I added. "A secret passed down to Pearl, who finally decided it was time to bring the truth to light through her Heritage Garden project. Unfortunately, by itself it isn't evidence of anything."

"Maybe if we find the journal, that will give enough context," Keone said.

I shrugged; none of what we were discovering so far was anything Lei could act on.

We photographed everything we found, careful to replace each document exactly as we'd found it. As I was returning the last folder to its drawer, I glanced at my watch and was shocked to see it was after 9:30 p.m.

"It's getting late," I said. "We should head back."

"Back to Ohia?" Keone asked, raising an eyebrow. "That's a thirty-minute drive, and we're both tired. My place is just five minutes from here."

I hesitated, suddenly aware of how exhausted I was—the stress of the investigation, the emotional weight of what we'd discovered, and the physical drain of two earlier swims that day had all conspired to make the thought of a drive home distinctly unappealing.

"We could grab your clothes in the swim bag from the truck tomorrow," Keone said. "You can borrow a T-shirt to sleep in. Get a fresh start in the morning."

"Practical as always," I said with a smile. "Alright, you've convinced me."

"Or maybe I just like having you in my bed," he teased, giving me a kiss too quick to respond to.

We carefully made our way out of the museum, locking the door behind us and leaving no evidence of our nocturnal research expedition.

The night had grown cooler, and the stars blazed overhead in a clear sky as we drove the short distance to Keone's cottage. Mango was gone from the little orchid-lined porch; that reminded me of Tiki and I shot off a quick text to Aunt Fae that I'd be gone overnight and to please feed the Feline Overlord.

"Make yourself at home," Keone said, flipping on lights as we entered. "I'll grab you a towel if you want to shower."

"That would be perfect," I admitted, suddenly aware of the dust clinging to my skin from the archives, along with dirt from under the plumeria tree.

While Keone rummaged in a linen closet for clean towels, I wandered to the kitchen and filled two glasses with water, gulping mine down greedily. I handed the other one to Keone. "Hydrate."

"Sure. Meanwhile, here you go." Keone handed me a fluffy towel and an extra-large, worn UH Hilo T-shirt. "Bathroom's all yours."

"Thanks," I said, accepting the items. "I won't be long."

The hot water was blissful, washing away not just the physical grime but some of the emotional heaviness as well. I borrowed Keone's shampoo, inhaling the familiar scent of coconut and something distinctly him I'd become happily familiar with. By the time I emerged wrapped in the oversized T-shirt, my hair swaddled in the towel, I felt almost human again.

I found Keone in the kitchen, assembling a plate of cookies and opening a bottle of wine. "Thought you might want a nightcap," he said, pouring two glasses. "Help process everything we learned today."

"You thought right," I agreed, accepting a glass and taking a sip.

The rich cabernet was exactly what I needed. "Do you think we should call Lei with what we found today?"

"Nah. None of it is time-sensitive," Mr. K said. "This is our time."

"I like the sound of that."

We moved to the lanai on the front of the house, settling onto comfortable chairs that faced the moonlit ocean. The rhythmic sound of waves breaking on the shore in the distance provided a soothing backdrop as we discussed what we'd discovered.

"So, Pearl's father was essentially a spy for the U.S. military while being processed for internment," I said, nibbling on a home-made chocolate chip cookie. "And Felix Santos was not only trying to steal the Yamamoto land but was taking valuables from detainees and potentially murdered someone who protested."

"And Pearl discovered all of this through her father's hidden journal and archival research," Keone added. "No wonder she was determined to create that garden as a memorial. It's not just about beauty and a legacy—it's about righting old wrongs."

We fell silent for a moment, the weight of history and present danger settling between us like a physical presence.

"You know," Keone said, his voice lighter, "there's something I've been meaning to ask you."

"Hmm?"

"When are you going to move in with me?" His tone was casual, but I could sense the seriousness beneath it. "You live here half the time anyway. Your toothbrush has its own holder in the bathroom."

I felt a familiar tightness in my chest; it was an involuntary response to commitment, to closeness, that had plagued me since childhood when I'd lost both parents in a traumatic car accident. "I don't know, Keone. It's a big step. Aunt Fae needs me. And where would Tiki..."

"It's okay." Keone set down his wine glass and moved to perch on the wide wood arm of my chair. "Kat, I'm not pushing. I just want you to know the option is there and that I'd like to move in that direction. Whenever you're ready."

I squeezed his hand, grateful for his patience. "I know. And I love you for it."

"Being anxious is normal," he said softly. "But so is moving forward. At your own speed."

The understanding in his gaze made my heart swell, and I set aside my wine glass to pull him down for a kiss. "How did I get so lucky?" I murmured against his lips.

"I ask myself that same question every day," he replied, kissing me with tenderness that quickly deepened into something more urgent.

Keone stood and pulled me to my feet. "I didn't shower yet," he said, his eyes dark with desire. "Care to join me? You'll be squeaky clean and it will save water for the cleanup afterward, you know. Very environmentally conscious."

I laughed, stepping into his arms. "You're not the only one who likes multitasking."

Later, wrapped in fresh towels and each other's arms, we made our way to his bedroom. As I drifted toward sleep, Keone's heartbeat was steady beneath my ear.

Some steps forward were worth the risk, especially when they led toward someone who understood your strengths, and your fears.

Tomorrow we would deal with the case and its decades of secrets.

Tomorrow we would continue the fight for Pearl and her garden.

But tonight, in this peaceful cottage by the sea, I would simply be present in the moment—safe, loved, and, for the moment at least, at peace.

10

THE NEXT MORNING at the post office, Pua hollered over her
shoulder to me. "Kat? There's a situation out here." Something in
her tone suggested this particular morning was taking an unwel-
come turn.

"What kind of situation?" I hollered back, gloved hands still
busily sorting mail. "Is the door stuck again?"

"It's ... it's Tiki," Pua replied. "And she's brought you a ... gift."

The hesitation in her tone was all I needed to know about what
kind of "gift" my cat had likely delivered. Tiki had, after all, brought
me the desiccated hand of the previous postmaster to kick off my
life in Ohia. Tiki was, despite her general disdain for any sort of
rules, an accomplished hunter with a flair for the dramatic, deliv-
ering trophies to those she deemed worthy. They always seemed to
arrive at inconvenient times.

"I'll be right there." I set aside the bundle of letters I was sorting, glad I was already wearing rubber gloves.

My scruffy calico feline sat proudly on the polished laminate
countertop next to a very dead gray Hawaiian roof rat.

The main area was empty of customers—a small mercy. Pua
stood rigid at her station uncomfortably near the scene of the

crime. Her face was a delicate mask of repugnance as she stared at Tiki and the aforementioned rodent. The corpse had been placed with what could only be described as artistic precision atop a Priority Mail form; its tail dangled off the counter.

"Tiki," I snapped. "I appreciate the rodent elimination effort, but—boundaries, please. Not at work."

Tiki blinked slowly, her yellow eyes radiating smug satisfaction, and licked her chops as if to emphasize the tastiness of her offering. She placed a paw on it and gave a little push in my direction. The rat—thankfully intact, rather than partially dismembered—was clearly meant as a bribe or a consequence, perhaps in response to last night's absence from home.

"Is it normal for her to bring you . . . presents?" Pua asked, maintaining her distance from both cat and rat.

"Only when she's feeling particularly generous—or grumpy," I replied. "Or when she wants to remind me of her superior hunting skills. Or when—heck, I have no idea. Tiki does what she wants, when she wants. As you know."

"This is unsanitary," Pua muttered. "To begin with."

"I'm aware." I scooped up the rat with a handful of tissues. "Thank you for the gift, Tiki, but the post office is not an appropriate place for you to bring me a present. Federal regulations." I gave Tiki a firm scratch behind the ears. "I promise to be home tonight."

Tiki's kinked tail twitched in what might have been amusement or disdain (with her, it was hard to tell.) Meanwhile, Pua trotted to our little kitchen area and returned with disinfectant spray, paper towels, and a ziplock bag. I dropped the rat inside and sealed it as Pua sprayed the laminate counter, all the way up to Tiki's paws. She glanced up at me. "Is she going to move?"

"Unsure." I gestured toward the door which was propped open to catch the ocean breeze and told Tiki, "Shoo. Go visit Aunt Fae or torment the birds at the park or something."

With the languid stretch that cats have perfected over millennia, Tiki rose from her regal sitting pose, arched her back, and leapt gracefully from the counter. She padded to the door, pausing to glance back with an expression that clearly said, "You're welcome."

Once Tiki had sauntered out into the sunshine, Pua opened the counter and trotted across the lobby to close the door behind her.

"I'll finish cleaning," she said.

"I've got it," I assured her. "Least I can do since my cat desecrated the workplace."

I quickly disposed of the rat in our outdoor trash bin before thoroughly scrubbing the counter. In spite of my disgust (maybe because of it?) my stomach let out an embarrassingly loud growl. I'd skipped breakfast in my rush to get to work after the late night at Keone's, and it was now well past my usual lunch time.

"Take your break early," Pua suggested. "I can handle things here. It's dead anyway." She raised a brow. "Pun intended."

Through the front window, I could see Tiki sitting in the dirt parking lot, her tail twitching as she stared at the general store.

"I think I will," I decided. "Seems like Tiki wants to visit Opal and Artie's place. Maybe they have that ahi tuna sandwich special today."

"The one with the mango aioli?" Pua asked wistfully. "If they do, could you bring one back for me?"

"Sure. Consider it a peace offering to make up for this morning's trauma," I said, stripping off my gloves and grabbing my wallet.

Outside, the sun was warm with a gentle trade wind. Tiki, spotting me, stood and stretched before trotting across the parking lot toward the general store in the lead, her tail held high as a furry flag.

"I'm coming, Your Feline Overlord Majesty," I called after her.

I glanced back at the glass doors of the post office. As I'd suspected might be the real reason she'd hustled me out, Pua was thoroughly disinfecting and scrubbing the entire counter again. "We may never get the place clean again, Tiki. Thanks a lot."

My cat did not deign to reply.

Opal and Artie's General Store occupied a building that had once been the town's first trading post. Its weathered wooden exterior had been lovingly maintained, while the interior had been modernized just enough to accommodate refrigeration and health department requirements without losing its creaky, squeaky, historic charm.

The bell above the door jingled as I entered. The store was filled with the eclectic mix of items that made the place interesting to tourists and indispensable to locals: groceries, fishing supplies, beachwear, homeopathic remedies, incense, local crafts, and the café counter serving Artie's daily lunch special.

Artie had started out featuring coffee and malasadas from a local bakery and homemade coffee cake on Sundays. Demand had led to creative expansion of his culinary talents into takeaway lunch items I'd come to count on, along with half the town of Ohia.

Tiki slipped past me to run toward Opal, who was arranging hand-woven *lauhala* pendants in a display case. Opal was dressed in flowing purple gauze pants and a tie-dyed top, her white hair wrapped in a turquoise scarf adorned with tiny sparkling mirrors. Around her neck hung no fewer than seven necklaces of varying lengths, each featuring crystals, symbols, or charms that clinked softly with her movements.

"Tiki!" Opal's voice rang out. "What cosmic timing! I was just thinking about your mama and wondering when she'd be by for the weekly ahi sandwich."

"You caught me," I said. "And Tiki's here to find any fish flakes that might have fallen through the cracks. She already terrorized Pua and me with a rat delivery."

"Ah, a gift from the hunting goddess." Opal nodded, as if dead rodents were perfectly acceptable offerings in polite society. "She's manifesting protective energy today."

Artie emerged from the back room, carrying a tray of wrapped sandwiches. Unlike his wife's bohemian appearance, Artie favored size XXL aloha shirts and cargo shorts, though his salt-and-pepper beard gave him a slightly wizardly look that complemented Opal's mysticism.

"Kat! Perfect timing," he said. He always seemed to recognize when I was in the room, blind or not. "Tuna special just finished. You want the works on yours?"

"Yes, please," I replied. "And one to go for Pua. She's holding down the fort at the post office."

"Coming right up," he said, disappearing through the connecting door to their adjoining home, where he made the store's daily offerings in their kitchen.

Opal crouched beside Tiki, who had settled regally on a cushion behind the counter that seemed to have been placed there specifically for her.

"She's agitated," Opal observed, bangle bracelets jangling as she stroked Tiki's fur. "The energies are shifting. She feels it."

I'd learned not to dismiss Opal's intuitions, despite their over-the-top packaging. Behind the crystals and cosmic terminology was a remarkably perceptive woman who noticed things others missed.

"We had a busy night," I said, leaning against the counter. "Keone and I found some pretty disturbing information about the Santos family's connection to Pearl's family's land."

Opal's eyes widened with interest. "The past reaching into the present," she said. "The runes have been restless."

Before I could ask what exactly constituted "restless runes," Artie returned with a plate bearing the most glorious tuna sandwich in existence—fresh ahi, lightly seared and chilled, on home-made focaccia with local greens, thin-sliced Maui onion, avocado, and the shop's famous lilikoi aioli that somehow balanced sweet, tangy, and savory.

"One for here," he announced, setting the plate before me, "and one to go for Pua." He placed a neatly wrapped package beside it. "On the house today. Consider it our contribution to the investigation."

"You don't have to do that." I reached for my wallet.

"We want to," Opal said firmly. "Pearl is ohana to us. She taught Artie to fold origami cranes when he was her student long ago."

At the mention of cranes, I paused with the sandwich halfway to my mouth. "Cranes? Like 'the crane will fly once more'?"

"You've heard the phrase," Opal said. It wasn't a question.

"It was in a note addressed to Pearl," I said, setting the sandwich down. "Keone and I have been trying to figure out what it means. We thought it referred to a statue in the garden her grandfather built before the war."

"That's part of it," Artie said. "But for Pearl, cranes have always been about more than the statue. They're her . . . meditation, I guess you could say."

"She folds them constantly," Opal said. "Hundreds, maybe thousands over the years. She gives them for special events, like weddings and graduations. Says each one carries a wish, a memory, or a truth that needs to be remembered."

I felt a tingle of excitement. "Where does she keep them? The paper cranes, I mean."

"All over," Artie shrugged. "Her house, her classroom at the community center—"

"The community center," I interrupted. "In Ohia State Park? Where she teaches origami workshops? I knew about that."

"She has a whole cabinet of supplies there. Paper in every color imaginable," Opal confirmed.

"And finished cranes," Artie added. "She lets the *keiki* take some home, but she keeps many of them there for her projects and gifts, too."

My mind raced. Maybe Pearl had left something there—a hidden message? The missing evidence? I had to find out.

The community center was a former gym in the state park. It had recently been enlarged through local fundraising efforts, and was used for classes, events, and cultural demonstrations.

Most importantly, I had keys to it—Aunt Fae and I served as

weekend caretakers for the park in return for rent, a position that mostly involved trash pickup on weekends, and making sure gates were locked and buildings secure after-hours.

"I need to check out that classroom," I said, taking a hurried bite of my sandwich.

The flavors of Artie's exceptional ahi creation exploded across my tongue, momentarily distracting my investigative instincts. "Oh man, that's good."

"Take your time," Artie chuckled. "The cranes will wait for you."

Opal reached into her pocket, her bracelets creating a melodic tinkling. "Before you go rushing off," she said, "perhaps the runes can offer guidance." She produced the small pouch she always carried with her.

"I'm not sure we have time for a full reading," I said, battling a sudden urgency as I munched another bite.

"Just three," she insisted, loosening the pouch's drawstring. "For direction."

Tiki, who had been grooming herself with single-minded focus, stopped and fixed her gaze on the rune pouch. Her attention seemed to confirm Opal's suggestion.

"All right," I agreed. "Three quick runes."

Opal spread a silk cloth on the counter and gestured for me to draw three kukui nut shells from the bag. I did so, placing them in a row.

"Past, present, future," she said, studying the symbols revealed.

The first curved, corrugated black shell bore what looked like an angular "P" shape. The second showed what resembled an "X" with the bottom right arm extended. The third displayed a simple vertical line.

Opal's fingers hovered over each in turn. "Wunjo reversed," she said, touching the first. "Joy inverted—a happiness that was stolen or corrupted. The foundation of this mystery lies in a joy that was transformed into sorrow."

Her finger moved to the second shell. "Nauthiz—need, necessity, hardship endured. The present moment requires perseverance through difficulty. The truth is buried but fighting to emerge."

Finally, she touched the third nutshell, and her eyes widened slightly. "Isa—ice, stillness, that which preserves. In the future position . . ." She paused, her brow furrowing. "Something preserved will reveal itself. A truth frozen in time."

"The journal?" I guessed. "We know Pearl found her father's journal recently."

Opal shook her head. "Something else. Something hidden in plain sight." Her gaze grew distant. "I see folded wings. Paper wings. The crane flies not with feathers but with truth."

A chill ran down my spine despite the warm day. "The origami cranes," I whispered. "She's hidden something in the paper cranes."

Tiki suddenly stood up on her cushion, stretched, and leapt to the counter, careful not to disturb the rune shells. She fixed me with an imperious stare that clearly communicated: *Get moving.*

"I need to go," I said, wrapping the remainder of my sandwich. "Opal, Artie—thank you."

"Take this," Artie said, handing me a small paper bag. "An extra sandwich for Keone. Tell him it's payment for fixing our generator last month."

I accepted the bag, then turned to Opal. "Do the runes say anything else?"

Her pale eyes refocused on me, sharp and clear. "Be careful. The crane may fly, but a serpent can strike from hidden places."

With that cheerful warning, I gathered my sandwiches and headed for the door. Tiki leapt down and followed, apparently deciding that her presence was required for this next phase of the investigation.

BACK AT THE POST OFFICE, Pua practically pounced on the sandwich I delivered. "You're a lifesaver," she declared, unwrapping it with reverence. "It's been a madhouse here."

I glanced around the conspicuously empty post office. "I can see that. Absolutely swamped."

"Well, Mr. Kekoa came in with fifteen packages for his mainland grandchildren, and Mrs. Palaunu needed help filling out customs forms for her daughter in Japan."

"Plus, that extra round of cleaning due to Tiki's 'gift,'" I said. "I get it. Listen, I need to take a longer lunch break. Something's come up with the investigation."

Pua's eyes lit up with interest. "What kind of something? Does it involve more lock-picking?"

"No more breaking and entering for you," I said. "I'm just going to check out the community center at New Ohia State Park. Totally legitimate—I have keys."

"Oh." Her disappointment was almost comical. I couldn't help remembering how Keone and I had broken into the museum the night before. Yep, I was treading on some thin ethical ice with this one, and I might as well continue.

"I could use someone to cover for me here. Tell anyone who asks where I am that I'm doing a special postal inspection at the park. Technically true, since I'll be checking if Pearl received any mail at her classroom there. Oh—and use the landline to call Sergeant Lei Texeira. Tell her I have some new information for the case, and if she's out on this side I'd like to catch up in person."

Pua brightened. "I can do that."

I glanced around. "Where is Tiki?"

Pua pointed vaguely outside. "She slinked past right when you came back. Probably plotting her next rodent delivery."

Knowing Tiki, she was more likely planning to meet me at the community center via whatever mysterious cat pathways she used to appear exactly where she was needed. I'd long since stopped questioning her uncanny access and timing.

"I'll be back before closing or I'll call," I promised, grabbing my car keys. "And Pua? Thanks."

She saluted with her sandwich. "Just doing my duty for truth, justice, and the postal service way."

THE NEW OHIA State Park was a swath of former pastureland at the edge of town. I'd been a part of wresting it from the grip of a crime family, who had been developing the area as luxury homes. Now it was a work in progress state park, featuring native Hawaiian plants, gentle hiking trails, and views of both mountains and ocean. The community center sat near the entrance—a single-story building with a pool everyone could use.

I parked in the parking lot, noting that it was nearly empty on this weekday afternoon. A few tourists wandered the nearby native Hawaiian healing garden Aunt Fae was helping develop with Josie as head. The community center, a recent expansion on the original clubhouse building, appeared closed today, its doors locked and windows closed.

My caretaker's ring jingled as I approached the main entrance, heavy with various keys for the park's facilities. I found the right one and let myself into the community center, flipping on lights as I entered the cool, dim interior.

The center was divided into several classroom spaces and a ballroom/gallery that displayed rotating exhibits of local art and cultural artifacts. Pearl's origami class was held in the smallest room at the back—an intimate space with large windows over-looking the rise of the hill behind the park's entrance.

I made my way to the room, footsteps echoing in the empty building. The classroom was neat and orderly, with low tables surrounded by cushions in the traditional Japanese style. Along one wall stood a large cabinet with dozens of small drawers—the type used in art studios to organize materials.

"This must be it," I murmured, approaching the cabinet. A loud mew from behind me told me Tiki had followed me in. "Don't know what you think you'll find here, girl, but Aunt Fae and I have a pest control service keeping these buildings rodent-free."

The drawers were labeled in Pearl's precise handwriting: different papers organized by color, weight, and pattern. But it was the larger bottom drawers that caught my attention. These bore labels like "Completed Works – Spring Collection" and "Demo Pieces – Advanced Class."

I opened the drawer marked "Personal Collection" and caught my breath. Inside were dozens—perhaps hundreds—of expertly folded paper cranes in every imaginable color and pattern. Some were tiny, barely larger than my thumbnail, while others were the size of my palm. They were arranged in neat rows, each one perfect in its complex folds.

"She must have been folding these for years," I said aloud, carefully lifting one to examine it. The paper was high-quality, and the crane was folded with such precision that every angle was crisp and clean.

But what struck me most was the weight. The crane felt slightly heavier than it should, as if something more than paper comprised its form.

Carefully, I began to unfold it, trying to minimize damage to the delicate paper. As the folds opened, I noticed tiny, precise handwriting covering the interior surface—dates, names, and what appeared to be monetary amounts.

"She wrote on them before folding," I realized. "The cranes aren't just art—they're her documentation."

A noise at the door made me jump, but it was only Tiki. She must have pushed the swing-style front door open. She strolled in as if she owned the place, leapt onto the nearby craft table, and began inspecting the unfolded crane I held with feline curiosity. She then walked over and pawed gently at a different crane in the drawer—this one folded from metallic red paper with gold accents.

Unlike the others, which were arranged in rows, this one sat slightly apart.

"That one, Tiki? Okay, I'll check it out." I carefully lifted the crane. Like the first, it felt weightier than expected. But the weight came not just from writing, but from something small and solid nestled within the folds. As the last crease came undone, a tiny metallic object fell onto the table.

"A data drive," I breathed, picking up the small device. It was no larger than my fingernail, one of those ultra-compact models designed for maximum storage in minimal space.

The origami crane's paper itself was covered in Pearl's handwriting, but these weren't just names and numbers. This was a message:

"To whoever finds this—if you're reading this, something has happened to me. The drive contains evidence of crimes committed by Felix Santos during the war and covered up by his family for generations. The origami cranes in this collection each document a stolen item and its rightful owner. This is my legacy of truth. May these cranes fly and bring justice. —Pearl Yamamoto"

My hands trembled as I held the tiny drive. Here was the evidence Pearl had collected, the proof she'd mentioned to Mr. Takahashi—all hidden in her origami classroom.

The sound of the community center's front door opening fully and hitting a wall echoed through the building. Footsteps approached—too heavy to be Keone's.

Tiki's ears flattened, and she let out a low growl, the fur on her spine rising.

I pocketed the drive and began refolding the cranes, refolding them to their original state and tucking them in my pockets. Whoever was coming, I didn't want them to know what I'd found.

"Ms. Smith?" A male voice called. "Are you in here?"

"Just a moment," I called, closing the drawer and moving to block the cabinet from view. "We're not open today."

My stomach tightened as I recognized David Santos, the

mayor's son, standing in the doorway. The planning department official who had been blocking Pearl's permits had tracked me down somehow. This couldn't be good.

David wore the casual-but-expensive polo shirt and chinos that seemed to be the uniform for government officials in Hawaii. His resemblance to his father was striking; he had the same square jaw and calculating brown eyes. His hair was dark while the mayor's had gone silver.

Tiki positioned herself between me and the door, her tail puffed to twice its normal size—a warning sign I'd learned to heed.

"The door was unlocked," David Santos said with a smile that didn't reach his eyes. "I saw your car and thought I'd see what brings the Ohia postmaster to the community center."

"Just checking on the facility." I forced a friendly tone. "Aunt Fae and I are the weekend caretakers. We like to make sure everything's in order mid-week too. We haven't met, but you seem to know my name."

"You're well-known in the community. And I'm David Santos. Planning Commission. Mayor Santos is my dad. Our paths were bound to cross sometime; it might as well be now." His gaze swept the room, lingering on the cabinet behind me. "Ah, Pearl Yamamoto's origami supplies. She's quite the artist, isn't she? Such a shame about her . . . illness."

"Yes, we're all hoping for a speedy recovery," I said. Tiki was advancing toward David, her body low to the ground in stalking position.

"Some things, once broken, can never be fully restored," he said, his voice taking on a philosophical tone. "Perhaps it's the same with health. And reputations."

"Reputations?" I needed to keep him talking; see what I could get out of him even as I gauged the distance to the door. This guy was blocking the only exit from the small classroom. I could take him, though, if I had to; my Secret Service hand-to-hand skills might be rusty, but they weren't gone.

"Family legacies are fragile things," he went on in the same musing tone. "My grandfather built ours from nothing. My father has maintained and improved it. And I . . ." he paused, his eyes narrowing . . "I won't allow it to be destroyed by old lies better left forgotten."

"I don't know what you're talking about." Best to play dumb a little longer.

"I think you do," David hissed. "You and your boyfriend have been busy. The museum archives. Pearl's property. You've been digging up the past, Kat Smith. That's dangerous work."

The threat was barely veiled now. "We're just trying to help Pearl." I stepped sideways, trying to put distance between us, but he matched my movement, advancing into the room.

"Did you send that anonymous text?" I asked, deciding direct confrontation might be my best option. "The one threatening me if I didn't stop investigating?"

A flicker crossed his face. "Text? No. But whoever sent it gave good advice." His hand moved to his pocket. I tensed, unsure what he might be reaching for.

Before he could withdraw whatever it was, Tiki launched herself at his legs.

That one eared, kink-tailed, yowling, twenty-pound calico streak of fury hit his thighs with her claws extended. David let out a startled howl, stumbling backward, as Tiki's claws connected with, and penetrated, his expensive pants.

"What the—hellcat!" he shouted, trying to kick or knock her loose without success. "Get off!"

I seized the opportunity to dart past him. A waft of sandalwood cologne, tainted with sweat, hit my nose. Tiki disengaged as quickly as she'd attacked, racing ahead of me down the hallway toward the entrance.

"Kat Smith!" David yelled after me, voice sharp with anger. "Stay out of our business! This isn't over!"

"It is unless you want serious injury from my cat!" I hollered over my shoulder. I pushed through the front door into the bright afternoon sunlight.

To my surprise, Lei's truck was pulling into the lot at that moment, her cop light flashing on the dash. She opened the door and stepped out, looking ready for action in slim black jeans and a tan cotton blazer. Sunlight winked off the detective shield on her belt. "Pua called and said you sounded excited about something at the community center."

"David Santos, the planning commissioner, is inside," I said. "He threatened me. And I found something—evidence Pearl hid in her origami cranes collection."

"Where is Santos now?" Lei asked, her hand coming to rest on the service weapon at her hip.

As if on cue, Santos emerged from the center, composure restored except for the distinct, blood-spotted claw marks visible on the rumpled chino fabric of his thighs.

He stopped short at the sight of Lei and me talking.

"Detective," he said. "I was just having a conversation with Ms. Smith about proper authorization for accessing park facilities."

"Really?" Lei said. "Because it sounded more like you were threatening her about our investigation into Pearl Yamamoto's attempted murder."

Santos's face remained neutral. "Ms. Smith misunderstood. I was just expressing concern about the dangers of spreading unfounded rumors about respected community members."

"Like your grandfather the war criminal?" I rapped out.

Something dark flickered in his eyes before he masked it with a politician's smile. "I should get back to the office. Permit applications to review." He nodded curtly and moved toward his car, giving Tiki a wide berth. "You're lucky I'm not lodging a complaint with animal control about that dangerous feline."

I rolled my eyes and bit my lip on any further comment—I actually didn't want to have to deal with something like that.

Lei watched the planning commissioner go, her expression

thoughtful. "I'll be following up with that man. Downtown in handcuffs, preferably."

I pulled the tiny drive from my pocket. "I found this hidden in one of Pearl's origami cranes. According to her note, it contains evidence of crimes committed by Felix Santos, David's grandfather, during the war. Crimes the family has been covering up for generations. We should go back inside and collect the cranes as evidence, now that he's out of the room."

"But how did he know you were here?" Lei frowned.

"Good question," I said. "Someone's keeping tabs on my movements. First the threatening text—which might have been him—and now this."

Lei held out her hand. "Let me see that drive. We need to find out exactly what Pearl discovered."

I placed the tiny device in her palm, feeling both relief at sharing the burden and reluctance to give up our key evidence. "We've got more info I haven't had time to update you on that speaks to motive."

Just then, the smoke alarm went off inside the building. A rush of apprehension tightened my gut as Lei and I ran to investigate.

Sure enough, David Santos had burned all of Pearl's carefully constructed cranes in the steel trash can inside the classroom. "Oh no!" I exclaimed. "I didn't even have time to photograph them!"

"At least we still have the drive," Lei said as I dumped a vase of water on the smoldering ash in the can. "Let's go to the Hana police station and see what's on it. And I'll need a statement from you about David's threats. Nice work, by the way," she added, glancing down at Tiki, who was now sitting serenely beside my vehicle as if she hadn't just assaulted a local official.

"Tiki has good instincts about people," I said, bending to stroke her. Tiki turned on a purr that sounded like a motorboat with a bad gas mix and wound around my ankles.

"Better than some humans I know," Lei said. "I'll take this back to the Hana station and see what's on the drive. If there's solid evidence, we might have enough to bring Santos in for questioning."

"I wish I could go with you, but the case has taken enough of my workday," I said regretfully. "Since I've got you though, let me catch you up on what Keone and I uncovered yesterday."

"Anything hard? Because I need something to tie all this historical stuff to the attack on Pearl."

"Afraid not, but it's still important." I filled her in on yesterday's events. "We're gathering quite a cache of motive."

"And it's getting the Santoses moving," Lei said. "Unfortunately, burning those cranes is nothing more than a minor fire violation, but I've got that in my back pocket to charge him with if I have to. Hopefully I find more evidence on the drive. Until next time—keep up the good work, Kat." Her gaze fell to Tiki, sitting at my feet, and an elusive dimple creased her cheek. "And cat."

11

SATURDAY MORNINGS WERE SACRED in my world—the one day a week when I allowed myself the luxury of sleeping past dawn. No postal regulations to enforce, no early mail trucks to meet, no schedule except the one dictated by my own body's need for rest.

At least, that was the theory.

In reality, Saturday mornings in our household involved Tiki's insistence that breakfast should be served at precisely 6:17 a.m., regardless of human preferences. This particular Saturday was no exception.

"Mrrrow."

I kept my eyes firmly shut, clinging to the remnants of a pleasant dream involving Keone, a deserted beach, and absolutely no investigations or postal emergencies.

"Mrrrrrow." The vocalization grew more insistent, accompanied by the gentle but deliberate press of kneading paws on my chest.

"Five more minutes," I mumbled, burrowing deeper into my pillow.

The weight on my chest shifted, and suddenly Tiki settled directly onto my pillow, her whiskers tickling my nose. I cracked one eye to find myself staring directly into an unblinking yellow gaze approximately two inches from my face.

"This is harassment," I informed her.

Tiki responded by placing one paw delicately on my cheek and patting, as if checking whether I was sufficiently awake to fulfill my breakfast-providing duties.

"Fine," I sighed. "But you should know this is an abuse of our relationship."

Tiki arched her back lazily, as if she hadn't been fully awake and pestering me and leapt gracefully from the bed. At the doorway, she paused to ensure I was actually getting up before proceeding downstairs toward the kitchen.

I glanced at the clock: 6:20 AM. "Argh!" At least she was consistent.

Shuffling downstairs in my oversized UH Hilo T-shirt (the same one I'd borrowed from Keone), I found Aunt Fae already at the table, a steaming mug of coffee in one hand and the latest issue of "True Crime Quarterly" in the other.

Aunt Fae had never worn a stitch of makeup ever, and had spent most of her life covered up from the sun in Maine. This was possibly why her skin was soft and smooth, taking a good ten years off her seventy-something age. She kept her salt-and-pepper hair in a no-nonsense bob she trimmed herself with nail scissors. Today she wore her usual outfit, a T-shirt advertising Ohia General Store (where she provided backup help for Opal and Artie) and a pair of jeans.

To me, she was one of the most gorgeous women I'd ever known—inside and out.

"Morning, sunshine," she greeted without looking up from an article that, judging by the visible headline, involved a dismemberment in Delaware. "Your furry alarm clock is right on time."

"Tiki's practicing psychological warfare," I muttered, making a beeline for the coffee pot. "I think she's mad that I didn't come home the other night."

"Cats and grudges," Aunt Fae said. "They go together like peanut butter and jelly."

I poured coffee into my favorite old *Do Not Speak to Me Until this Mug is Empty* cup, a relic from when I'd moved into the shack behind the post office.

I then set about appeasing Tiki with gourmet cat food—the expensive kind that claimed to be "wild-caught sustainable seafood medley" but smelled suspiciously like regular miscellaneous fish parts, but with better marketing.

Misty, a delicate gray tabby with white paws and Tiki's daughter, rose languidly from her basket and came to eat as well. With a much mellower personality than her mother, she seemed to benefit from cruising in her parent's more turbulent wake. With Tiki so firmly claiming me as her human, Misty had attached to Aunt Fae. All of this was part of a harmonious home I was hesitant to break up, even for something as appealing as Mr. K in bed every night.

"Any developments in the investigation into Pearl's poisoning?" Despite her casual tone, I could see genuine concern in Aunt Fae's blue eyes; Pearl was a friend to us both.

"A lot has been happening. I found evidence hidden in Pearl's origami cranes," I said, leaning against the counter as Tiki, after her earlier demands, picked fussily at her breakfast. "A computer drive with documentation about Felix Santos's crimes during the internment period."

Auntie's eyebrows shot up. "In paper cranes? That's a proper use of crafts. I approve."

"I went back to the Hana police station with Lei to have a look at it yesterday, but it was encrypted. Lei has the drive now. She's having the tech department at the main station go through it." I sipped my coffee, savoring the rich warmth as I took a seat beside Auntie. "David Santos confronted me at the cultural center yesterday. It got . . . tense."

"Define 'tense,'" Aunt Fae said, setting down her magazine and going into the kitchen. "This calls for banana bread." She took a loaf off the counter and cut a generous slice for each of us, popping them in the toaster oven.

"I'll sum it up. He made veiled threats, Tiki attacked him, I escaped, and Lei showed up just in time to prevent further escalation."

"Tiki attacked him? That's my girl!" She reached down to offer Tiki an approving scratch, which the cat accepted as her due before returning to her breakfast.

"But the worst thing is, he burned Pearl's cranes. The ones where she'd documented the evidence she'd gathered."

Aunt Fae expression hardened even as the fragrant aroma of warm banana bread surrounded us in a comforting perfume. "This is serious business you're mixed up in. Attempted murder—it's like something straight out of my magazines, except it's happening to my niece."

"I'm being careful," I said.

"Hmm. Is 'careful' what we're calling breaking into museums after-hours now?"

I choked on my coffee. "How did you—"

"Pua called looking for you yesterday evening," Aunt Fae explained with a mischievous twinkle. "She mentioned something about whether I thought it was hypocritical of you to scold her for breaking into your office when you'd done the same thing at the museum."

"Someone must have seen Keone and me," I muttered. "Dang it."

"I assured her that ethical consistency is overrated when solving this kind of case," Aunt Fae said cheerfully. "Besides, I was the one who taught you how not to need keys. Remember that time we got locked out of our Maine cabin during a snowstorm?"

"You told me it was an essential life skill," I said, smiling despite irritation with Pua's tattling. "And that particular time it was."

"Wasn't I right?" She grinned. "Look how handy it's been for your Secret Service, then criminal investigation career!"

"But I'm a postal worker now."

"A postal worker who solves crimes in her spare time," Aunt Fae said. "I rest my case."

Before I could formulate a suitably witty retort, my phone rang from somewhere in my bedroom upstairs. "That's probably Keone," I said, heading toward the stairs. "We're supposed to go hiking today if nothing breaks in the investigation."

"Tell him I've got extra banana bread if he wants to stop by for breakfast first," Aunt Fae called after me. "And home cured bacon from the Namura family."

"He wouldn't want to miss that!"

But my phone's screen showed not Keone's name, but Lei's. A call from the detective this early on a Saturday made my heart speed up. "Lei? What's happened?"

"As you may have heard, Pearl was moved back to our Maui hospital. She woke up briefly today, around four a.m." Lei's voice was clipped, professional, but I could hear the underlying strain. "Someone tried to get to her. Kawika, her caregiver, was attacked."

"What? Is he okay? Is Pearl safe?" My heart had jumped so hard I lay a hand on my chest.

"Pearl's safe. Kawika has a concussion. I'm at the hospital now. I need you and Keone to come out as soon as you can."

"We'll be there ASAP," I promised, already moving to my dresser to grab clothing. "Maybe Keone can fly us out—you know how long the drive takes. What exactly happened?"

"Pearl regained consciousness briefly and managed to say a few words to Kawika. Then someone hit him. He came around quickly though and was able to give me a call."

"And Pearl?" I asked, my heart racing.

"Unharmed. The nurses had just given her scheduled medication, so she was drifting back to sleep when the attack occurred. She's sedated now, and I have a uniform outside the door."

"Did Kawika say what Pearl told him?"

"Something about '1942' and 'crane box.' Does that mean anything to you?"

"1942 was when the processing center was operating on her family's land," I said, quickly pulling on jeans while holding the phone against my shoulder. "And the crane box is what we've been looking for—a sandalwood box with a crane carved on it that supposedly contains her father's journal."

"Well, now we know it's important enough for someone to risk attacking a man in a hospital to prevent him from sharing what Pearl said." Lei's voice hardened. "I've got officers stationed outside Pearl's room. No one gets in without clearance."

"We'll be there in a couple of hours unless Keone can fly us," I said, hunting for a clean shirt. "In which case it'll be a lot sooner. Have you called him?"

"Keone's next up. I wanted to reach you first."

"Thanks, Lei. We'll be there as soon as we can." I ended the call and quickly finished dressing, my mind racing.

Pearl had woken up—that was the good news. But someone had been watching and waiting for precisely that moment—and had tried to silence her again by coming at her caregiver.

Returning to the kitchen, I found Aunt Fae and Tiki waiting for me expectantly. I quickly told them about Lei's call.

"Good lord. The Santos family isn't messing around, are they?" Aunt Fae scowled. "I never liked either of those men. Just a little too slick, and not just their hair pomade."

"We don't know who it was," I cautioned. "But Lei has officers guarding Pearl now."

"You be careful," Aunt Fae said firmly. "And take this for Kawika." She handed me a wrapped loaf of banana bread as well as the slices she'd toasted for me. "Hospital food is terrible."

I accepted the bread. Trust Aunt Fae to think of comfort food in a crisis. "I'll call you with updates," I promised, heading for the door.

Tiki trotted after me. "Oh no, you don't," I told the cat firmly.

"Hospital security is tight enough without trying to smuggle in a cat." Tiki sat, wrapping her tail around her paws, and fixed me with a look that suggested she would magnanimously allow me to go without feline supervision this time. "I'll be back soon," I told her. "Keep an eye on the house for me." Addressing her like this had stopped feeling silly a long time ago.

As I got into Sharkey, as I'd nicknamed my white SUV, I called Keone. He had already heard from Lei.

"Meet me at the Hana airport," he said. "We'll take the project plane to Kahului."

"That's what I was hoping you'd say." Keone had a tiny three-seater personal aircraft he'd built himself from a kit. I'd ridden all the way to Oahu in it and lived to tell the tale. "That'll shave off a few hours."

I put the pedal down for max speed to the airport; fortunately the famously windy and narrow Road to Hana was deserted this early on a Saturday morning. The sun was climbing higher, casting long shadows across the tarmac and illuminating the ocean and lush greenery that lined the coastal highway. This was the kind of perfect Hawaiian morning that normally would have me feeling grateful and peaceful.

Instead, all I could think about were the few words Pearl had said—"1942" and "crane box."

What old secrets were hidden there that someone would risk attempted murder, twice now, to keep buried?

THE MAUI MEMORIAL Medical Center was bustling with activity when we arrived in a rideshare from the airport and hurried inside.

At the information desk, I identified myself to an officer I recognized from community events—Officer Palakiko, a young Hawaiian man whose usual friendly demeanor looked strained. "Detective Texeira is expecting you two. I need to see ID though."

We showed our IDs. "ICU, third floor," the officer directed.

The elevator ride to the third floor seemed interminable, but holding Keone's hand made it better. When the doors opened, I could see Lei and an officer in conversation through the glass windows of a small waiting area.

"How's Kawika?" I asked Lei as we approached.

"Conscious but hurting," Lei answered, joining us. "Doctor says he has a concussion and needed stitches where he was struck. He's in the room next to Pearl's, under guard as well."

"Can I speak to him?" I asked.

Lei nodded. "Briefly. I was about to get his official statement."

We followed Lei down the corridor to a private room where another officer stood at attention. Inside, Kawika lay propped against pillows, a large bandage visible. His normally robust complexion was pale, but he managed a smile as we entered.

"The investigative team arrives," he said, his voice hoarse. "Sorry about the dramatic summoning."

"Save your strength, cuz," Keone said, moving to stand beside the bed. "Lei said you spoke to Pearl before the attack?"

Lei took out her phone. "I'm going to record this for your statement, okay?"

Kawika nodded, then winced at the movement. "Yes. Okay." He sighed and closed his eyes. "Pearl opened her eyes around four a.m. I was half asleep in the chair beside her bed. At first, I thought I was dreaming when I heard her."

"What exactly did she say?" Lei asked.

"She seemed confused, like she wasn't sure where she was. I told her she was in the hospital, that she'd drunk some tea that was tampered with. She got agitated then, tried to sit up." He paused, gathering his strength. "She grabbed my hand and said, 'The truth is in the crane box. 1942. They'll destroy it.'"

"Did she say who 'they' were?" Lei asked.

Kawika shook his head, then groaned at the movement. "I asked her, but she was fading. The last thing she said was, 'Protected the land once. Will again.'"

"That's when you called Lei?" I asked.

"Yes. I stepped into the hall to make the call—didn't want to disturb Pearl. After, I stepped back into the room. That's the last thing I remember clearly." Kawika frowned. "Someone must have been watching, waiting for Pearl to wake up. They heard me on the phone and acted quickly."

"The security footage confirms that someone in scrubs and a surgical mask entered Pearl's room right after Kawika stepped out. Can't make out details or gender, even. The camera angle doesn't show the attack itself, but based on timing, they must have followed Kawika back into the room and struck him from behind." She refocused on Kawika. "Did you recognize anything about your attacker? Height, build, anything distinctive?"

He closed his eyes briefly, concentrating. "I never saw them. But I remember . . . a smell. Right before I was knocked out. Something distinctive."

"What kind of smell?" Lei was making a handwritten note on a small spiral pad.

"Sandalwood," Kawika said, opening his eyes. "Strong. A cologne or aftershave."

"Did the security cameras catch the person leaving?" Lei asked.

"Yes, but they kept their head down and face turned away from the cameras. They knew where the cameras were positioned." Lei's full lips firmed into a line. "They were waiting for Pearl to regain consciousness."

"Which means they have someone at the hospital keeping them informed," I said. "An inside source."

"I've thought of that," Lei said. "I've restricted access to Pearl's medical information by having her name changed in the computer. I've switched out the security detail to officers from outside— people with no ties to Hana or the Santos family."

Kawika shifted uncomfortably, his face tightening with pain. "What about the crane box? Do you know what Pearl meant?"

I explained what we'd learned about the sandalwood box carved with a crane that supposedly contained Takeo Yamamoto's journal documenting Felix Santos's crimes during the internment period.

"That's why I brought you and Keone out here," Lei said. "I wanted to speak in person and tell you we need to find that evidence before anyone else does. I've turned the drive over to our tech department, but I'm worried there's something specific in that box that's crucial."

A nurse appeared in the doorway, her expression making it clear that our time with Kawika was up. "Mr. Pali needs rest," she said firmly. "Doctor's orders."

Kawika looked ready to protest, but pain was evident in every line of his face. "Find the box," he said as we prepared to leave. "Pearl risked everything to protect that evidence. Don't let it be for nothing."

"We won't," I promised. "You focus on recovering." I remembered the loaf of banana bread, extracted it from my backpack, and placed it on his bedside table. "From Aunt Fae. She says hospital food is terrible for healing."

The ghost of a smile crossed his face. "Wise woman. Tell her thanks."

As we left Kawika's room, Lei led us to an empty waiting area where we could speak privately. "I've got officers canvassing the hospital staff who were on duty last night, trying to identify our fake nurse," she explained. "My gut tells me we're dealing with a professional, possibly hired help."

"The Santos family has connections," Keone said. "And they're not the type to do their own dirty work."

"Except for David," I said. "He was willing to confront me personally at the cultural center and burn those cranes. And what about Pearl?" I asked Lei. "Can we see her?"

Lei shook her head. "Doctors have her sedated for now. They say the brief period of consciousness is a positive sign, but they want to keep her calm and monitored."

"We'll focus on finding the crane box," Keone concluded. "Any ideas where to start?"

"Pearl's house," I suggested. "We've already searched the cultural center. The logical place for something that personal would be her home."

"Did you search the house, Lei?" Keone asked.

Lei nodded. "I have a warrant and I did a quick sweep, looking for anything that spoke to motive. Took all her teas and medicines into evidence to make sure they weren't tampered with. But I never found a crane box."

"Then that's our next stop," I said.

"I have to stay on this side of the island," Lei said. "But I'll get you authorized to do a more careful search out at her property."

As Lei made the call, Keone pulled me aside, his expression serious. "Kat, we need to be careful. Whoever attacked Kawika won't hesitate to come after us if they think we're close to finding the box."

"I know. But we can't back off now."

"Just promise me you'll stay close," he said, his eyes holding mine. "No solo heroics."

I decided not to remind him I was the former Secret Service agent trained for combat; he was feeling protective, and it was sweet. "Same goes for you," I replied, squeezing his hand. "We're in this together."

Lei rejoined us, tucking her phone away. "Officer Mahelona will meet you at Pearl's house. He's been instructed to give you full access and assistance."

"Thanks, Lei," I said. "Any word on the drive's contents?"

"Too early yet." Lei's wildly curly hair was escaping its ponytail. She pulled an elastic band off her wrist and bundled it tighter on top of her head. "I've put a rush on it, but it might be hours before we know what's on there."

"Then we focus on the crane box," I said. We took a further moment to fill her in on our research at the museum and discovery of the military ID hidden under the plumeria tree.

"This is all pointing to motive and something larger in play, but I still don't have anything hard I can act on," Lei said. "Keep me updated. And watch your backs. Whoever did this is still out there, and they're getting bolder."

12

PEARL'S BEACH house looked different to me by the time we got back to Hana in Keone's tiny plane and then drove to Ohia. The lush, peaceful gardens seemed to hide shadows as we approached, while the ocean breeze carried chill whispers. I bit my lip, using the tiny pain to remind myself not to get too fanciful.

Officer Mahelona, Lei's contact, met us at the front door. His imposing uniformed frame blocked the entrance until he verified our identities. Young but serious, he had the hypervigilant demeanor of someone determined not to let anything happen on his watch. "Detective Texeira briefed me," he said, stepping aside to let us enter. "Full access to the house, but I'm to stay with you to protect the chain of evidence retrieval."

"Understood," Keone said, with a nod of professional respect as all three of us donned latex gloves. "We're looking for a specific item. A wooden box with a crane carving. Likely sandalwood, probably old."

"Size?" Mahelona asked.

"Small enough to hide," I said. "Maybe the size of a jewelry box or a thick book."

The interior of the house was immaculate, showing Kawika's careful attention during Pearl's absence. Everything seemed precisely arranged, from the stack of gardening magazines on the coffee table to the row of orchids blooming serenely on the windowsill.

"Where should we start?" I asked, feeling overwhelmed by the tall cabinets and packed shelves. Pearl had lived in this house for decades. A small box could be hidden anywhere.

Keone tipped his head back and closed his eyes, musing. "If I were hiding something important, I'd want it close, but not obvious. Somewhere I could access it or check on it regularly without drawing attention."

"Her bedroom," I decided. "Let's start there."

Pearl's bedroom was as meticulously kept as the rest of the house. The four-poster bed was made with hospital corners, a colorful silken spread smoothly draped across it. Family photographs lined the dresser—Pearl as a young woman with her parents, Pearl at her teaching retirement ceremony, Pearl with various groups of students over the years, Pearl with her husband.

I started with the dresser drawers, carefully pulling out and examining each one without disturbing the perfectly folded contents. Nothing seemed unusual or out of place. Keone checked the large walk-in closet.

Officer Mahelona checked beneath the bed and behind the headboard, his movements efficient. "Nothing here," he reported.

We expanded our search to the en suite bathroom, the hall closet, the guest bedroom. Each space yielded nothing but more evidence of Pearl's organized, purposeful life.

"This isn't working," I said after an hour. "We're thinking too conventionally. Pearl is cleverer than this."

"You're right," Keone agreed, rubbing the back of his neck. "She hid evidence in origami cranes. She wouldn't just stick the box in a cabinet."

"But we know she used to keep it in her desk. Before it held important evidence. So it's probably here in the house." I stood in the center of the living room, trying to think like Pearl. "If I had a precious family heirloom containing evidence that could destroy a powerful family, where would I keep it?"

My eyes swept the room, taking in details I'd overlooked before: traditional Japanese calligraphy scrolls on the walls. A collection of ceramic figures arranged on a shelf. The small Buddhist shrine in the corner with incense holders and a photograph of Pearl's parents.

"The shrine. It's perfect." I moved toward the elevated table in the corner. On top sat a framed photograph of Pearl's parents and husband, incense holders, and a small bell. What I had initially taken to be a decorative base was a wooden rectangle marked with intricate carving.

"That's it," I breathed, kneeling on the low padded bench before the shrine. I removed the items atop the box carefully and set them aside. Then I removed the sandalwood box and held it, examining the exterior as Keone and Officer Mahelona came close to observe.

The sandalwood's rich reddish color had deepened with age and regular handling. The top was carved with an exquisite flying crane, wings outstretched in flight, every feather detailed with remarkable craftsmanship. It was heavier than it looked, suggesting contents beyond the merely ceremonial.

The box didn't have a conventional closure, but rather a clever wooden sliding mechanism that required a specific sequence to open. I examined it carefully, noting worn spots where fingers had pressed over many years.

"May I?" Keone asked, extending his hands.

I passed him the box. He turned it with his fingers exploring the mechanism with sensitivity. "It's a Japanese puzzle box," he explained. "My grandfather had one. You have to slide the panels in the right sequence."

His fingers moved deliberately across the box, sliding small sections of wood in a pattern that seemed random to my untrained

eye but clearly followed some internal logic. After some manipula-
tion, there was a soft click, and the top panel shifted slightly.

"Got it," Keone said, gently sliding the top open.

Inside, nestled in faded silk, lay a small leatherbound journal,
its cover cracked with age and handling. Beside it was a folded
document that looked like a map or diagram, and a small cloth
pouch tied with a faded red cord.

"This is it," I said softly. "Takeo Yamamoto's journal."

Keone carefully lifted the journal from the box, handling it with
the reverence it deserved. He opened it to reveal pages filled with
neat Japanese characters interspersed with sections in English.

"I can't read the Japanese parts," he said after a minute of scanning, "but the English sections seem to be Takeo's observations
about the processing center."

I leaned closer, reading over his shoulder:

"*August 12, 1942 - Tanaka-san confronted Santos today about the
missing family ceremonial sword. Santos claimed all confiscated items
were documented and would be returned after the war, but I have seen
his private collection growing. When Tanaka-san demanded proof of
documentation, Santos ordered him removed from the mess hall. Later, I
heard shouting near the storage buildings. When I investigated, I saw
Santos strike Tanaka and push him. He fell to the bottom of the loading
dock stairs. When I called for help, Santos claimed he had fallen, but
there was blood on Santos's uniform cuff that he quickly covered.*

Tanaka-san died an hour later without regaining consciousness."

"This is direct eyewitness testimony of Felix Santos's involvement in Tanaka's death," Keone said grimly. "No wonder the family
was desperate to prevent this from coming to light."

I continued reading the next entry:

"*August 13, 1942 - During the confusion after Tanaka-san's death, I
managed to retrieve several items from Santos's private collection in his
office—a list of 'confiscated' valuables with their estimated worth, and
Santos's military ID which he lost during the struggle with Tanaka-san. I
have hidden these items where they will be safe until they can serve as*

evidence of his crimes. If anything happens to me, this journal will guide my family to the truth."

"The ID tag we found under the plumeria tree," I said. "Takeo took it as evidence. But we didn't find any list."

"Maybe whoever was digging under the tree before us got it first," Keone said. "Let's see what else is in here." He unfolded the document that had been stored alongside the journal.

It was indeed a map—a detailed drawing of the Yamamoto property showing the original Japanese garden, the processing center buildings that had been erected during the war, and various landmarks, including the plumeria tree. Small 'X' marks with dates appeared at several locations around the property.

I whipped out my phone and took photos of everything. "He buried evidence in multiple spots," I exclaimed. "The ID tag was just one piece."

"Look at this," Keone said, pointing to a notation near what was now Pearl's garden shed. *"August 15, 1942 – Full inventory list and photographic evidence."*

"We need to check that location," I said, excitement building. "If the full inventory still exists—"

"It would prove systematic theft, not just isolated incidents," Keone finished.

"And we could get those items back to the families who lost them," I said.

"This box is a treasure trove of evidence," Keone said, carefully returning the items to their places. "Not just about historical wrongs, but about the motive for Pearl's poisoning."

I closed the box reverently, the puzzle mechanism clicking back into place. "We need to get this to Lei immediately."

"I'll get an evidence bag and take it to the station once backup arrives," Officer Mahelona said, reaching for his radio. "Something this important shouldn't travel without proper security."

As he stepped away, my phone buzzed with an incoming text. It was from Pua: *"Ok, I did it again. I'm at your house. Aunt Fae and I* steamed open Pearl's letter. Seriously, you need to see this. Historical Preservation Society confirms grant for Tea Garden BUT it's cc'd to Councilman Akana as project sponsor. Thought Ilima was sponsor? Something is weird here."

I showed the message to Keone. "Why would Councilman Akana be listed as the project sponsor for Pearl's garden? I thought Ilima was handling the political side of things."

"Good question," Keone replied, his expression thoughtful. "Akana is on Ilima's campaign team, right? The third member alongside Pearl?"

"Yes, but he's been pretty much in the background. We haven't heard much about his involvement with the garden project specifically." I typed a quick reply to Pua: "Hold the letter. Coming to see it soon. Don't mention to anyone else."

I called Lei directly to brief her on what we'd found in the crane box. Her reaction was measured but optimistic. "This could be what we need," she said. "The journal provides motive, and the map might lead us to even more evidence. Good work, both of you."

"There's something else," I said, explaining Pua's message about Councilman Akana being listed as the project sponsor on the historical preservation grant.

"Interesting," Lei's voice took on a thoughtful tone. "Akana's been pushing for development in the area for years. His construction connections are well-known."

"Could he have his own motives for wanting to control the Heritage Garden project?"

"It's worth looking into," Lei said. "Follow that lead. I have to focus on preparing for Mayor Santos's interview. He's not going to be happy to be called in; lawyers are bound to be involved."

Backup arrived. The crane box was carefully logged as evidence, placed in a protective container, and taken away with the solemnity it deserved by Officer Mahelona and his partner.

"Let's get to my house," I said to Keone as we watched the police cruisers disappear down the driveway. "I want to see that letter myself."

THE HOUSE WAS quiet when we arrived. Aunt Fae and Pua sat in loungers out on the back deck. "Finally!" Pua exclaimed. "I've been sitting on this all morning. It came in yesterday's late delivery."

"Well hello to you, too," I said, joining the two older women as Keone paused on his way to the kitchen to get us drinks. Tiki and Misty ambled out from under the potted palms to circle my ankles in greeting. "This looks comfy."

"Except for the reason I'm here." Pua produced an official-looking envelope with the Hawaii Historical Preservation Society logo from her Chanel bag. The letter had been opened—a fact I chose not to comment on, given my own recent adventures in ethical flexibility.

The letter was indeed a grant confirmation for the Heritage Tea Garden project, allocating $250,000 for the initial phase of plans development. What caught my attention immediately was the recipient line: "*Project Sponsors: Pearl Yamamoto and Councilman Roger Akana.*"

"Why is Akana listed as cosponsor?" I wondered aloud.

Keone had arrived with a tray bearing four glasses of lilikoi juice tinkling with ice. He set it down and we each grabbed one. I handed him the letter.

He read as I guzzled the tart-sweet drink. "Look at this paragraph: '*As discussed in our meeting on May 15, the revised project scope will incorporate elements of the proposed Hana Cultural Corridor, creating synergy between the Heritage Tea Garden and future development projects in adjacent areas.*'"

"Cultural Corridor?" I echoed. "I've never heard of that."

"I have," Pua said. "It's Councilman Akana's pet project. A planned development that would create a tourist-friendly 'cultural experience' along the coast, with shops, restaurants, and an exclusive thematic resort."

Keone and I exchanged a glance. "Seems like Akana has been positioning himself to incorporate Pearl's garden into his larger development plan," Mr. K said.

"And without Pearl's knowledge," I added. "She's been fighting for this garden as a memorial to internment victims, not as part of a commercial tourist attraction."

"We need to know more about Akana's connection to all this," I said. "Pua, thanks for flagging this, even though it's against regulations to have opened that letter, obviously. I've let Lei know he might be involved after you texted me. We have to be careful. Akana's got a long reach, just like Santos. Let's keep this between us. No coconut wireless updates, please."

"My lips are sealed." Pua was clearly thrilled to be part of the investigation. She made a zipping gesture beside her mouth, turning an imaginary key.

Keone checked his watch, a fancy thing with multiple dials, a compass, and an altimeter. I'd given it to him for his birthday and seeing it on his wrist still gave me a little *ping!* of happiness. "We should call Lei and update her soon, but I want to swing by the general store. If anyone knows the local gossip about Akana's development plans besides you, Pua, it's Opal and Artie."

"Good thinking," I agreed.

"Grab me some of their weekend malasadas while you're at it," Aunt Fae hollered at our departing backs.

"You got it!" I said over my shoulder.

"If we don't eat them all first," Keone said out of the side of his mouth, and I elbowed him affectionately.

ARTIE AND OPAL'S General Store was busy with the Saturday late lunch crowd when we arrived. The food service area was filled with tourists and locals enjoying lunch and buying drinks and ice cream. Opal held court near the crystal counter, apparently reading runes for a circle of brightly dressed tourists.

We waited for a break in the traffic and when it had cleared out a bit, we approached Artie. "Kitty Kat!" Even blind, Artie always seemed to be able to recognize me coming.

"Keone and I would like some malasadas," I said.

"And some of your *mana'o* wisdom," Keone added.

"Malasadas are gone, but you can help me restock the chili and cornbread special and I'll try give the other," Artie said. We followed him into the back of the store, where a small pass-through storage room led into the Pahinui's kitchen.

Once inside the cozy, yummy-smelling kitchen area, Artie said, "Opal can deal with any stragglers out there." He closed the connecting door to afford some privacy. "Must be serious."

"It is," Keone said. "We need information about Councilman Akana's development plans. Specifically, anything you folks know about something called the Hana Cultural Corridor."

Artie's eyebrows shot up and he blinked rheumy eyes. "Now there's a controversial topic. Councilman Akana's been trying to get that project off the ground for years. Most locals are against it—too commercial, too much traffic for Hana and Ohia. But he's persistent."

"What exactly is he proposing?" I asked.

"A 'cultural experience' along the coast," Artie explained, making air quotes around the euphemism. "Shops, restaurants, cultural demonstration areas—all designed to look 'authentically Hawaiian' while being commercial."

"Where exactly would this corridor be located?" Keone asked. I suspected we both knew the answer.

"It would start just south of Pearl's property and extend up the coast," Artie confirmed. "Originally, he wanted to include her land, but she refused to sell. That's when he shifted to a partnership approach, trying to convince her that her Heritage Garden could be the 'cultural anchor' for the larger development, which would include the Santoses' five-acre parcel she wants for the garden."

"And she agreed to this?" I asked skeptically.

"Ha!" Artie snorted. "Pearl was adamant that her garden would be a place of reflection and education, not a tourist trap."

"So why is he listed as cosponsor on her historical preservation grant?" Keone asked.

Artie's expression registered surprise, then he frowned. "Ah, now I see where this is going. Akana sits on the board of the Historical Preservation Society. He could have influenced the grant process, perhaps even modified the application."

"Without Pearl's knowledge," I said. "Except someone issued her a letter disclosing it. That's how we found out."

"It wouldn't be the first time Akana's operated that way," Artie said. "His development company, Anuenue Enterprises, has a reputation for aggressive tactics. They've bought up several properties along that stretch of coastline over the past decade, sometimes using questionable methods."

"Questionable how?" I asked.

Artie glanced toward the door, lowering his voice further. "There have been rumors about properties experiencing 'mysterious' problems just before Anuenue makes an offer. Water line breaks, electrical issues, vandalism, even a stream drying up in a pasture."

"Definitely sounds shady," Keone said.

"There's one more thing you should know. Anuenue Enterprises doesn't operate alone. They have a financial partner that provides much of their capital—Santos Investment Group."

The connection hit like a thunderbolt. "Mayor Santos's family investment company," I said. "Of course."

"The Santos and Akana families have been business partners for decades. The mayor's father and Akana's father started working together in the 1960s, developing some of the first tourist accommodations in Hana."

"That means we have two families with historical connections," Mr. K summarized, "both with financial interests that would be threatened by Pearl's garden project, both with motives for wanting to control or stop it."

"And both with connections to the historical injustices Pearl was preparing to expose," I added.

"I'm just sharing what I've heard," Artie said, spreading his hands. "What you do with that information is up to you."

"That's why we came to you, Uncle Artie," I said, and gave him a kiss on the cheek. "This helps a lot."

We helped Artie carry a fresh pan of cornbread and hot pot of chili out to restock the lunch counter after hastily packing a ration for ourselves to take back to the shack to eat while we updated Lei.

"We need to look into Anuenue Enterprises and its connection to the Santos Investment Group," Keone said as we neared the shack and set our lunch on the rickety table. "If Akana and the Santos family are business partners, they could both have motives for stopping Pearl's project."

"But which one poisoned her?" I wondered. "Or are they working together?"

"That's what we need to find out," Keone said.

We sat down and hastily consumed our to-go bowls of chili and hot buttered sides of cornbread. Once the needs of the body were taken care of and my teeth had been brushed, I called Lei on the landline and put her on speaker. "It's Kat and Keone checking in," I said. "We have new information about Councilman Akana's connection to all this."

"Interesting timing," Lei replied. "Akana just called asking to be present during Mayor Santos's interview, claiming 'community interest.' I denied the request, of course."

"They're working together," I said. "Akana and Santos are business partners. There's a financial connection between their families going back decades."

"Talk fast," she instructed. "Mayor Santos is waiting in the interview room, and I don't want to give him time to get comfortable."

We quickly briefed her on everything we'd learned from the letter, Artie, and our earlier discoveries at Pearl's house.

"We have two potential suspects," Lei summarized. "Mayor Santos, with a historical motive to suppress evidence of his grandfather's crimes, and Councilman Akana, with a financial motive to control Pearl's property for his development plans. And they're business partners."

"Which complicates determining who actually poisoned Pearl," Keone noted. "Though we still don't know who could have been at Pearl's premises the day of the tea party."

"Meanwhile, the tech department has broken the encryption on the thumb drive you found in the origami crane. It contains financial records—documentation of payments from Anuenue Enterprises to various officials over the past five years."

"That's hard evidence!" I exclaimed.

"Not quite," Lei said.

"Bribes?" Keone interjected.

"Let me finish. The payments are labeled as 'consulting fees' but the timing corresponds to key zoning decisions and permit approvals. Pearl was documenting modern corruption, not just historical crimes."

"Which gives both Santos and Akana motive to silence her," I said.

"I'm going to interview Santos now. I will live stream the interview via button cam to you, through our phones. Your knowledge of the case might help you spot things I miss."

"Thanks for including us, Lei," I said fervently.

I didn't ask if this was protocol for a police interview because I was pretty sure it wasn't.

WE FOLLOWED LEI'S PERSPECTIVE, watching on my phone in a slightly fish-eyed distortion view, as she walked into the interview room. Mayor Santos sat stiffly in a chair at a shiny metal table, his coiffed salt-and-pepper hair a little wilted, his face shiny. Apparently, the air-conditioning wasn't working. Beside him sat a sleek blonde woman in an expensive suit—his attorney, based on the protective way she leaned toward him.

Lei set a folder on the table before taking a seat across from Santos.

"Thank you for coming in, Mayor," she began. "This is an informal interview. You're not under arrest, and you're free to leave at any time, as your attorney has surely advised you."

The lawyer nodded. "My client is here voluntarily to assist your investigation in any way he can. We understand a respected community member has been harmed, and naturally, the mayor wants to help resolve the matter."

"Naturally," Lei echoed, her tone neutral. "Let's start with your relationship with Pearl Yamamoto. Tell us about that."

Santos shifted slightly in his seat. "Pearl and I have known each other for many years. We've had our disagreements on certain community matters, but I've always respected her dedication to education and cultural preservation."

"These disagreements," Lei said. "They wouldn't happen to involve her Heritage Tea Garden project, would they?"

"I have expressed concerns about the project's scope and potential impact on traffic patterns," Santos said. "But these were professional disagreements, nothing personal."

"Nothing personal," Lei said. "Even though the garden was specifically designed to commemorate the Japanese internment period, including events involving your grandfather, Felix Santos?"

A muscle twitched in the mayor's jaw, but his expression remained neutral. "Ancient history is rarely relevant to modern civic planning, Ms. Texeira."

"You can call me Detective Sergeant Texeira, thank you. What about Pearl's request that you donate the five-acre lot adjoining hers as part of the garden? A piece of land that, according to records we've uncovered, was taken from her family by your grandfather for a fraction of its worth."

"I told Pearl the lot was not available as a donation," Santos said. "However loudly she played the guilt fiddle." He ran a finger around his buttoned collar, tugging at it. "Can you adjust the temperature in here?"

"I apologize, Mayor, the air-conditioning is out in this section of the building," Lei said smoothly. "Let's move forward quickly so we can get you out of here." She flipped open the folder. Keone and I leaned forward, and our heads bonked; we were looking at a series of Lei's handwritten notes, nothing more. "Now, some evidence has come to light regarding your ancestor, Felix Santos. Apparently, according to historical records, he didn't just swindle the Yamamotos out of their land. He stole valuable items from other detainees and was involved with a homicide."

The attorney leaned forward. "Detective, is there a specific question here? My client cannot be held responsible for unsubstantiated rumors about events that allegedly occurred over eighty years ago."

"Of course," Lei said. "I'm more interested in his response to evidence of those events being made public now. Perhaps through Pearl Yamamoto's garden project and the educational materials she was preparing."

"I have no control over Ms. Yamamoto's educational materials," Santos said stiffly. "But I will take prompt legal action to prevent slander such as you're describing."

"That tells me you have a significant interest in preventing certain historical revelations," Lei said. "Revelations that might damage not only your family's reputation, but your reelection campaign."

"This is absurd," the attorney interjected. "A fishing expedition."

"I'm simply exploring motives that might tie the mayor, or his son, who is, coincidentally, on the planning commission, to the attack on Ms. Yamamoto," Lei said. "Let's just say there's a lot there. Now let's discuss your business relationship with Councilman Roger Akana. Tell me about that."

The sudden change of direction clearly caught Santos off guard. He blinked rapidly before regaining his composure. "Councilman Akana and I have several mutual business interests, as do many community leaders."

"Specifically, through Santos Investment Group's partnership with Anuenue Enterprises," Lei clarified. "A partnership that has financial interests in developing the coastal area near Pearl Yamamoto's property."

"All completely legitimate business arrangements," the attorney piped up.

"Though I'm curious about a series of payments from Anuenue Enterprises to various officials, documented in files recently discovered in Pearl's possession. Payments that coincide with favorable zoning decisions for your joint projects."

Santos paled visibly and unbuttoned his collar. "I'm not involved in the day-to-day operations of Santos Investment Group. You would need to speak with our financial officers about any specific transactions."

"I intend to," Lei said. "But first, I'd like to know where you were on the morning Pearl Yamamoto was poisoned."

"This is becoming an interrogation," the attorney protested.

"It's a simple question," Lei countered. "One an innocent man should have no trouble answering."

Santos cleared his throat. "I was at a breakfast meeting with the tourism board just outside Ohia. From 7:30 until approximately 9:45 a.m."

"Interesting," Lei said. "Because Pearl was poisoned during that window of time, according to medical estimates. Her house is less than ten minutes from there."

"Are you suggesting I slipped away from a meeting with a dozen witnesses to poison an elderly woman's tea in front of even more people?" Santos asked incredulously. "I heard she drank the bad tea at a social gathering."

"I'm suggesting it would have been physically possible," Lei said. "Just as it would have been possible for you to hire someone else to do it."

The attorney stood abruptly. "This interview is over. My client has cooperated fully, but I won't allow these unfounded accusations to continue."

Lei remained seated, her expression calm. "One more question before you go, Mayor Santos. Where were you at approximately 4:15 a.m. this morning?"

Santos froze halfway to standing. "What?"

"This morning," Lei repeated. "Around 4:15 a.m.. Pearl Yamamoto regained consciousness briefly and spoke to her caretaker, Kawika Pali, whereupon someone attacked Mr. Pali in Pearl's hospital room. I'm wondering if you can account for your whereabouts during that time."

"I was at home, asleep," Santos said, his voice strained. "As any normal person would be at that hour."

"Can anyone verify that?" Lei pressed.

"My wife," Santos replied. "Not that I need an alibi for something I had nothing to do with."

Lei nodded, closing her folder. "Thank you for your time, Mayor Santos. We'll be in touch if we have further questions."

As Santos and his attorney left the interview room, Keone and I gazed at each other, eyes wide. "She rattled him," Keone said. "Especially with that last question about this morning."

Lei called us a moment later. "He's definitely hiding something, but I'm not convinced he's our poisoner."

"What about the hospital attack?" I asked.

"The timing doesn't quite work," she said. "We have security footage of the hospital parking lot. No vehicle matching Santos's entered between 3:30 and 5:00 a.m., nor were there any suspects entering matching his physical description."

"That means either he has an accomplice, or . . ."

"Or Councilman Akana might be more directly involved than we initially thought," Lei finished. "Or the mayor's son, David. I need to bring him in for questioning next, but I don't have enough cause. Let's keep digging."

We ended the call.

I stood up, stretching to my full height. I wiggled my whole body to discharge the tension collected in my muscles. "I need exercise. This has been the most intense 'day off' I've had in a while."

Keone stood and stretched as well. I admired the slice of tanned, toned abs revealed when his shirt rode up. "We could go over to the beach for a swim, or . . . perhaps . . .?" He glanced meaningfully at the Murphy bed attached to the wall and raised a brow.

I smiled, slow and catlike, channeling Tiki at her most feral. I leaned forward over the table, letting my cleavage (what there was of it) do the talking. "I'll take the 'or perhaps,' Mr. K," I said. "And it better be a workout."

WELL, we broke the old Murphy bed.

Yep, that happened. The thing was long past its expiration date, but still—that was a dramatic finish to our afternoon delight.

After laughing our butts off when we landed naked on the floor, there was nothing for it but to throw on our suits and go for a cool-off swim in the ocean. By the time we'd swum laps, come back to the shack and showered, we were both feeling hungry—the chili hadn't made much of a dent in our healthy young appetites.

"Where should we get food?" I asked. "I require sustenance."

"Me too. Maybe Aunt Fae is cooking as we speak," Keone said optimistically.

"Anyone but me in the kitchen," I said.

He moved in for a kiss. "I'll take you in the kitchen," he murmured in my ear.

Suddenly, the K & K landline rang.

I glanced over at the ID screen and frowned. "It's your mom. Why would she be calling here?"

"This can't be good," Keone said, and lunged for the handset.

13

"Mom?" Keone said, as he picked up the phone and hit Speaker. "Everything okay?"

"No," Ilima's voice was tight with tension. "Someone just called my home phone. A disguised voice—you know, one of those nasty distorter things? They told me to drop out of the mayoral race if I 'know what's good for me and my family.'"

"Hi, Ilima. You're on speakerphone," I said as my skin prickled with alarm. "When exactly did this happen?"

"Less than five minutes ago," Ilima said. "I tried calling Sergeant Texeira, but her phone went to voicemail. Neither of you were picking up your phones—again! That's why I called your office."

"Listen, Mom, this is serious. Is anyone with you?" Keone's knuckles showed white where he leaned on them on the table. "I need to know you're safe."

"Your cousin Frankie is outside mowing. I'm fine." Ilima sounded more annoyed than worried.

"I'm calling Lei right now," I said. "In the meantime, stay home, keep your doors locked, and write down everything you remember about the call—exact words, background noises, anything distinctive about the voice even through the disguiser."

"Already did that," Ilima said. "But . . . this can't be a coincidence, can it? With everything happening with Pearl and the investigation?"

Keone shook his head even as I said, "No. There's actually been an escalation. Kawika was attacked at the hospital while watching over Pearl. They're both under police protection now."

Ilima gasped. "Is Pearl okay?"

"Yes, though still in the ICU," I said. "It's all connected. The Santos-Akana partnership is feeling the pressure from multiple directions."

"What Santos-Akana partnership?"

"Things have been moving fast, Mom. I'll catch you up," Keone said. "It's getting to be dinnertime—can Kat and I come by to eat, and catch you up in person?"

"Of course. I'll put something on right away."

"Meanwhile, stay safe, Ilima. Get Frankie to stay until we arrive," I said.

After Keone ended the call, I immediately dialed Lei's cell, using the direct number she'd given us for emergencies. To our relief, she answered on the third ring, her voice tired but alert.

"Kat? What's happened now?"

I quickly explained about the threat to Ilima. Lei's exhaustion seemed to evaporate as she processed this new escalation.

"I'll have Hana PD do a sweep by her house," she said. "And let's see if we can trace that call, though if they used a voice disguiser, they probably took other precautions too."

"It has to be connected to Santos and Akana," I said.

"I agree," Lei said. "But proving it is another matter." Lei's frustration was evident even over the phone. "The evidence from the crane box is compelling but historical. The data from the drive is . . . inconclusive, unless we can connect it to something criminal. We're still building the case for the modern corruption and trying to find a physical connection to Pearl's poisoning."

"And now, let's add threats against a mayoral candidate," I said.

"Right now, we need to focus on keeping Ilima safe and finding evidence that connects Santos or Akana to these threats," Lei said.

We ended the call and locked up the shack, leaving the broken bed in disarray on the floor.

"I'll fix that later," Keone said. "What else are Sundays for? Now for the big question: your vehicle, mine, or both?"

If we took one vehicle, I'd end up at his place for the night—and that was just fine with me.

"Yours," I said. "You can bring me back with the tools to fix the bed tomorrow. Now let's get rolling to your mom's."

"I like where this is heading," said Mr. K with one of his patented twinkles, and dang if my heart didn't do one of those silly bebops romance novels talk about.

My phone pinged as we pulled out of the parking lot with a text from Lei: *"Call to Ilima was traced to payphone near county building. Officers checking security cameras now."*

I read the message to Keone, who was navigating a hairpin turn as we headed for Hana. "A payphone? Who even uses those anymore?"

"Someone who knows cell phones are easily traced," Keone said. "The county building is right next to Santos's office."

"Pretty brazen to make the call from there, though," I said. "It's practically leaving a signature."

"Or it's meant to look that way," Keone said. "What if this is another attempt to create obvious evidence pointing to Santos?"

As we drove and hit a corner with cell service, another notification popped up on my phone—a news alert from the Maui Sentinel app: *"Breaking News: Mayor Santos Announces Heritage Tea Garden Project 'On Hold Pending Review'."* I opened the article to find a press release issued by the mayor's office, stating that due to "concerns about historical accuracy and potential environmental impact," the Heritage Tea Garden project would be placed on indefinite hold pending a comprehensive review by Maui County authorities.

"He's making a move," I said, summarizing the article for Keone. "With Pearl hospitalized, Santos is using his authority to block the garden project, and I'm sure his son David is the neck turning the head on this one."

"Damage control," Keone agreed. "He's trying to buy time, maybe permanently shelve the project before the evidence in Pearl's journal becomes public. He and Councilman Akana probably have a plan to take over the whole project for their tourist trap."

"We can't let him get away with this," I said, anger building. "Pearl and her family have waited long enough for justice, and she's fought hard for this garden—which will benefit the whole community."

"Between the journal, the financial records, and now the escalating threats, we're building a case he won't be able to escape," Keone said.

Sadly, I wasn't so sure. Powerful people often got away with things lesser mortals wouldn't dare.

SUNDAY MORNING FOUND me waking in unfamiliar surroundings, momentarily disoriented until I registered the sound of waves breaking on the shore outside, and remembered I was at Keone's cottage. I stretched, smiling as I spotted the bedside clock, which read 8:15 AM.

I'd slept in, past when the feline alarm clock in my life would allow. "Ha, Tiki. You can't wake me up here."

I smelled the fragrance of fresh Kona coffee and heard Keone moving around in the kitchen; if I played my cards right, I might even get breakfast in bed.

I rolled onto my side and shut my eyes—but found myself going over the evening's events instead of drifting off.

Ilima had been in feisty mode when we arrived at her house,

stomping up and down and waving her spatula as she declared war on Mayor Santos. We had eaten dinner with her and filled her in on developments. The Red Hats and her campaign manager had arrived before our dishes could be removed from the table; she'd mustered the troops for a campaign planning session.

We were able to escape to Keone's next-door cottage after that, where Lei called to let us know that street security footage from near the payphone showed a figure in a hooded sweatshirt and baseball cap—impossible to identify with certainty, though the build suggested a man of average height.

Mayor Santos, meanwhile, had doubled down on his decision to halt the Heritage Garden project, giving an interview to an Oahu TV station in which he expressed "deep concern about rushing into a project with historical implications without proper vetting. Valuable properties like the ones involved would be better used to bolster the local economy."

Councilman Akana had been standing at the Mayor's side throughout the whole thing; together they were advancing their agenda for the tourist trap corridor.

"Dang it." I wasn't going to be able to play lady of leisure after all; my brain was too busy. I slipped out of bed and into Keone's robe, which hung on the back of the bedroom door. It was loose on me, but it was soft and carried his scent—a comforting blend of soap and man.

In the kitchen, I found Mr. K at the stove, flipping Portuguese sausage in a cast-iron skillet. A bowl of fresh papaya slices sat on the counter alongside a plate of toasted sweet bread.

"Morning." Mr. K greeted me with a smile as he cracked eggs into the sausage grease. A whiff of fatty fabulousness hit my nose. "Coffee's ready. Sleep okay?"

I stepped close to slip my arms around his waist and kiss his slightly bristly jaw. "You know I did. Thanks to a couple of rounds of physical therapy, as you called it."

"And here I thought I was keeping you from developing traumatic memories of the bed breaking and dumping us on the floor," Keone said.

"A noble effort." I detached, and poured myself a cup of coffee, adding a splash of coconut milk from the refrigerator. I sniffed the air as Mr. K stirred the contents of the skillet. "And you already know, the way to this woman's heart is through her stomach."

"I'm working every angle," he said. "Are you ready to move in yet?"

"Ha." I smiled, settling onto a stool at the kitchen counter. Despite the stress of the case, this domestic moment felt surprisingly right—as if we were glimpsing what life might be like if I took the leap and moved in permanently. "Keep up the good work, babe. I'll let you know."

Keone transferred the sausage slices to a serving plate covered in paper towels. "Lei called while you were asleep. Kawika's condition has improved. They're talking about releasing him if his MRI looks good. Pearl's improved too."

"That's good news," I said.

"I got the impression Lei's hoping we might talk to him. Says he's been asking about the case."

"Then we should visit him at the hospital. Pearl too," I said. "I'd like to check on them both."

"Sounds like a good activity for a Sunday. We can take the project plane into town again." Keone set a plate of food in front of me: Portuguese sausage, eggs, papaya, and sweet bread toast—the perfect Hawaiian breakfast. "Lei also mentioned that the manager of First Hawaiian Bank left her a message. Something about Pearl's safety deposit box."

"What safety deposit box?" I frowned.

"Apparently the manager recognized Pearl's name from the news about her poisoning. When he heard she was hospitalized, he contacted Lei because of some recent activity involving her box."

"What does that mean?" I spoke through bulging cheeks as I dug into the delicious breakfast.

"That's what we're going to find out when Lei does," Keone said, joining me at the counter with his own plate. "She said they were meeting first thing Monday morning at the bank."

"Too bad we've both got work or we could join her," I said.

We ate in companionable silence for a few minutes, the only sounds the clink of cutlery against plates and the distant crash of waves outside. It was a peaceful moment, like the calm at the eye of a hurricane—a brief respite before returning to the swirling chaos of our investigation.

"This feels nice," I said quietly, not quite meeting his eyes. "Waking up here. Breakfast together, like this."

Keone's hand covered mine on the counter. "It could be like this more often, you know."

"I know," I acknowledged. "And I'm . . . working on it. Being here is a step in that direction."

"A step at a time works for me." He smiled, but his eyes were a little sad.

My heart flopped like a gaffed fish. I stopped the sensation with a mouthful of Portuguese sausage. "We better get going. This case isn't going to solve itself."

14

AFTER BREAKFAST, we dressed and headed for the airport after making sure Ilima was well chaperoned by her minions.

The comfortable domestic bubble of the morning gave way to seriousness; but there was no way not to find the plane ride from Hana to Kahului in Keone's little aircraft anything but enchanting.

The morning was still, bright and clear, the kind of perfect Maui day that made air travel close to the rugged, green bluffs and valleys of the east side of the island especially stunning. I leaned my forehead on the window and watched for whales in the aqua-blue ocean below as we flew alongside velvety cliffs and waterfalls.

Maui Memorial Medical Center in Kahului felt different on a Sunday—less frantic than during our last visit, though the police presence remained. Officer Palakiko nodded to us in recognition from his position near the entrance before directing us to Kawika's new room on the regular medical floor.

While we were on our way, Lei texted that the meeting at the bank had been moved up to today; she had prevailed upon the manager to come in and meet her on the premises due to the urgency of the case. *"Join me if you can,"* her text read. I texted back that we'd try.

We found Kawika sitting up in bed. Color had returned to his face, though a large bandage still covered his head. He was eating what appeared to be hospital oatmeal with the resigned expression of someone who knew complaining wouldn't improve the quality.

"If it isn't the detective duo," he greeted us, setting aside his spoon. "Please tell me you brought real food."

"Sorry," I apologized. "Next time."

"I hope there won't be a next time, and they let me out of here tomorrow."

"How are you feeling, cuz?" Keone asked, pulling up chairs for us.

"Like someone tried to crack my skull open," Kawika said. "Better than yesterday, though. The doctor says I'll have a headache for a while."

"Any more memories of the attack?" I asked.

Kawika's expression sobered. "Fragments. I remember the sandalwood smell more clearly now—definitely cologne, not natural wood."

I frowned, remembering a flash of fragrance. David Santos had smelled of a sandalwood cologne.

"And . . . the attacker said something right before they hit me."

"What did they say?" Keone asked, leaning forward intently.

"Something like 'nothing personal' or 'just business,'" Kawika frowned with the effort of remembering. "It was a man's voice, I'm sure of that now."

"How's Pearl?" I asked. "Have you seen her?"

"Briefly, this morning. They took me to her in a wheelchair." A smile softened his features. "She's weak but definitely Pearl. First thing she did was scold me for not ducking fast enough."

We chuckled—it was exactly the sort of thing Pearl would say, her concern masked by practical admonishment. "Can we visit her, do you think?"

"The doctors are keeping her quiet. They don't want her agitated. Family only," Kawika said. "Though there's no family here on the island, I get an exemption as her Power of Attorney and caregiver."

"Did she say anything about the case?" Keone asked. "About the evidence or the Santos-Akana connection?"

"Not directly," Kawika lowered his voice, though we were alone in the room. "She asked if I could retrieve the temple box."

My brows rose. "Temple box?"

"Apparently, there's a second sandalwood box," Kawika said. "Similar to the crane box, but kept at the Buddhist temple at Iao Valley where Pearl has meditated in the past. She said I should retrieve it before 'they' realized it existed. I wonder if you could do that for me."

"Of course," I said. "I've always meant to visit that temple. This is a great excuse."

"Pearl was clever," Keone said. "She spread her evidence in multiple locations, ensuring that even if one cache was discovered, others would remain. Did she say what's in this temple box?"

Kawika shook his head, then touched his temple with a wince at the movement. "Only that it was 'the other half of the truth.' She gave me this—" He reached for the drawer of his bedside table and withdrew a small key on a red silk cord. "She kept it around her neck. She said it opens the temple box. The head monk, Venerable Sonam, is expecting someone to come and claim it."

I accepted the key, examining its small size and brass gleam in my palm. "We'll go check on it right away."

"One more thing," Kawika added. "Pearl mentioned that the 'final piece' is still waiting to be found. Something about 'what's buried isn't always in the ground.'"

"More cryptic guidance," Keone said, with a slight eye roll.

"She's protecting information that people have already tried to kill for," Kawika said, a little frosty in Pearl's defense. "Caution seems warranted."

We didn't stay much longer, aware that Kawika needed rest and we had a busy morning ahead. As we were leaving, he caught my hand.

"Be careful," he said. "Whoever did this," he gestured to his bandaged head, "won't hesitate to try again if they think you're close to the truth."

"We'll be careful," I assured him. "You focus on recovering. We'll handle the rest."

Outside, in the hallway, Keone checked his watch. "It's early. Maybe we can make it to the temple and still meet Lei at the bank if we hurry."

"Let's split up," I suggested. "You meet Lei at the bank, and I'll go to the temple for the box. We'll cover more ground that way."

Keone's expression darkened. "After everything that's happened, you want to go alone?"

"The Buddhist temple is hardly a high-risk location," I pointed out. "It's a public place, in broad daylight, with monks and visitors present. Besides, we need to know what's in both the temple box and the safety deposit box as soon as possible."

I could see the internal struggle playing out on his face—the logical investigator acknowledging the efficiency of my plan versus the protective boyfriend wanting to ensure my safety. I chose not to remind him I was also a trained former Secret Service agent and knew a dozen ways to disable an attacker with or without a weapon.

Why cut him off at the knees?

I guess I was learning a thing or three about relationships —finally.

"Okay," he said at last. "We'll take separate rideshares. Call me the minute you have the box and are on your way to Lei's office at the police station."

"Deal," I said, and gave him a quick kiss. "I got this. You got this. We both got this."

∾

THE IAO VALLEY BUDDHIST TEMPLE was a serene oasis nestled among tropical foliage near the park at the end of the Valley. I loved the drive back through the sparsely populated valley with its steep, corrugated green walls sculped by time, erosion, and seasonal waterfalls. As usual, puffy clouds caught on the dramatic peaks. One even sported a rainbow.

We soon pulled up to the Temple. Its graceful architecture—a blend of traditional Asian design and modern elements—created a harmonious presence that seemed to exist slightly outside the normal flow of time.

As I approached the main entrance, removing my shoes as custom dictated, I was greeted by a young monk in maroon robes.

"Welcome," he said with a slight bow. "How may we assist you today?"

"I'm here to see Venerable Sonam," I explained. "About an item left by Pearl Yamamoto."

Recognition flickered in the young man's eyes. "Please, follow me."

He led me through the main sanctuary, where several people sat in silent meditation, and into a small garden courtyard. There, tending to a miniature rock garden with a small rake, was an elderly monk whose serene presence seemed to radiate calm.

"Venerable Sonam," my guide said softly, "this visitor has come regarding Pearl Yamamoto."

The elder monk looked up, his weathered face creasing into a smile. "Thank you, Tenzin."

As the younger man departed, Venerable Sonam gestured for me to join him on a stone bench beside the rock garden. "You are Pearl's friend," he stated rather than asked.

"Yes," I said. "My name is Kat Smith. Pearl is in the hospital, and her caregiver, Kawika Pali, sent me to retrieve something she left in your safekeeping."

"The box of memories. Pearl has meditated here on and off monthly for twenty years. She told me someone might come with the key." He studied me with surprising intensity for one so seemingly gentle. "Do you have it?"

I showed him the small key on its red cord. Sonam nodded again, apparently satisfied.

"Pearl is a woman who carries many burdens," he said softly. "The weight of history, of justice delayed, of truth buried. She always returns to her path of revealing what has been hidden." He rose with vigorous grace for his age. "The box is in our meditation room. Please, follow me."

I followed the elder monk through a side door into a small, dimly lit room with cushions arranged in a circle on the floor. A simple altar stood against one wall, bearing incense holders, a small Buddha statue, and several photographs of what appeared to be previous temple leaders.

Venerable Sonam approached the altar and reached behind it, producing a wooden box similar to the crane one we'd found at Pearl's house, though slightly smaller and carved with a different design—a lotus flower in full bloom rather than a flying crane.

"The lotus rises from the mud, pure and beautiful despite its origins," he said, noting my interest in the carving. "Pearl chose this symbol for what this box contains."

He placed the box in my hands with ceremonial care. "She said the contents would help right an old wrong, but might cause pain in the process."

"Yes," I said, feeling the weight of both the box and the responsibility it represented. "We're trying to find the truth about what happened to Pearl and why."

"Truth and justice are worthy pursuits," the monk nodded. "But remember that they sometimes arrive with unexpected consequences." With those words, he bowed slightly and gestured toward the door. "You may use this room to examine the contents if you wish. Privacy and peaceful reflection may be beneficial."

"Thank you," I said sincerely. "For keeping this safe for Pearl."

"It was a small service for one who has given much to our

community," he replied simply, then left, sliding the door closed behind him.

Alone in the quiet meditation room, I sat cross-legged on one of the cushions and placed the lotus box before me. The key fit perfectly into a small lock on the front, turning with a soft click that seemed loud in the stillness.

The box opened to reveal contents quite different from the crane box. Instead of a journal and maps, this one contained what appeared to be old photographs and letters, carefully preserved in tissue paper. I lifted out the first photograph—a black and white image of a Japanese family standing proudly in front of a traditional garden. The back bore a date: "Yamamoto Family, 1939."

The next several photos documented what appeared to be the construction and operation of the Japanese garden that had preceded the internment camp on Pearl's property. In one, a man I assumed was Pearl's grandfather stood beside the crane statue that had been the centerpiece of the garden.

The letters were in Japanese, which I couldn't read, though some had English translations attached. They seemed to be correspondence between Pearl's father and various officials after the war, documenting his efforts to reclaim the family property and seek justice for what had happened at the processing center.

While clearly of historical value, nothing in the box seemed to provide new evidence about the Santos-Akana conspiracy or direct proof connecting them to Pearl's poisoning. It was an important historical archive, but not the smoking gun I'd hoped for.

Disappointed, I carefully replaced the items, wondering if I'd missed something. Pearl had called this "the other half of the truth," suggesting it contained crucial information. Yet all I saw were historical documents that essentially confirmed what we already knew.

As I prepared to close the box, something caught my eye—a slight irregularity in the wood grain at the bottom of the interior.

Looking closer, I noticed that what appeared to be the bottom panel didn't quite match the side walls in color and texture.

"A false bottom," I murmured, remembering Keone's comment about the crane box being a Japanese puzzle box. This one likely had a similar hidden compartment.

I examined the box carefully, looking for any indication of how to access the secret space. After several minutes of unsuccessful attempts, I noticed a small, almost invisible seam near one corner. Pressing it yielded no result, but when I applied pressure to the opposite corner simultaneously, I heard a faint click.

The false bottom lifted slightly, revealing a hidden compartment beneath. Inside lay a single item: another key, larger than the one for the box itself, with a small tag attached. The tag bore a name and a number: "*First Hawaiian Bank, Box 722.*"

A safety deposit box key. This had to be related to the box Lei was investigating at the bank! I quickly secured both the lotus box and the safety deposit key in my bag, then called Keone as promised.

"The temple box contained old photographs and letters, plus a hidden compartment with a safety deposit key for First Hawaiian Bank, Box 722. Is that the same box Lei is looking into?"

"Yes," Keone confirmed, his voice tense with excitement. "Lei's with the manager now. Apparently, someone tried to access Pearl's box yesterday using fake identification. The manager got suspicious and refused access, then called Lei this morning when he made the connection to her case."

"I'm on my way." I was already heading for the door. "I'll be there in ten minutes," I said, thanking Venerable Sonam with a quick bow as I hurried through the main sanctuary.

The drive to First Hawaiian Bank was supposed to take up to twenty minutes in a rideshare and took ten more to arrive, so I was later than I'd hoped.

The bank occupied a modern building in downtown, its glass and steel architecture a stark contrast to the traditional temple I'd just left. I knocked on the locked glass doors, and Keone let me inside, giving me a quick hug. "You're just in time. Things are getting interesting. Follow me."

I trailed his broad-shouldered silhouette through the unlighted lobby to the manager's office, where I found Lei seated across from a nervous-looking man in his fifties whose shiny nameplate identified him as "Gregory Kwan, Branch Manager."

"Glad you made it, Kat," Lei greeted me. "Mr. Kwan was just showing us the security footage from yesterday's attempted access."

"And I have the key to Pearl's safe deposit," I said, producing the safety deposit key from my pocket.

Mr. Kwan's eyebrows rose. "I haven't seen that in a while. Ms. Yamamoto has maintained this box for over thirty years, with very infrequent access—only a few times in the past decade."

"May I see the footage too?" I asked, taking a seat beside Keone.

Mr. Kwan turned his computer monitor so we could all view it.

The footage showed the bank's safety deposit viewing area, where a man in a business suit was speaking with a bank employee. Though the angle wasn't ideal, I immediately recognized the visitor.

"That's David Santos," I exclaimed. "The mayor's son."

"Kat had a run-in with him recently. He confronted Kat at the cultural center, and he's been blocking Pearl's permits for the Heritage Garden project," Keone said.

"The documents he presented seemed authentic at first glance," Mr. Kwan said. "Authorization from Ms. Yamamoto allowing her 'nephew' to access the box in her absence. But something felt off about the interaction. And when I asked for additional identification, he became agitated, then left."

"What tipped you off?" Lei asked.

"Two things," the manager replied. "First, I've known Ms. Yamamoto as a client for many years, and she's never mentioned any nephew here on the island. Second, the authorization document had yesterday's date on it, but I knew from the news that Ms. Yamamoto has been hospitalized and is still alive."

"What happens now?" I asked. "Can we access the box with the key I found?"

Mr. Kwan looked uncomfortable. "Normally, we would require Ms. Yamamoto's presence or a legally executed power of attorney."

"Pearl is still out of commission, but let's call Kawika!" I exclaimed. "He's her POA and he asked me to find the box that held the key. He did that at Pearl's request."

It was only the work of a few minutes to get Kawika on video phone, showing his ID from his hospital bed and authorizing the opening of the box in Pearl's stead.

After that, Mr. Kwan led us to the safety deposit vault, a secure room lined with metal doors of various sizes. Using a master key along with the one I'd found in the temple box, we opened Box 722 —a medium-sized container that he placed on a private viewing table in an adjacent room.

"I'll be right outside," he said, leaving us alone with the steel container.

Lei lifted the lid, revealing several carefully organized items inside. On top was an envelope addressed simply "In Case of Emergency" in Pearl's precise handwriting.

Lei opened it and read aloud:

"If you are reading this, something has happened to me. The contents of this box provide definitive evidence connecting the Santos and Akana families to historical crimes and ongoing corruption. The USB drive contains financial records documenting bribes disguised as consulting fees, alongside evidence of their joint attempts to acquire my property through both legal and illegal means. The recorded conversation was provided by a friend and it documents a meeting where both families discussed 'removing obstacles' to their development plans—with me specifically named as the primary obstacle. May justice finally be served. —Pearl Yamamoto"

Beneath the letter lay a small USB drive, a micro recorder, and a manila envelope containing what appeared to be property documents and financial records.

"This is it," Keone said softly. "Proof of their corruption and conspiracy."

Lei carefully bagged each item as evidence. "If we're lucky. But I hope we are. With this, we can finally bring charges against both Akana and Santos."

"But which one actually poisoned Pearl?" I frowned. "And who attacked Kawika?"

"The recorded conversation might tell us," Lei said. "But we'll need to analyze everything back at the station before drawing conclusions."

As Lei finished securing the evidence, my phone rang with Kawika's number flashing on the screen.

"Kawika?" I answered. "We got into the safe deposit box and it contains the kind of proof Lei needs to bring a case."

"That's good," Kawika said, but his tone said something else wasn't.

"Is everything okay?" I put the call on speaker so Lei and Keone could hear.

"Not exactly," Kawika replied, his voice tense. "I just had a visit from Mayor Santos himself. He claimed he was there to wish me well, but he spent the entire time fishing for information about what Pearl might have told me and where we are in the case. When he was leaving, he said something . . . disturbing."

"This is Sergeant Texeira and you're on speaker," Lei rapped out. "Speak."

"He said, 'Tell Pearl when she wakes that the Heritage Garden was a mistake. The holes we dig to plant in can end up as graves.'"

"He's trying to intimidate you. This evidence we've just uncovered could end his career and possibly send him to prison," I said.

"I'll check in with the guard on Pearl's door and make sure

everyone is on high alert," Lei said. She stepped aside to make the call.

"There's something else," Kawika said. "After Santos left, one of the nurses mentioned seeing someone matching David Santos's description at the hospital yesterday morning—around four a.m., right before someone attacked me."

"That would make sense," I said. "I think David wears a sandal-wood cologne, too. I smelled it when we had our confrontation at the community center. Stay safe." We ended the call.

"Pearl's secure," Lei said. "No activity on her floor." Keone told her the additional snippet Kawika had added. Lei frowned. "More vague sightings. Still no hard evidence, though hopefully the contents of the safety deposit box give me what I need. Meanwhile . . . what do you think Akana's role is in all this?"

"Partner or pawn," Keone said. "He's connected through the business dealings and the Cultural Corridor project."

"Let's get back to the station and go through these materials," Lei said. "If we can establish a direct link between either Santos or his son and the poisoning or attack, we can make an arrest. Mean-while, between his confrontation with Kat and being spotted in the hospital, I have enough to bring David Santos in for questioning."

As we put away the empty box, Mr. Kwan returned with the necessary documentation for the evidence removal.

On our way to help Lei review the new evidence at the station, I mulled over what we'd uncovered so far.

Pearl had methodically created a web of evidence deposits: the crane box at her home altar, the drive and clues at the community center, the lotus box at the temple, the safety deposit box at the bank. Each cache contained pieces of the puzzle, strategically placed to ensure that, even if one was discovered and removed, others would remain to tell her story.

It was the careful planning of a woman who knew she was in danger but refused to be silenced. Thanks to her foresight, we were closing in on the truth.

But would what we had be enough to bring any of these powerful players to justice—let alone rectify the past? "We have to try," I whispered.

15

THE KAHULUI POLICE Station was quiet on a Sunday afternoon. The faint scent of a cup of Lei's coffee, forgotten and gone cold in a mug decorated with the Maui Police Department shield, mingled with the lemony disinfectant that permeated all government buildings. Keone and I were stationed in Lei's tiny cubicle office. The small space was growing increasingly stuffy, despite a ceiling fan that rotated lazily overhead. The blinds were half-drawn against the sun, creating stripes of golden light across the scattered files covering the desk.

Lei had installed us in her office with the cache we'd recovered from the bank and then shot out to try to pick up David Santos for questioning. She'd gone to his address in Kahului, only to find he'd vanished. She'd put out a Be On Look Out, but so far, no luck. She was now at the airport, impressing on the security forces there the need to detain Santos if he tried to get off the island.

Every now and then Keone or I would get up from the records we were reviewing to stretch. I liked leaning back to look at the colorful corkboard on Lei's partner Pono Kaihale's side of the cubicle; it was chock-full of family photos and colorful with artwork from his kids. Keone's cousin was on vacation, which was why he hadn't been around to leaven the investigation with his big laugh and bold presence.

Lei's side of the cubicle was utilitarian, a montage of wanted posters and police bulletins. Only one framed photo of her, her husband Michael Stevens, their two children and a pair of Rottweilers, gave any glimpse into her personal life.

"Still nothing from the Coast Guard about a sighting of David Santos," Officer Palakiko said, poking his head into the cubicle. Sweat beaded on his forehead, evidence of the humid day outside that the building's struggling air-conditioning couldn't quite combat. "But they verified there are no boats registered to the Santos family here on the island."

"What about him getting out on a chartered vessel?" I rubbed my eyes, dry and tired from hours of scrutinizing small print and trying to understand what I was looking at. "David Santos would have access to something like that, with his family's resources."

"I'll add that to our search," the officer said, wiping his brow with a grubby handkerchief. "But that's a lot of boats to track."

"Keep on it," I said. "If he's trying to leave the island without using the airport, a private boat is his most likely option."

As Palakiko departed, the squeak of his leather duty belt fading with distance, I turned to Keone. "Don't you think we should listen to that recording from the safety deposit box? Maybe it will tell us something."

Keone frowned. "I know Lei wanted to play it right away, but she thought she'd pick up David Santos and question him first—which has turned out to be a bigger project than anticipated. But won't she be pissed if we play it without her?"

We both glanced over at the small recorder in its plastic evidence bag.

"Yep, she'd be mad," I said reluctantly.

"Why don't you call and see if we can listen to it with her on speaker?" Keone said.

"Good idea." I called Lei and she was agreeable. I set my phone on the desk and hit the button while Keone carefully removed the recorder from the evidence bag. "You're on speaker, Lei. We're ready to play the recording."

"Go ahead," she said.

Keone pressed 'Play'. A series of clicks and shuffling sounds filled the small office before voices emerged.

". . . need to move forward with the development plans," a man's voice said, his tone clipped and businesslike. "The council vote is next month, and we need to ensure it passes."

"And what about the old woman?" another voice asked. "She's gathering those documents. If she goes public with them . . ."

"Pearl Yamamoto is becoming an obstacle," a third voice said. A chill ran over me, raising the hairs on my arms: I recognized it immediately as David Santos. "We've invested too much to let her derail everything with her Heritage Garden nonsense. Those old internment claims need to stay buried."

"I agree," said another voice—softer, more measured. "It's unfortunate, but we can't let sentiment interfere with progress."

My heart skipped a beat. That measured, reasonable tone was also familiar. I gripped the edge of the desk, trying to keep my expression neutral—I didn't want to alarm Keone.

"And if she doesn't back down?" the first voice asked.

"Then we remove the obstacle," David Santos replied, his voice hardening. "One way or another."

"There are ways to handle this discreetly," the measured voice said. "She's elderly. No one would question a health crisis."

"That's how you can repay your debt," the first voice said. "But it better look natural."

The recording continued with discussion of property values and council members to pressure, but I barely heard it. My mind was racing, piecing together all the times I'd interacted with the owner of that voice.

When the recording ended, there was silence in the office, broken only by Lei's voice coming through the speaker.

"Well, that's certainly enough for questioning of those involved," she said grimly. "Did either of you recognize any of those voices?"

Keone cleared his throat. "I thought I recognized Mayor Santos, his son David, Councilman Akana . . ." He trailed off and gazed at me questioningly. "And one other. I'm not sure of the fourth voice. All male speakers, though."

I nodded and swallowed hard, buying myself a moment to think, because I was certain I'd heard both David Santos and *Kawika Pali*.

But what if I was wrong?

What if it just sounded like him? The recording wasn't the best, and the thought of falsely accusing someone who'd been attacked, who'd cared so loyally for Pearl, who might be innocent . . . I hesitated to speak his name aloud.

But if Kawika really was involved, he was still at the hospital with Pearl.

Right now.

With easy access to her, helpless in her bed.

"Kat?" Lei prompted. "You went quiet. Did you recognize someone?"

"One of them was David Santos," I said. "That's all I could swear to. The recording quality isn't great."

"I have some ideas about who's on that recording, but David Santos is definitely our priority," Lei replied. "I'm heading back to the station now."

"See you soon," I said, my voice steadier than I felt.

As I ended the call, Keone leaned forward. "You recognized someone, didn't you?"

I hesitated. "I'm not sure. I need to get some air," I said abruptly, standing up.

Keone looked at me with concern. "You okay?"

"Yeah, just . . . cramped in here. And worried about Pearl." I grabbed my purse, trying to appear casual. "Actually, I think I'll swing by the hospital to check on her. I'd like to get eyes on her myself."

"Want me to come with you?" Keone asked, half rising from his chair.

"No, you stay, please," I said quickly. "Someone needs to keep going through these records. I'll just pop in for a quick visit and be back in an hour."

Keone frowned. "Call me if anything seems off, okay?"

"Of course," I promised, already heading for the door.

THE HOSPITAL CORRIDOR was quieter than usual for a Sunday afternoon. I'd stopped at the gift shop downstairs, picking out an arrangement of anthuriums and orchids, hoping they'd brighten Pearl's room. The flowers gave me a perfect cover; I was just a concerned friend making a visit. Hopefully I could drop Lei's name and make it past the officer at her door.

As I approached the elevator, I froze. Through the glass walls of the hospital café, I spotted David Santos. The man we'd been hunting all day was calmly sitting at a table, deep in conversation with a man in light blue scrubs, whose back was to the window. They were huddled close, Santos gesturing emphatically while the medical staffer nodded.

I ducked behind a large potted palm, nearly dropping my flowers. Santos was supposed to be running, trying to flee the island—not chatting in the hospital cafeteria. I peered around the foliage for another look at the man in scrubs. I couldn't see his face, but something about his build seemed familiar.

My hands trembled as I pulled out my phone and dialed Lei.

"Detective Texeira," she answered crisply.

"It's Kat," I whispered. "I'm at Maui Memorial, and David Santos is here."

"What?" Lei's voice sharpened. "What are you doing at the hospital?"

"I decided to check on Pearl," I said. "Lei, Santos is in the café talking to someone in scrubs. They look . . . intense."

"Do not approach," Lei ordered. "I'm ten minutes out. Stay where you are and keep eyes on him if you can do it safely. But Kat, do not engage. This man may have tried to kill Kawika—and Pearl."

"Understood," I said, my gaze fixed on Santos. "And Lei? I think the person he's talking to works here. At the hospital. Where Pearl is, need I remind you. He's wearing scrubs."

"Keep them in visual," Lei said. "I'm calling for backup and I'm on my way."

I tucked the phone into my pocket as I positioned myself behind the palm where I could watch without being obvious. Santos and the medical staffer were now examining something on a tablet, their expressions serious.

Pearl's room was three floors up. That Santos and his accomplice were here couldn't be a coincidence. I clutched the bouquet tighter, the wax-paper-wrapped stems crushing under my grip as I watched and waited, praying Lei would arrive before the men made a move.

But Santos and the man in scrubs stood up from their table. The staffer tucked the tablet under his arm and nodded once to Santos before turning toward the elevator bank. He wore a blue medical mask and a paper hair covering; I couldn't recognize him in that getup.

Santos remained in the café, steam from his untouched coffee curling upward as he pulled out his phone.

They were splitting up. A chill ran through me, jump-starting my heart.

I fumbled for my phone, my fingers slipping against the smooth case. I redialed Lei, the ringtone echoing in my ear once, twice, three times before rolling to voicemail.

"Lei, it's Kat," I whispered urgently, ducking further behind the broad leaves of the plant. "David Santos is here in the café, but the guy he was meeting in scrubs is heading to the stairs right now. I think they're going after Pearl. Third floor, room 312. I'll try to beat him by taking the elevator. Please hurry."

As I ended the call, I watched the man in scrubs hit the staff door to enter into the stairwell. The fluorescent light from the elevator briefly illuminated his forehead and nose, but his face was effectively hidden by the mask and hair covering. The door closed behind him.

I rushed to the elevator and jabbed the button, the plastic cool under my fingertip. Fortunately, it was waiting, and chimed as the doors parted, releasing a wave of antiseptic-scented air. Inside, the space smelled of hand sanitizer. I pressed the button for the third floor, watching the numbers glow one after another as the elevator ascended.

When the doors finally opened on the third floor, harsh fluorescent lighting made me blink after the dimness of the elevator. The corridor stretched before me, beige walls and speckled linoleum floor gleaming under the unforgiving illumination. The squeak of rubber-soled shoes and the distant murmur of a television provided a soundtrack for my racing heart.

The air on this floor was cooler, chilling me further as I moved down the hall. As I rounded a corner, scanning for Room 312, beeping and low voices at the nurse's station filled the air, enhanced by the scent of industrial floor cleaner.

My stomach tightened as I spotted an empty chair outside Pearl's room, abandoned as if its occupant had left in a hurry. A half-finished cup of coffee sat on a small side table, a thin skin formed on its surface, the Maui PD logo visible on the plastic drinking vessel.

The officer who was supposed to be guarding Pearl was gone.

Pearl's door stood slightly ajar, a sliver of muted light spilling into the hallway. From inside came the rhythmic beeping of monitors—too fast or too slow, I couldn't tell, but the electronic pulse underscored my urgency. My precious size 11 Nike shoes squeaked against the polished floor as I pushed the door open with my shoulder, wincing at the pneumatic whine of the hinges, which I made sure closed all the way behind me.

The room was dim, its blinds drawn against the hot sun. Pearl lay still, white sheets pulled up to her chest, her small frame barely making a dent in the hospital blankets. The machines around her blinked and hummed, green and red lights casting an eerie glow across her pale face. The air smelled of disinfectant and loneliness.

I moved quickly to the bedside, my gaze scanning the monitors and registering the regularity of Pearl's heartbeat. "Whew. You're alive." I set the flowers down on Pearl's nightstand, the waxy wrapper crinkling loudly in the quiet room.

"Pearl?" I whispered, gently touching her arm. The skin beneath my fingertips was paper-thin and cold. "Pearl, it's Kat."

Her eyelids fluttered, dark lashes against pale cheeks, before opening slowly. Confusion clouded her sunken eyes momentarily before recognition dawned, her gaze sharpening in the dim light as she focused on my face.

"Kat," she said, her voice like dry leaves crackling. "What are you doing here?"

"I came to check on you." I kept my voice low, the words barely carrying over the persistent beeping of the monitors. "Pearl, has anyone been in your room in the last few minutes? A man in scrubs?"

She frowned, the movement creating new lines in her already creased face. "The nurse was here a little while ago. Checking my IV." She lifted her hand slightly, drawing my attention to a tube taped to her skin, the clear liquid dripping steadily from the bag hanging above.

"Was it your regular nurse?" I asked urgently.

Pearl's brow furrowed. "No . . . I don't think I've seen him before. He said my regular nurse was on break."

A sudden tightness in my chest made it difficult to breathe, the room's recycled air feeling thin and insufficient. I glanced at the IV dripping into Pearl's arm, then at the door. Whoever had been in here might have tampered with her IV.

I couldn't leave it connected. I'd rather be sorry than wrong. "You might be in danger. I need to get this thing out."

Pearl blinked in confusion but made no protest as I grasped her delicate hand. "This might hurt a bit," I warned, carefully peeling back the tape securing the IV to Pearl's skin. Her arm was mottled with bruises and the needle left a tiny bead of red as I eased it out. Pearl winced but didn't make a sound. I pressed a tissue from the bedside table against the mark.

"Hold this," I said, pressing her fingers over the tissue. "Keep pressure here."

The machines around us continued their rhythmic beeping. I located the power cords and followed them to the wall, unplugging them one by one. The monitors went dark, their electronic eyes closing, the beeping silenced mid-note.

"What about the call button?" Pearl asked, her voice stronger now, fueled by adrenaline. "I can call for help."

"We don't have time," I said, moving to the foot of the bed. I found the brake release pedal and pressed it with my foot, feeling the mechanism give way with a metallic click. The bed shifted slightly, no longer anchored to the floor.

"Hold on to the side rails," I instructed, positioning myself at the head of the bed. I gripped the metal frame, heavy and solid beneath my hands. "I'm going to push you out of here."

Pearl nodded, her knuckles white against the bed rails. Her eyes darted to the door, then back to me. "Where will we go?"

"Somewhere safe," I promised, though I had no idea where that might be. "Just stay quiet."

The door swung open as the bed approached it.

Kawika, dressed in scrubs and a hair covering, stood in the doorway, a small bouquet of flowers in his hand. A mask was pushed down under his chin.

"It was you," I breathed—and hoped he hadn't heard me.

Surprise registered on his face as he took in the scene—Pearl in her mobile bed, me pushing it, the darkened monitors.

"Kat? What are you doing?" he asked. "Pearl, are you alright?"

The moment he spoke, I recognized him for sure: that measured, reasonable voice had agreed with Santos on the recording. The calm tone that had suggested a health crisis for Pearl.

I forced my expression to remain friendly, even as every nerve ending screamed a dangerous rage.

"Kawika," Pearl exclaimed, relief evident in her reedy tone. "Thank goodness it's you. Kat thinks someone might be trying to hurt me."

Kawika's expression gave way to something harder, more calculating, before smoothing into a sympathetic frown so quickly I might have imagined the transition. "That's terrible," he said, stepping into the room. The door closed behind him. The soft click of the latch engaging sounded like a gunshot in the quiet. "What makes you think that, Kat?"

His eyes met mine, dark and unreadable. The flowers in his hand, the same bouquet as mine—trembled slightly, the only indication that he wasn't as calm as he appeared.

"The police officer is gone outside the door," I said. "And Pearl said a nurse she didn't recognize was in here, messing with her IV."

"I checked with the nurse's station. The officer stepped away to take a call because his cell phone wasn't picking up in here. And the nursing staff has been changing shifts." Kawika moved closer, setting his flowers next to mine on the nightstand—going back to buy them must have been why he was behind me in reaching the room. "Why disconnect everything? Were you going to move her?"

The question hung in the air between us, innocent on the surface but loaded with implications.

"I was worried," I said. "I'm former Secret Service. Protecting is my training."

"Of course," Kawika agreed in that calm, reasonable voice. "But Pearl should stay here where the doctors can monitor her, don't you think? I'll get a nurse to help get everything reconnected."

He reached toward the call button on the wall, his finger hovering over it.

"No!" I said, too quickly. "I mean, we need to find her regular nurse. The one who knows her case."

I was trapped—caught between continuing the pretense and revealing what I knew, which could escalate the situation and put Pearl in more danger.

The room suddenly felt smaller, the air thicker.

I glanced down at Pearl's frightened face, then back at Kawika.

The weight of indecision lifted suddenly, replaced by cold clarity. Playing along wasn't going to save us.

"I heard you," I said firmly. "On the recording from the safe deposit box."

Kawika's eyes revealed a flicker of surprise before he composed himself. "What recording?" he asked, his voice softer than before.

"Someone recorded a meeting between you, David Santos and his father, and Councilman Akana," I said, stepping around the bed to position myself between him and Pearl. He would have to get through me to touch her. "You and David Santos discussed removing Pearl as an 'obstacle.' You suggested a health crisis."

Pearl's sharp intake of breath was the only sound for a long moment as the two of us locked eyes.

"I just saw you with David," I continued, my voice tight. "Downstairs in the cafeteria. You were both looking at something on a tablet. Planning your next move."

"Kawika!" Pearl exclaimed, her voice a breathy thread of shock.

"You poisoned her tea at the ceremony," I said. "And now you're here, dressed as medical staff, to finish what you started."

"Kawika?" Pearl's voice quavered. "Is this true?"

Kawika gazed at Pearl. Then Kawika's shoulders sagged, his confident posture giving way to something heavier. For the first time since entering the room, his hard demeanor changed, showing a face aged suddenly, etched with conflict and regret.

"It wasn't supposed to be like this," he said, his voice barely above a whisper. "You weren't supposed to suffer."

Pearl's arms trembled as she clutched the bed rails. "No. Please say it isn't true."

Kawika tugged at the scrubs he wore, as if suddenly uncomfortable in the disguise. "Santos told me to dress in these. Said it would be easier to access your room, to adjust your medications." He stared at the window, shame writ large in his stance. "When I got up here and saw the officer gone, when I realized it was really happening . . ."

"You were just with Santos," I said, not swayed by his apparent remorse. "I watched you both talking not fifteen minutes ago. And how did you get injured? A difference of opinion with Santos?"

"Yes," Kawika said, clenching and unclenching his hands. "He decided I was a liability. He thought I was losing my nerve. But I didn't rat him out. Downstairs, he was giving me final instructions. Showing me Pearl's chart, which medications to increase." His voice grew quieter. "He's waiting in the cafeteria for me to text him when it's done."

"And were you going to do it?" Pearl asked, her gaze searching his face.

"I don't know," Kawika said honestly. His voice cracked. "I've been drowning in debt. And guilt."

"Then help us," I said, seizing the moment of vulnerability. "Santos is downstairs. The police are looking for him. Help us stop this whole thing now. It will help your case."

Kawika scowled. "You don't know what he's capable of. What

they're all capable of. The development means too much money, too much power."

"And what about what's right?" Pearl asked, her frail voice finding strength. "What about justice for the families who were interned? The records prove what happened, what was taken from us."

"I know," Kawika's voice was hollow. "I've thought about that every day since . . ." He couldn't finish the sentence. "They said the past should stay buried, that it would only hurt people to bring it all up again. They made it sound reasonable at first. Then they made it sound necessary, when they bought my gambling debts." He gestured at the scrubs he wore. "They made it clear I didn't have a choice."

"There's always a choice," I said. My hand had crept down into my pocket to hold my phone. "And you're making one right now, with every second you stand between us and that door."

"Santos has people throughout the hospital," Kawika said finally. "Security, nurses, maybe even doctors. You think that officer just happened to disappear from his post?"

"Help us get out of here," Pearl said, her voice gentle but firm. "Help us and then tell the police everything you know. It's the only way to make this right, Kawika."

His face reflected his internal struggle—fear, shame, and something like hope battling for dominance. Finally, he reached into his pocket and pulled out his phone.

"Santos is expecting me to text him when it's done," he said, his decision visible in the straightening of his shoulders. "I can help you get out of here, and we can send him straight to the police." He glanced down at the scrubs he wore with an expression of disgust. "I never wanted any of this." He gazed at Pearl. "I was wrong. So wrong. I'm sorry."

"Show us, then," Pearl said simply. "With actions, not words."

Kawika nodded, a new resolve settling over his features. "I know a service elevator that leads to the parking garage stairs. I can text Santos to meet me there. Tell him it's done. He'll believe that."

"And Lei can find him there," I said, hope surging.

"Yes," Kawika said, moving toward the bed. "But we need to move Pearl in case he decides to take action himself or send someone. He'll come up here, and he's armed." Kawika moved to the bed. "We need to move quickly and quietly and hide her. There's an empty room at the end of this hall—used for storage. No one will find us there."

I nodded, positioning myself at the foot of the bed while Kawika took the head. Together, we guided Pearl's bed toward the door, the wheels gliding silently. I peered into the hallway; it was empty, the abandoned coffee cup still sitting on the small table outside.

"Clear," I whispered, and we maneuvered the bed through the doorway. I winced at the soft squeaking of the wheels against the linoleum floor.

The corridor stretched before us, eerily quiet. Kawika pushed us away from the nurses' station, toward a deserted area. The overhead lights hummed softly, casting long shadows as we moved swiftly but cautiously down the hall. Pearl lay still in the bed, her expression alert despite her frailty, one hand clutching the rail while the other pressed the tissue against the spot where I'd removed her IV.

"In here," Kawika said, stopping at a door marked 'Equipment Storage.' He pulled a key card from his pocket—part of his disguise—and swiped it through the reader. The lock clicked open, and he pushed the door wide.

The room was dim, filled with shelving units stacked with supplies—extra bedding, unused monitoring equipment, boxes of gloves and masks. A small window high on the wall let in just enough light for us to navigate the space.

We wheeled Pearl's bed into the center of the room, and I immediately began scanning for anything we could use to barricade the door. Kawika seemed to read my mind, dragging a heavy metal storage cabinet toward the door.

"Help me with this," he grunted, and I moved to assist, the cabinet scraping against the floor as we positioned it in front of the door.

Kawika pulled out his phone. "I should text Santos. Keep him here until the police can find him."

I nodded, and he quickly typed a message. "Done," he said, sliding the phone back into his pocket. "I told him to meet me in the north stairwell in ten minutes."

With the door secured, I pulled out my phone, relieved to see I had service. This time when I dialed Lei, my fingers were steady, my purpose clear. The phone rang once, twice.

"Where are you, Kat?" Lei answered, her voice crisp and professional.

"I'm with Pearl. We're hiding in a storage room on the third floor, east wing."

"Kat, what the heck . . ."

"David Santos is down in the cafeteria," I interrupted. "And we have Kawika with us. He was working with Santos—he's the one who poisoned Pearl's tea. But he's helping us now, and he's willing to testify."

I heard Lei's sharp inhale. "Are you safe? Is Pearl okay?"

"Yes, for the moment. We've barricaded the door. But Santos is waiting for Kawika to . . . to finish the job." I glanced at Kawika, who was checking on Pearl, adjusting her pillows with gentle hands that belied his earlier intentions. "Santos doesn't know Kawika has switched sides. He's told Santos to meet him in the north stairwell into the parking garage."

"I've got units three minutes out," Lei said, and I could hear her moving, the jingle of metal in the background. "I'm less than five minutes away myself. We'll lock down the hospital and find Santos. Do not open that door for anyone but me, understand? I'll identify myself when I arrive."

"Got it," I said, relief washing over me. "Hurry, Lei."

As I ended the call, I turned to find Pearl and Kawika deep in conversation, their voices low but intense. I moved closer, catching Pearl's words.

"... doesn't excuse what you did, but I understand the pressure you were under," she said, resting her hand on Kawika's arm. "Mayor Santos has always known how to manipulate people, even back when his father ran things."

Kawika shook his head, unable to meet her eyes. "I should have been stronger. Told you about my troubles, my debts. You trusted me, mentored me. And I betrayed that trust in the worst possible way."

"Yes, you did," Pearl was gentle but unflinching. "But you're trying to make it right now. That counts for something."

"How can you even look at me?" Kawika asked, his voice breaking. "After what I did? I could have killed you."

"And I'm angry about that—angrier than I've been in a long time. But I've lived long enough to know that people are complicated, Kawika. Good people can do terrible things when they're scared or confused."

A tear slipped down Kawika's cheek; he swiped it away angrily. "I don't deserve your forgiveness."

"Probably not," Pearl said. "But it's mine to give, and I choose to give it. What matters now is what you do with it."

The distant wail of sirens filtered through the small window, growing louder by the second. I moved to peek through a crack in the blinds and saw police cruisers pulling up to the hospital entrance, lights flashing against the afternoon sun.

"They're here," I said, relief flooding through me. "The hospital will be on lockdown soon."

Belatedly, I remembered Keone, waiting for news in Lei's cubicle. I composed a text telling him what was going on, then didn't send it. Better to inform him after we were safe.

We fell into tense silence then, listening to growing commotion outside—raised voices, hurried footsteps, the muffled announce-ments. Pearl closed her eyes and dozed off, exhaustion finally catching up with her. Kawika sat down on an overturned bucket and dropped his head into his hands, the weight of his actions visibly pressing down on him.

Minutes stretched like hours until finally, a firm knock came at the door.

"Kat? Pearl? It's Sergeant Texeira."

"Lei?" I approached the barricade cautiously as Kawika rose to his feet.

"It's me," she confirmed. "Santos is in custody. We caught him in the north stairwell, just where Kawika said he'd be. It's safe to come out now."

Kawika and I exchanged a glance, then moved aside the heavy cabinet. The door swung open to reveal Lei, her badge visible on her belt. Her gaze landed first on Pearl, checking that she was safe, then moved to Kawika, hardening instantly.

"Kawika Pali," she said formally. "I'm placing you under arrest for the attempted murder of Pearl Yamamoto." She reached for her handcuffs. "Turn around, please."

Kawika complied without protest; his shoulders slumped in resignation.

"He helped us," I said quietly as Lei secured the cuffs.

"I know," Lei said. "And that will count in his favor. But he still has to answer for what he has done."

She recited his rights, then leaned closer. "Just so you know," she said quietly, "I recognized your voice on that recording even before Kat confirmed it. It's a good thing for you that you chose to help Kat and Pearl. You were never getting away with anything. It's kind of ironic that you were the one who helped us get into the safety deposit box."

"Meant to be, I guess." Kawika nodded, accepting this. As Lei led him toward the door, he turned back to look at Pearl one last time. "I'm sorry," he said simply. "For everything."

Pearl, now awake and watching the scene unfold, nodded once. "I know you are," she said. "Make it right, Kawika. Tell them everything and take down those other men."

Lei guided him into the hallway where two uniformed officers waited to escort him out. As they disappeared down the corridor, I sank onto a box beside Pearl's bed. The adrenaline was draining away, leaving me shaky and exhausted. I sent a text to Keone telling him what happened and that everything was fine, now.

And it was.

Or maybe would be.

I wheeled Pearl back to her room. We called for a nurse, and one she knew showed up, along with a different officer to monitor the door. I was glad to see it was Officer Palakiko. We conferred for a moment as I caught him up on recent events. "Hopefully too much has gone down for the suspects to make another move," I told him. "But I'm glad you're here, anyway."

"Proud to do my part for a *kupuna* like Pearl Yamamoto," he said.

Back in the room, I made sure she was settled, tucking in her blanket. I handed her a plastic cup of water with a straw; she drank thirstily. "Thanks, Kat. You solved this."

"I had a lot of help, and I'm just glad it's over," I said, squeezing Pearl's fragile hand gently. "You're safe now. There's no reason for Mayor Santos or Councilman Akana to move against you with Kawika in custody. The jig is up, as they say." I studied her face, worried about the impact of Kawika's betrayal on her health. "Do you really forgive him? Kawika?"

Pearl was quiet for a moment, her gaze distant. "Forgiveness isn't the same as forgetting," she said finally. "I forgive him because holding onto anger would only poison me. But I won't forget. The garden will stand as a reminder—not just of what happened to our families all those years ago, but also of what happens when people choose to let power corrupt them."

Outside, the sun was lowering, casting long golden rays through the window when I raised the blind. In the warm glow Pearl closed her eyes, instantly falling asleep in the way of very old people and babies. Her pale lined face looked peaceful, now that the danger had passed. The truth would come to light after decades in shadow; we had set everything in motion.

My job to serve and protect was done here; but there would be others.

For now, Keone was waiting for me.

16

I woke to the sound of vacuuming in the hallway, and the warm press of Keone's body against mine. For a moment, I kept my eyes closed, savoring the simple pleasure of safety and comfort after the chaos of the past few days. The Hampton Inn's bed was soft and the sheets luxurious, and I'd slept deeply.

When I finally opened my eyes, sunlight was streaming through the partially open curtains, highlighting the rumpled sheets. Keone was still asleep beside me; his face was relaxed in a way I rarely got to see.

I reached for my phone on the nightstand, careful not to disturb him, and saw a text from Lei:

"Team meeting at MPD in an hour to review the case. I'll let you know the outcome."

"Need us to come in?" I typed back. *"To fill in any blanks."*

"Nope. Got it handled. Enjoy that hotel room."

Maui Police Department had paid for the room as a case-related expense after the takedown of David Santos and Kawika Pali yesterday. Mayor Santos and Councilman Akana were also under arrest.

I smiled and typed back: *"Not a chance I'm getting out of this bed anytime soon. Keep us posted!"*

Setting the phone down, I nestled against Keone, who stirred and draped an arm over my waist. We'd called in to work, and both of us had today off.

"What time is it?" he mumbled into my hair.

"Almost nine," I replied. "Lei's heading into a meeting with the MPD brass about the case."

"Mmm," he acknowledged, his eyes still closed. "Good thing we've got personal time off."

"Very good thing," I agreed, turning in his arms to face him. "Though I wish I could be a fly on the wall in that meeting."

Keone's eyes opened then. "You okay with all of it?"

I considered for a moment, turning my face to rest my cheek on his warm, bare chest. "Yes. The authorities will take the case where they can, and it will be what it will be. And honestly, I need some distance from all of it right now."

"How about we get breakfast downstairs and eat on the lanai, then spend some time at Makena Big Beach after that?" He nuzzled my neck. "Have to make the most of time off on this side of the island."

"Perfect," I said, I'll get dressed and be ready in just a few minutes.

By the time we made it to the balcony with our coffee and breakfast, it was nearly ten. We settled onto a single lounger, sides pressed together, plates balanced on our laps as we watched tourists dotting the pool's deck below.

My phone buzzed again with a text from Lei: *Press conference later. Captain Omura is putting it all out there. Pretty sure Ilima will be measuring curtains in the Hana-Ohia mayor's office by the end of the week.*

I showed the message to Keone. "Justice for Pearl, and a new beginning for Hana-Ohia."

"Santos may weather criminal charges, but his career is over,"

Keone said, taking a sip of his coffee. "And Mom and Edith will make sure the Heritage Garden becomes everything Pearl dreamed it could be."

I leaned against him, feeling the weight of the past few days begin to lift. "History preserved, truth acknowledged, and oleander reserved strictly for ornamental purposes."

As we relaxed and ate, my mind drifted to the meeting happening across town.

I could picture Lei sitting at the conference table, her files and evidence neatly arranged before her. Captain Omura would be there—I'd met her once at a community outreach event, a petite Japanese woman with an air of quiet authority that made even the tallest officers straighten when she entered a room. District Attorney Hiromo would be there too, and he had a reputation for meticulous preparation that was legendary on the island.

I imagined them going through the evidence piece by piece— the recording from Pearl's safety deposit box, the toxicology reports confirming oleander poisoning, Kawika's detailed confession implicating both himself and David Santos in the attempt on Pearl's life. I could see them laying out the complex web of connections: Mayor Santos orchestrating the whole thing with Councilman Akana, using David as their on-the-ground enforcer, pressuring Kawika until he broke.

All to get their hands on Pearl's land—the final piece they needed for their "Cultural Corridor" development that would have made them millions while erasing a crucial piece of island history.

The irony wasn't lost on me. They'd wanted to bury the past— the records proving that Pearl's family's land had been illegally seized during the Japanese internment and never properly returned. Instead, they'd managed to bring that history into the spotlight, ensuring it would now be preserved and remembered.

"What are you thinking about?" Keone asked, breaking into my thoughts.

"Just how things have a way of coming full circle," I said.

"Santos and Akana wanted to erase history, but they'll end up preserving it instead."

"And paying a price for trying to bury it," Keone added.

My phone buzzed again—another text from Lei:

Omura is taking no prisoners. She told the police commissioner her parents were interned at Manzanar. This is personal for her. They're talking about claiming the five-acre parcel from the Santos family using eminent domain—and paying them the same pittance for it that they paid the Yamamotos. Looks like it will be part of the Heritage Garden for sure.

"Captain Omura's parents were interned," I told Keone. "No wonder she's going hard after the Santos-Akana cabal."

"The department doesn't usually dig in on a case where the primary target—Pearl—survived and the main perpetrators are already in custody," Keone said.

"But it's bigger than that. It's about acknowledging what happened decades ago and making sure it's not forgotten or repeated."

Press conference scheduled for 10am tomorrow. They're going to lay out everything—the attempted murder, the development scheme, the historical context with the internment records. Sticking to what we can prove but making the connections clear enough for even the densest voter to follow.

"Wow," I said, showing Keone the message. "They're really doing this."

"Good," he said. "The public deserves to know the truth."

I nodded, thinking of Ilima, who had stood by Pearl from the beginning, championing the Heritage Garden against the Santos-Akana Cultural Corridor plan. With this scandal breaking, her mayoral victory was all but guaranteed.

"You know what this means for your mom," I said.

"Mayor Kaihale has a nice ring to it," Keone agreed. "And I bet her first official act will be to secure historical landmark status for

Pearl's garden." Despite everything—the poison, the conspiracy, the betrayal—Pearl had won. Her garden would be preserved, her family's history acknowledged, and the truth about what had happened during the internment period would be known.

The thought filled me with a quiet satisfaction.

"We should call her," I said suddenly, reaching for my phone again.

"Pearl?" Keone asked.

I nodded. "She should hear about the press conference from us, not the news."

I dialed the hospital room. "Hello?" Pearl's voice came through the line, stronger than it had been the day before, but still carrying the tremor of age and illness.

"Pearl, it's Kat," I said. "I have some news about the case."

As I filled her in on the upcoming press conference and what it would mean for the future of her garden, warmth flooded me.

Pearl had been knocked down but never defeated. She was always ready to begin again, to fight for what mattered. To preserve the past while building something new for the future.

When I hung up, Keone was watching me with a soft expression.

"How is she?" he asked.

"Stronger," I said. "And very pleased about the press conference. She said she'd try to watch it from her hospital room."

Keone nodded, then gestured toward the view before them: sunshine, waving palms, sparkles on the pool and the sea beyond. "So, what do you say? Ready to face the world again?"

I looked out at the ocean beyond Kahului Bay—endless, washing away the old, always creating something new. Much like our beloved island of Maui, where the past and future were forever in conversation.

"Not quite yet," I said, settling back against him on the lounger and turning to give him a kiss. "Let's stay here a little longer." Sometimes the most important thing you could do was simply be present —to witness, to remember, and when the time was right, to help others do the same—with some kissing in the sunshine to spice things up.

17

TWO WEEKS LATER:

Late afternoon's warmth slanted through the sliders of our former model home in New Ohia State Park, bathing the assembled company in warm golden light. The wide deck had been arranged with additional seating to accommodate our expanded group, while the adjacent living room buzzed with conversations, and in the background, Artie Pahinui skillfully plucked the strings of his guitar in a slack-key melody.

Tiki and Misty had claimed the prime sunny spot on the bay window seat of the living room, their combined gray and calico fur gleaming as they observed the human proceedings with characteristic feline detachment—occasionally accepting offerings of cheese bites from Rita, who remained convinced that all cats required constant supplementary feeding regardless of their obvious health.

At the center of the gathering sat Pearl Yamamoto, her diminutive frame dwarfed by what she called her "command center," a state-of-the-art wheelchair that gleamed with polished titanium and custom details. Despite the toll the poisoning had taken on her body, Pearl's dark eyes remained bright and sharp beneath her silver hair, which was perfectly styled and adorned with delicate jade combs.

Standing behind Pearl's wheelchair, next to Keone, was Lani Nakasone, her caregiver of two weeks. Lani was a part-time waitress at the Hotel Hana, which had been slow lately, allowing her time to work with Pearl and provide her care. She and Keone had dated in the past; their relationship had ended amicably, but seeing them together still triggered a tiny, irrational twinge of something I refused to call jealousy.

Especially since Lani was genuinely kind, and exactly what Pearl needed right now. I actually liked her. I just didn't like her next to my man, which was where she was standing right now.

Keone laughed at something Pearl told the both of them as I moved between the kitchen and the deck, balancing a tray of iced tea glasses while navigating around the Red Hat Society ladies. They had commandeered the most comfortable seating, and their vibrant purple outfits and signature red hats added a festive air to what was essentially an informal debriefing session following the most significant corruption case in our area's recent history.

"Here, let me help with that," Keone said, intercepting me before I could attempt to distribute drinks single-handedly.

"Thanks," I smiled, releasing the tray to his more stable grip. "I think Aunt Fae invited half the town instead of just the key investigation participants."

"She does love to throw a gathering," Keone said. "Why have an intimate debrief when you could host a community forum complete with color-coordinated refreshments?" He nodded toward the dining table, where Aunt Fae and my friend Elle had arranged an impressive spread of finger foods organized by color— a rainbow of culinary offerings that was as visually striking as it was delicious.

"At least she restrained herself from printing commemorative T-shirts. Though I wouldn't put it past her to have them on order for the Heritage Garden groundbreaking ceremony," I said as I finished handing out the glasses of iced tea.

"Too late." Keone grinned as he set down the empty tray to reach into his pocket. He produced his phone and showed me a mock-up image Aunt Fae had sent him that morning: a proposed T-shirt design featuring a stylized crane in flight above the text "Truth Rises: Ohia Heritage Garden Now."

"Oh wow," I groaned, though I couldn't help smiling. "Please tell me you talked her out of it."

"Actually, Pearl loves the design," he replied. "Says it captures the spirit of the project. They're discussing color options and sustainable fabric choices and planning to have it on the Heritage Garden website, along with other swag."

"I insisted on organic bamboo fabric for any of the Heritage Garden merchandise we're planning." Pearl must have overheard us, because she chimed in, her voice carrying its characteristic blend of authority and humor. "If we're going to commemorate justice with clothing, it should at least be ethically and sustainably sourced."

Lani leaned down to adjust Pearl's shawl, a handwoven piece in shades of purple that complemented her cream-colored dress. "You have strong opinions about fabric," she said with an affectionate smile. "I've learned a lot about textiles in the last two weeks."

"That sounds about right," I said, making my way over to them. "How are you feeling today, Pearl? I hope this isn't too much."

Pearl waved away my concern with a beringed hand. "After so long in that hospital room, being surrounded by friends feels like medicine." Her gaze swept the room and she smiled with evident satisfaction. "Besides, how could I miss the victory celebration?"

"We're calling it a 'case review,'" I reminded her. "Lei was very specific about not labeling it a celebration while some aspects of the case are still proceeding."

"Semantics," Pearl said dismissively. "When justice begins to unfold, after so many years of waiting, I reserve the right to consider it celebration worthy, regardless."

Before I could respond to this characteristically Pearl-like proclamation, Lei appeared from the kitchen. Her curly brown hair was down, a plumeria decorated her ear, and she'd exchanged her gun and badge for casual jeans and a linen blouse. She looked pretty, young, and relaxed.

"Your aunt's pulled out the good stuff for the 'official debrief,'" she informed us, carrying a small tray with glasses of champagne and tumblers of amber liquid. "For those who are in the mood for a little day drinking. Fae says we've earned it after navigating 'the most convoluted conspiracy since Watergate'—her words, not mine."

"Hear, hear!" exclaimed Edith, snatching a tumbler of Scotch off the tray. Josie, beside her, claimed a glass of champagne, as did Rita and Opal.

My good friend Elle went for a Scotch. "It's been a while since I've done any day drinking," she said.

"I'll take mine with ice, please," Pearl said, extending a slightly tremulous hand. When Lei raised an eyebrow, Pearl added, "Dr. Patel cleared me for one medicinal drink per day. I've been saving today's allotment for this precise moment."

Lei carefully placed a glass in Pearl's hand and steadied it, while Lani fetched the ice bucket and added a few cubes with a pair of tongs. I smiled at the sight, because the two of them reminded me of courtiers waiting on a queen.

"Aunt Fae has been binge-watching political documentaries again," I explained to the group, accepting my own glass of champagne. "Last month it was lunar landing conspiracies. The month before that, it was cold cases from the 1970s. Her subscription queue is a journey through humanity's darkest and strangest moments."

"Keeps the mind sharp," Aunt Fae declared, appearing behind Lei with another tray, this one holding a bowl of tropical fruit cubes speared with toothpicks for easy eating. "They provide excellent inspiration for my mystery writing group."

"How are the 'Poison Pen Pals' doing these days?" Keone asked, using the formal name of Aunt Fae's writing circle—five women, some right here in the room. They met monthly to craft murder mysteries that were, according to their own description, "demographically underrepresented in the genre."

"Thriving," Aunt Fae replied with satisfaction. "Edith's working on a serial killer novel featuring a retirement community gardening club as the investigative team. Rita's crafting a locked-room mystery set in a knitting circle and in a house full of cats—imagine the tangles, ha! And I'm outlining a true-crime-inspired thriller based on—" she lowered her voice conspiratorially, "—recent local events, with names and identifying details changed to protect the guilty and to avoid libel suits."

"I didn't hear that," Lei said, a dimple in her cheek betraying amusement. "As the detective of record on those 'recent local events,' I am not endorsing any fictionalized accounts of real events, particularly those featuring elected official cover-ups or plant toxins."

"Who said anything about plant toxins?" Aunt Fae asked, though her blue eyes were mischievous. "Now that you mention it, there are some fascinating recipes involving oleander . . ."

Pearl's soft laugh turned into a cough, and Lani immediately produced a glass of water and swapped that for the Scotch. "Perhaps we should avoid detailed discussions of the substance that nearly killed me," Pearl said, after taking a sip. "Though I like the idea of transforming my near-death experience into a mystery novel."

"Uncovering the plot certainly was convoluted enough for one," I said. "And that's my cue to redirect this conversation." I raised my glass slightly and tapped the side of it with serving tongs to get attention. "Shall we move to the actual debriefing portion of this gathering? I believe everyone who should be here has arrived."

Indeed, our core group had settled in: Lei was sitting comfortably in one of the Adirondack armchairs, Keone and I moved over to claim the porch swing, Artie and Opal were together on the padded bench near the palms, Pearl had positioned her chair in the middle where she could see everyone, with Lani standing behind her. Aunt Fae perched on the wide arm of Lei's Adirondack chair with the air of a co-host at an official proceeding. The Red Hat Society members—Josie, Edith, Clara, and Rita—formed a vibrant semicircle of purple and red on the settees arranged around a low table, while Ilima sat slightly apart in the second Adirondack, her expression thoughtful, with Elle perched beside her on a stool.

The special election following Mayor Santos's removal from office had concluded just last week, with Ilima winning in a landslide that surprised no one. Her transition from community activist to mayor-elect of Hana-Ohia had been swift, but already the office seemed to suit her well, adding a new gravity to her already dignified persona.

"First," Lei began, setting her champagne glass on the small table beside her, "I want to thank everyone here for their contributions to this investigation. What began as a seemingly straightforward poisoning case expanded into something far more complex."

"And that poisoning wouldn't have been detected if not for Tiki," I said, as my one-eared, kink-tailed former feral feline pranced through the gathering to jump on my lap. "She was the one who knocked the fatal dose of tea right out of Pearl's hand."

Everyone clapped spontaneously until Pearl made an imperious gesture. "Now, Sergeant Texeira, please continue with your update. Some of us are operating on limited energy reserves and would like to hear the official status before requiring a nap."

Lei smiled. "Of course. I'd like to update everyone on where things stand legally, and then perhaps our mayor-elect can share the latest developments regarding the Heritage Garden project."

Ilima nodded in acknowledgment, inclining her head for Lei to go on.

"David Santos is in custody and has been formally charged with attempted murder, conspiracy to commit murder, and evidence tampering," Lei said. "The recording from Pearl's safety deposit box, combined with Kawika Pali's confession and testimony, has provided us with compelling evidence of his direct involvement in planning Pearl's poisoning and the conspiracy to stop the Heritage Garden from going forward."

Pearl's expression remained neutral at the mention of Kawika's name, but I noticed her fingers tighten on the armrest of her wheelchair. Lani placed a gentle hand on her shoulder, a gesture of support that Pearl acknowledged with a slight nod.

"What about Mayor Santos?" Clara asked, leaning forward with interest, straightening her graceful violet *muumuu*.

"Former Mayor Santos," Ilima corrected, the emphasis meaningful.

"Former Mayor Santos," Lei continued with a nod, "is currently facing multiple charges related to corruption and his role in the conspiracy. While we don't have direct evidence linking him to the poisoning, financial records and communications uncovered during our investigation show he was working with Councilman Akana to block the Heritage Garden project in favor of their Cultural Corridor development."

"Which would have made them millions," Keone said.

"Exactly," Lei nodded. "The plan, as we understand it now, was to wait until Pearl passed away—either from natural causes or with some 'assistance'—and then move forward with the Cultural Corridor project once Kawika was in control of Pearl's estate. The mayor and Akana had already lined up investors and started preliminary planning, all while publicly claiming to support the Heritage Garden."

"And Kawika?" I asked. His betrayal still felt fresh despite the time that had passed. "What's happening to him?"

Lei's lips firmed. "Kawika Pali has provided a full confession. He admitted to poisoning Pearl's tea at the ceremony under direction from David Santos, and to planning to finish the job at the hospital. His testimony of the master plan they concocted to gain control of Pearl's estate has been invaluable in building the case against both David and the former mayor. He's in jail but his sentence will be mitigated by his cooperation."

A weighty silence fell over the room. Pearl took a small sip of water, which Lani had given back to her, her eyes momentarily distant before she refocused on the group. "I've requested to go visit him," she said quietly, causing several surprised glances. "Not immediately, but eventually. There are questions that only he can answer about how this unfolded over time."

"Are you sure that's wise?" Ilima asked gently. "He's my nephew, but I'm not going anywhere near him. The betrayal was profound, and seeing him might—"

"Might what?" Pearl interrupted, a flash of her old fire evident. "Upset me? I'm already upset. Might reopen wounds? The wounds haven't closed. I have forgiven the boy, but I need to understand how someone I trusted with my life, someone whose life has been connected to mine for so many years, could make this kind of choice." Lani adjusted Pearl's shawl again, the simple action seeming to ground the older woman. "It's part of my recovery," she said at last. "Coming to terms with Kawika and what he did."

"Speaking of recovery," I said, wanting to steer the conversation toward more positive developments, "how do you feel about the Heritage Garden project moving forward? Lei mentioned there have been significant developments."

Pearl's expression brightened, the tension in her shoulders easing. "The project has received official approval from the county planning commission," she announced, her voice stronger than it had been moments before. "With Mayor Santos removed from office, the commission evaluated the proposal purely on its merits and historical significance."

"One of my first official actions as mayor will be to formally designate the Heritage Garden as a protected historical site," Ilima's voice carried the authority that was a natural part of her. "The paperwork is already prepared for signing on my first day in office."

"Wonderful news," Aunt Fae said. "When will construction begin?"

"Preliminary site preparation starts next month," Pearl replied, nodding toward Ilima. "I'll be present for the groundbreaking ceremony, even if it means attending in this rolling contraption." She patted the arm of her wheelchair.

"The garden design has evolved in some meaningful ways," Edith Pepperwhite contributed, reaching into a capacious bag to withdraw a rolled set of plans. She spread them on the central table as we gathered around.

The design was beautiful in its elegant simplicity—a series of garden rooms flowing into one another, each representing a different aspect of the Japanese-American experience in Hawaii. The central feature remained the reconstruction of Pearl's grandfather's original garden, including a crane statue under the huge plumeria tree, positioned exactly where the original had stood before the internment.

"The most significant addition," Pearl explained, gesturing toward a circular structure near the garden's entrance, "is this memorial and education center. It will house permanent exhibits documenting both the historical internment period and the subsequent land disputes. I believe it's essential that the full story be told —not as sensationalism, but as acknowledgment of how difficult and complicated the path to justice can be."

"Including recent events?" Josie asked, glancing at Pearl.

"Especially recent events," Pearl said. "The attempted silencing of the narrative is part of history—a continuation of the same forces that have tried to bury this embarrassment for decades. Excluding it would be incomplete."

"The garden will also include a community gathering space," Edith continued, indicating a terraced area designed for outdoor events. "Pearl wants the project to serve not just as a memorial, but as an active, living space where the community can come together."

"A place for both remembrance and renewal," Opal nodded approvingly.

As the conversation continued and sunlight faded to the golden hour, I noticed Pearl beginning to tire, though she was clearly making an effort to conceal it. Lani noticed too, subtly checking her watch and making eye contact with me. Understanding the unspoken message, I began to think about how to wind down the gathering without making Pearl feel she was the cause.

As the conversation shifted to logistics for the garden's groundbreaking in a few months, I noticed Lani checking her watch more pointedly. She caught Keone's eye, and he nodded slightly, understanding the message.

"I think we should probably start wrapping up," Keone said diplomatically. "It's been a full afternoon."

"Indeed," Pearl said, not bothering to hide her fatigue any longer. "As much as I've enjoyed this gathering, my body is reminding me rather insistently that I'm still recovering."

This announcement prompted a flurry of goodbyes and well-wishes as the guests began to gather their things. Pearl accepted each farewell with grace, though I could see the strain of maintaining her composure as tiredness overtook her.

After Pearl and Lani departed, with promises to reconnect as the event for the Garden was planned, the gathering quickly disbanded. Lei left, citing early court appearances the next day, but promising updates as they occurred.

Eventually, only our core group remained: Keone and I, Aunt Fae, Ilima, and Artie and Opal, who seemed in no hurry to conclude the evening.

We moved inside as the air cooled, settling in the comfortable living room where Tiki and Misty had already claimed prime sleeping spots on the couch and had to be dislodged.

"Pearl seemed stronger than I expected," Artie observed,

accepting a cup of punch from Aunt Fae. "Given how serious her condition was just a few weeks ago."

"She's determined to recover in time for the garden groundbreaking," Ilima explained. "The doctors are amazed by her progress, though they warn she may never regain her previous stamina."

As the evening drew to a natural close, Keone and I prepared to leave. Tiki, sensing our imminent departure, stretched languidly before leaping from her spot to twine around my ankles.

"We should get going," Keone said, checking his watch. "Tiki gets cranky if her dinner is too late, and it's been a long day."

"Such a demanding creature," I said fondly, as Tiki purposefully headed toward the door ahead of us. "Give me a hug, Aunt Fae."

"Aw, girlie. I miss you," she whispered in her ear. "But I'm happy if you're happy."

"I'm happy," I whispered back. I'd moved in with Keone the previous week, and we were all still getting used to things.

She kissed my cheek. "Good. Then you won't mind if I move a gentleman caller into your old bedroom next to mine, will you?"

I laughed. "Getting onto the dating websites, are you, Auntie?"

"I've still got tread on my tires," she said, and winked. "Drive safe."

Outside, the night was clear and star-filled, the ocean visible as a darker expanse beyond the trees surrounding the park.

Keone drove us along the coastal road toward the cottage with Tiki curled contentedly in her carrier in the back seat. Soon, the familiar shape of Keone's seaside cottage came into view, nestled beside his mother's larger home.

The two properties shared a garden that sloped to a steep bluff overlooking the ocean. This was now illuminated by solar-powered path lights that cast a warm glow across the native plantings of fruit and flowers.

"What are you thinking about?" Keone asked, glancing over at me as we pulled into the driveway.

"Everything, really," I admitted. "How Pearl is managing to move forward despite what Kawika did to her. How the Heritage Garden is finally becoming reality after all these years. How different things might have been if we hadn't found that final piece of evidence in her safety deposit box."

Keone nodded, parking the truck in the lean-to garage. "It's been an intense few months."

"That's an understatement," I smiled, reaching back to unbuckle Tiki's carrier. "When Tiki uncovered Pearl's poisoning, I had no idea where it would lead."

"A case like this reveals the connections that were always there, just beneath the surface," Keone said as we made our way up the gently lit path to the cottage door. "Between past and present."

"Like Pearl's clever use of carved boxes," I said, setting down Tiki's carrier outside the cottage's screened porch. Mango, Ilima's old cat, had long since been driven off by my much fiercer calico, who exited the carrier and went up the steps ahead of us. "The truth was waiting for the right alignment of light and perspective to become visible."

"Poetic way of looking at detective work," Keone said, opening the screen door and holding it for Tiki and me. We crossed the orchid-lined porch and went inside—no one locked their doors here.

Tiki immediately headed for her food bowl in the kitchen, meowing indignantly about the delayed dinner service. "Yes, your highness, right away," I said, setting down my bag and moving to the kitchen to attend to her demands.

Keone switched on lamps around the living room, casting a warm glow over the space we now shared. Through the window, I could see lights on in his mother's house next door. Ilima had been working late most evenings, preparing for her transition to the mayor's office.

"Mom's going to be up awhile," Keone said, following my gaze. "Probably reviewing budget documents. She's determined to understand every aspect of the town's finances before she officially takes office."

"She'll be an amazing mayor," I said, measuring out Tiki's food. "Hana and Ohia couldn't ask for a better leader right now."

"Agreed," he said, moving to the refrigerator. "She's already talking about establishing a community reconciliation commission to address lingering issues from the corruption investigation."

"That balance seems to be Pearl's core message throughout all of this," I observed, watching Tiki attack her dinner with enthusiasm, forgoing her usual prissiness. All that socializing at Aunt Fae's must have helped her work up an appetite. "Acknowledging painful truths without becoming defined or consumed by them."

Keone poured us each a glass of water and led the way to the house's front lanai, where we often ended our days listening to the waves and watching the stars. Night air carried the salt scent of the ocean mixed with the sweet fragrance of blooming ginger from the garden.

"It's still hard to believe how much has changed," I said, settling into one of the comfortable chairs. "Your mother becoming mayor, Pearl's garden finally being approved, the Santos family facing justice after generations of corruption."

"And you," Keone added, his voice softening as he sat beside me. "Moving to Ohia for a fresh start, getting pulled into one major investigation after another."

"And finding you," I said. "That wasn't exactly in my plan when I took the postmaster position."

"A fortunate side effect," he smiled, reaching for my hand. "Though I maintain it was inevitable."

"It's a pretty small dating pool out here," I agreed. "Now we've got to find someone for Aunt Fae."

We fell into comfortable silence, listening to the rhythmic sound of waves breaking on the shore below. Through the open door, I could hear Tiki moving around inside, probably settling into her favorite spot on top of the refrigerator, after completing her evening meal.

The lights in Ilima's house eventually went dark as we sat there, discussing the plans for the garden and our own future within this community that had become home in ways I never expected.

"This is home," Keone said, as we finally rose to go inside, the word carrying meanings beyond the physical cottage we shared. "And I'm glad you're with me."

"You read my mind," I said, following him through the door. "And I like that."

18

THREE MONTHS LATER:

The morning air carried the sweet perfume of plumeria blossoms mingled with the darker notes of freshly turned earth. Mount Haleakalā stood in majestic silence against the cloudless blue sky, its massive presence watching over the ceremony like a benevolent ancestor. The ocean stretched beyond the grounds in an impossible palette of blues: cerulean near the shore gradually deepening to cobalt and finally indigo at the horizon, where it met the sky in a seamless transition stitched together by clouds.

Three months had passed since Kawika's confession and the subsequent legal proceedings that had transformed Hana-Ohia's political landscape. Today, the land upon which the Heritage Garden would soon grow hummed with anticipation as community members gathered for the official groundbreaking ceremony.

White folding chairs arranged in neat rows faced a simple wooden platform decorated with ti leaves and colorful origami cranes—hundreds of them, folded by schoolchildren, seniors at the community center, and others who had embraced Pearl's invitation to contribute to the ceremony. The paper birds caught the morning light, their vibrant colors dancing in the gentle breeze that swept in from the ocean.

I stood near the back of the seating area, watching as Elle, bright as a cardinal in a fitted red sheath dress, directed the final arrangements with characteristic precision. Elle had thrown herself into coordinating the groundbreaking with the same enthusiasm she brought to all her events, transforming what might have been a simple ceremony into a meaningful celebration.

"Elle's really outdone herself this time," Keone observed, appearing at my side with two cups of the lilikoi punch being served at a refreshment table. He was splendid in a bronze-toned silk aloha shirt that brought out the gold in his skin and eyes. He handed me one of the cups, his fingers brushing mine in a casual toast.

"She's been planning this one for months, and there were a lot of bosses to please," I said, sipping the drink. The unique sweet-tart flavor of passion fruit burst across my tongue, perfectly balanced with a hint of ginger. "I think she's revised the seating chart at least four times to ensure the best possible 'energy flow'—her words, not mine."

"I notice the Red Hat Society has prime positioning," Keone nodded toward the vibrant splash of purple and red in the front rows. Aunt Fae, naturally, had added her own flourish to the standard ensemble—her red fedora sported a wire contraption from which a cascade of tiny origami cranes bobbed with every movement of her head.

"Elle's smart enough to know that community power brokers require strategic placement. Edith, for instance." I gestured with my cup. "And your mom."

The diminutive lawyer had pride of place with a chair beside the podium on one side, and Ilima Kaihale, the new mayor, on the other. None of those dignitaries had taken their seats yet; only Artie Pahinui occupied the wooden platform at the moment, rocking gently to and fro on his chair and keeping the beat with a bare brown foot as he played an intricate slack-key melody that welcomed us.

A gentle hush fell over the gathering as Pearl trundled in her fancy wheelchair toward the ceremonial area with Lani and her nieces, Sandy and Windy Nakasone, trailing behind. For today's occasion, Pearl had adorned her chair with flowing loops of lei in the garden project colors—jade green, soft yellow, and red. The Nakasone girls tossed plumeria down on the grassy aisle leading to the seats, a sweet touch.

Ilima walked beside Pearl, resplendent in a formal *muumuu* of deep blue, her mayoral sash gleaming against the fabric. Ilima had won the special election following Santos's removal and dressed the part like a natural.

Bringing up the rear of the little cavalcade was Edith Pepperwhite, smiling to the right and to the left, cradling a fancy scroll and large pair of scissors that would be part of the ceremony.

The crowd rose in spontaneous respect as Pearl navigated her wheelchair along the accessible path that led to the platform. Once on the platform, she activated the chair's elevation mechanism, rising gracefully to a standing position—a moment she had practiced repeatedly for this occasion, determined to stand symbolically as she addressed the community.

Moved to see her there, surrounded by such dear friends and community, I grabbed Keone's hand and squeezed it as we hurried to find our seats. The oleander poisoning had left lasting effects on Pearl's nervous system, but her mind was as sharp as ever, and her spirit seemed undaunted even after facing betrayal and near death.

I blinked back unexpected tears. The journey from her hospital bed to this moment had been filled with physical pain, emotional processing of Kawika's betrayal, and exhausting legal proceedings that had required Pearl's testimony on multiple occasions. Yet here she stood, embodying the resilience that had characterized her life.

"Welcome," Pearl said. Everyone sat, including her entourage. "*E komo mai.*"

Her voice carried clearly across the bowl of open space. "Welcome to this special day that marks the conclusion of decades of concealment and the beginning of acknowledgment and healing through the Heritage Garden project."

Pearl spoke of her family's experience during internment, the subsequent struggles to reclaim their property and dignity, and her vision for a garden that would serve as both a memorial and a community gathering place. Edith got up next, unrolling her scroll to highlight the project's design and timeline. Finally, Ilima made a fiery and passionate speech about truth, justice, and the Hawaiian way of aloha that left me patting my nonexistent pockets for tissues. Thankfully, Keone handed me a handkerchief. "Your mom is just getting started in politics," I whispered. "Next stop, the governor's mansion."

Next up, Pearl snipped a scarlet ribbon staked around a small *ohia lehua* tree in a pot. Heads of families directly affected by the historical land seizures—Japanese-American families whose properties had been taken during internment, and descendants of Native Hawaiian families who had experienced earlier dispossession, all helped plant the tree, placing handfuls of soil around its base. The *ohia*, positioned near the entrance, symbolized shared commitment to remembrance and reconciliation.

"This garden will tell many stories," one elderly *nisei* man said, brushing the soil from the planting from his hands. "Some painful, some inspiring. All necessary." Many others followed, reading poems, showing photos and a letter to family from the camps. The Nakasone girls each propped a sweet drawing against the fragile trunk of the sapling at the end. I smiled to see the grounds' ancient gardener, Takahashi, standing by with a watering can to apply love to the little tree when the hoopla was over.

The crowd's applause rippled across the grounds when the ceremony was over, replaced by the sound of distant waves and Artie's guitar playing, this time accompanied by an *ipu* drum.

Guests moved out from the chairs and planting site to explore the flag-marked pathways that outlined the garden's future layout, or to examine the architectural renderings displayed on easels near the refreshment area. The news van which had been filming focused in on Wendy Watanabe, a local reporter, holding forth.

I spotted Elle moving efficiently through the crowd, clipboard in hand. She caught my eye and flashed a quick thumbs-up before directing the catering staff on the dispersal of *pupus* being served.

Keone took my hand. "Let's do a walk-through." We wandered along the future pathways, stopping occasionally to study the small flags indicating where specific features would be installed. Careful planning was evident everywhere—accessible paths designed to accommodate Pearl and others with mobility challenges, seating areas positioned to capture both ocean views and mountain vistas, smaller spaces for contemplation, and bigger ones designated for educational gatherings.

"Pearl's thought of everything," I said as we paused by a marker indicating the future site of a Japanese-inspired stone garden. "Every detail has meaning."

"Speaking of meaningful places," Keone said, "there's something I'd like to show you while everyone is distracted with the reception food."

Curiosity piqued, I followed as he led me along a pathway that curved through what would eventually become a traditional Japanese meditation garden. The path ended at the massive old plumeria tree—one that had been carefully preserved in the garden's design due to its age and beauty—and where, on paper, it would shelter a reproduction of the garden's original crane statue.

Caution tape encircled the site, but Keone gave my hand a tug and led me to slip under it. "We have special dispensation from Pearl."

The tree's fullest bloom had passed, and its nearly bare branches arched overhead, architectural against the sky, budding at the tips into leaf. A few white and yellow blossoms still released their sweet perfume from above and below as fallen flowers dotted the ground in contrast of gold and cream against the dark earth.

The setting was almost ethereally beautiful as morning light filtered through the branches to create dappled patterns around us, highlighting the sculpture on a stone dais directly before us.

"Oh, wow," I said, gazing at the crane in its spot near the tree's trunk. A six-foot-tall rendering in bronze, the bird exuded peace; its neck arched in a graceful curve as it tucked its bill beneath a wing. The metal seemed to glow; it hadn't yet acquired the patina of age.

"This spot is for a stone bench to sit and contemplate," Keone said, pointing to a cement pad that faced the sculpture and the tree.

"The statue is gorgeous, and this spot will be perfect for reflection once the garden is complete," I said.

"I thought so too." Keone's hand moved to his pocket. "Which is why I asked Pearl's permission to bring you here today."

My heart speeded up as Keone withdrew something from his pocket—not a box, but an origami crane folded from iridescent paper that shifted between blue and green as it caught the light.

"Did you make this?" My voice was unsteady as I accepted the delicate paper bird.

"I did." His warm brown eyes gleamed. "They've become a symbol of our journey together. Open it."

I unfolded the crane with trembling fingers. Each released fold revealed words.

Keone had written in his distinctive handwriting: *"Some loves reveal themselves slowly and deepen with each passing day. Some questions can only be asked when the moment is right."*

As I released the final fold, something small and metallic rolled into my palm—a ring of vintage design, featuring a central pearl surrounded by tiny diamonds set in intricate gold filigree.

"This was my grandmother's," Keone said as I stared at the ring. "She gave it to me before she passed, saying I would know when and with whom to share it."

I gulped. My knees wobbled. "I wish that bench was finished so I could sit down," I muttered.

Keone took my free hand, his touch steady despite the emotion evident in his eyes. "Kat, you've become essential to me. My partner in investigation and in everyday moments, my favorite person to share everything—and a cat—with."

That he mentioned Tiki in that moment made my eyes well up; I was doing okay until then. I sniffled loudly, blinking. "Dang it."

Sun caught in the pearl's surface, revealing subtle variations of cream and pink within its depths as Keone continued, dropping to one knee before me.

"I'm asking if you'll share life's journey with me, as my wife. Will you marry me?"

The question hung in the fragrant air between us.

The distant sound of celebration from the main party area provided a gentle backdrop to the moment.

I stared down at the ring in my palm, its beauty undeniable, the weight of its significance even more so. Familiar tightness strangled my breath; the same constriction I'd felt at every major emotional crossroads since I was nine years old and lost both my parents in a single moment on an icy road.

"Keone—" I coughed, choking on joy and fear. Longing and hesitation. Desire for connection, and an instinctive self-protection that had become second nature.

Keone stood back up. "It's okay. Just think about it," he said.

His graciousness released my paralysis.

"I love you," I blurted, the words coming easily because they were undeniably true. "And I want a future with you. But marriage feels like tempting fate somehow."

"Because of your parents?"

I nodded, grateful for his perception. "I was so young when they died, but the lesson I learned was crystal clear: loving deeply means risking devastating loss. Every time I've gotten close to someone since then, that fear resurfaces."

"I know," Keone said. "It's okay. I thought it might be too soon to ask you." I finally had the courage to gaze into his warm brown eyes. I could see that he understood. "Loss has shaped both of us in different ways. Losing my dad, and seeing my parents' loving marriage, made me determined to wait, and be sure of, the right person to spend my life with."

"I know it's not rational," I said. "I know that loving someone doesn't cause them to be taken away. But the fear is so deeply ingrained that sometimes it feels like a protective spell—if I don't fully commit, maybe I can prevent history from repeating itself."

"What would make you comfortable right now? Not what you think you should feel, or what would make *me* happy—but what feels right for you?"

I stared down at the ring, then back at his face. This man had shown me time and again that he understood my complexities and respected my needs.

"I want to be with you," I stated, the certainty of that a solid foundation beneath the shifting sands of fear. "I want to build a life together. I'm just not ready for a traditional engagement with all the trappings." I slipped Keone's grandma's heirloom onto the ring finger of my right hand. "Would it be okay if I wore it here for now?"

"Perfect," he said, taking my hand and pressing a kiss to the ring that now adorned it. "This relationship is about finding what works for us."

"Are you sure?" I searched his handsome face for any sign of hidden disappointment. "Most people would expect a straightfor-ward yes—or no."

"I'm not 'most people,'" he reminded me. "And neither are you. We've never done anything the conventional way. Why start now?"

Relief and gratitude washed through me. "Thank you for understanding."

"I'd rather have you genuinely where you are, than pretending in any form."

I stepped forward and wrapped my arms around his shoulders. We were both the same glorious six-foot-one in height. We fit like two bookends measured for each other. We kissed for a long time. So long, in fact, that I forgot where I began and he ended.

It was Tiki, winding around our ankles with a loud "Mrrrow!" that made us break apart. I gave a breathless laugh and reached down to pet her. When I straightened back up, I met Keone's gaze, and he was twinkling his eyes at me. "I love you," I said.

"I love you, too, Trouble," he said. "Maybe that ring will stay on your right hand forever, and that's just fine. There's no expiration date for us."

We kissed some more. Tiki sat down on my feet, registering her presence. She eventually applied talons to my calf, letting me know she wanted sustenance.

"We should probably head back," I said, pulling away from his embrace. "Elle will send out a search party if we're missing too long."

Keone plucked a fallen plumeria blossom from my hair. "What do you want to tell people? My mom is sure to notice that ring."

"That we're engaged, but not yet planning the wedding," I said. "I'll know when I'm ready for the next step. I'll move the ring to my left hand, then."

"Perfect," he said, and it felt that way to me, too.

As we walked back toward the main gathering, following Tiki's sassy kinked tail, I was acutely aware of the ring on my right hand. Wearing it there was a promise to myself as much as to Keone: a promise to keep working through the fear that had shaped so much of my life, to move toward love rather than away from it, even when that was at my own careful pace.

The celebration was in full swing when we returned, with Elle efficiently directing the flow of guests between refreshment stations and informational displays about the garden's future features, as a full band now occupied the stage, and a younger crowd danced where the chairs had been.

Elle spotted us immediately, her eyes narrowing as she assessed our clasped hands and slightly rumpled appearance. "I was wondering where you'd got to," she said.

"Keone wanted to show me the plumeria tree that's being preserved in the garden design," I explained, which was true, if incomplete.

Elle's gaze dropped to my hand, where the vintage ring's pearl gleamed in the sunlight. Her expression softened into a smile. "I get it," she said. "Congratulations to you both!"

Before I could respond to her perceptive assessment, Elle was pulled away by a catering question. With a quick squeeze of my arm, she was gone, weaving through the crowd toward the refreshment tables.

I instinctively tucked my hand behind my back, suddenly self-conscious.

Keone noticed. "We don't have to tell anyone today if you're not ready," he said.

Before I could respond, Aunt Fae and Ilima approached us, engaged in what appeared to be an intense discussion. Aunt Fae's crane-adorned hat bobbed emphatically as she gestured toward one of the architectural renderings.

"All I'm saying is that the meditation space should incorporate elements from both Japanese and Hawaiian traditions," she explained. "A true reflection of the community's intertwined—" She broke off abruptly as she noticed us. "There you two are! We were wondering where you'd disappeared to."

I kept my hand behind my back, but the gesture only drew Aunt Fae's attention. Her sharp eyes narrowed with suspicion. "What are you hiding, Kat?" she asked directly, in the way that had both exasperated and comforted me throughout my life. "You've got that same guilty look you had when you were twelve and accidentally broke my heirloom vase."

"I don't have a guilty look," I protested, and brought my hand from behind my back. The sunlight caught the pearl's surface, gleaming with iridescence that both women noticed. Aunt Fae gasped dramatically while Ilima's eyes widened with surprise and delight.

"My mother's ring!" Ilima exclaimed, recognizing the family heirloom instantly. "Keone, you finally asked her."

"I did," Keone moved closer to my side and slid an arm around my waist. "And Kat has agreed we're engaged, just not setting a date yet."

Aunt Fae grabbed my hand and examined the ring. "Ah," she said, with uncharacteristic restraint. "On the right hand. You're not quite ready."

"We're easing into it. That feels right for now," I said. "I'm not ready for the trappings, but I'm ready to show our commitment."

"The most important promises are the ones we make in our own hearts, not the ones society prescribes," Ilima said, embracing first her son and then me. "I couldn't be happier to welcome you to our family, Kat—whenever and however that unfolds."

"What's happening over there?" Opal called. She'd gone all out with sparkling splendor for the event, wearing a caftan embroidered with tiny crystals and a red feather headdress; she towed Artie along, and Pua bobbed in their wake.

"What did we miss?" my curious co-worker exclaimed.

Aunt Fae, never one for subtlety, pointed at my hand. "Keone proposed. These two are engaged."

My cheeks burned with embarrassment, and I cast Keone a pleading glance as Opal and Pua joined the excitement and exclamations. "So glad," Artie said simply, his gentle smile conveying genuine happiness. "I wish I could see that ring, but I'll have to imagine it."

Opal took my hand in hers, her numerous bracelets jingling with the movement. "It's a vintage ring with a pearl, Artie," she said, examining the ring. "It fits her perfectly."

"You're not surprised I'm wearing it on my right hand?" I asked.

"Not at all," Opal said. "You've always needed to find your own path."

Artie nodded in agreement. "As long as you two are on it together, good things are ahead."

At this blessing from our resident psychics, also my "*hanai*" parents since I moved to Ohia, tears welled in my eyes. Artie and Opal had never tried to tear my emotional walls down; instead, they had patiently built love and acceptance around them until the walls melted away.

"What's all this?" Josie's voice carried across the gathering as she approached with the rest of the Red Hat Society in tow. "Is there news?"

"Kat and Keone are engaged!" Aunt Fae hollered before I could respond.

The Red Hats descended upon us in a flurry of scarlet, purple, and enthusiastic congratulations. Edith immediately began discussing potential botanical arrangements for "whatever ceremony you choose, dear, traditional or otherwise." Clara insisted on examining the ring, pronouncing it "perfect." Rita, ever practical, asked about our living arrangements and seemed pleased to confirm we were already settled in Keone's cottage. "Maile can come visit you there sometime," she said with a wink.

"This calls for a toast!" Josie declared, waving vigorously to Elle, who quickly arranged for champagne flutes to be distributed.

"I didn't plan for a toast," my friend said as she poured sparkling wine into a raft of glasses on a tray. "When you have the actual wedding, I'll be able to show my full range of talents."

"I wouldn't have it any other way," I said. "But it won't be for a while."

Pearl, having noticed the gathering, navigated her wheelchair toward us. "I see the news is out," she observed. "The plumeria tree was a suitable location after all."

I elbowed Keone. "So that's why you got special permission to cross that caution tape."

"I may have made certain suggestions," Pearl said, the controls of her wheelchair humming as she adjusted her position. "The plumeria tree has witnessed both destruction and renewal. It's the perfect place for a proposal, and I'm so happy for you both."

As Elle distributed bubbling champagne flutes, Ilima stepped forward, her natural authority commanding our attention.

"If I may," she said, raising her glass, "I'd like to propose a toast. To Keone and Kat, who have found in each other not just love, but true partnership. May your journey together be as unique and authentic as you both are."

"To Keone and Kat!" the group echoed, raising their glasses.

My cheeks burned at being the center of attention, but the genuine warmth from this community—now truly my *'ohana*—made the attention bearable.

Keone's hand found mine and squeezed it as we acknowledged the toast. "Thanks, everyone. Now I think my fiancée has had enough of the spotlight." He pointed with his glass toward his truck, parked in the lawn area ahead. Tiki sat on the hood like a big ornament. "And our feline overlord is saying it's time to go home."

We headed out in a flurry of goodbyes; I leaned into the arm Keone had wrapped around me. "Thanks for the rescue, Mr. K."

"The first of many. I've got your back, Trouble."

As the impromptu celebration continued without us and we backed away in Keone's vehicle with Tiki in her carrier, I noticed Opal and Ilima exchange a significant glance. Opal stepped away to examine one of the architectural renderings more closely. Pearl followed, her wheelchair bumping across the grass. The three women's expressions, visible in profile, were serious and focused—a stark contrast to the celebratory atmosphere surrounding us.

Keone noticed my distraction. "What is it?" he asked quietly.

"Something's going on with Pearl, Opal, and your mom," I

murmured. "They're huddled over that rendering like it contains classified information."

"It probably does," Keone said. "Pearl never does anything without multiple layers going on."

"They're hiding something," I observed as we pulled away from the Heritage Garden site, Mount Haleakalā standing magnificent against the cloudless sky behind us.

"Probably," Keone agreed, reaching across to take my right hand, his thumb brushing lightly across the ring's surface. "But that's tomorrow's problem."

As we drove along the coastal road toward Keone's cottage—our little home, with its view of the ocean and proximity to Ilima's house next door—I was filled with a sense of deep joy.

Whatever mystery Pearl, Opal, and Ilima were contemplating could wait.

Today was for celebrating how far we'd already come: a garden beginning to take root, justice being served, and a future unfolding with possibilities, hope, and love.

WANT to keep up with the next book in the series (because there will be more!) and be informed of specials and giveaways? Sign up for my newsletter HERE and get a free full-length mystery, TORCH GINGER, starring Lei Texeira, the detective you met in this book and the original heroine who kicked off the Paradise Crime World!

Need another FREE book in the Paradise Crime World? Download WIRED ROGUE, a Paradise Crime Thriller set on Hawaii, FREE. A great introduction story to get to know the CEO of Security Solutions, Sophie (Ang) Smithson and her complicated life and loves.

If you enjoyed this story and my voice on the page, you might also like my memoir FRECKLED: a Memoir of Growing up Wild in Hawaii, my personal (award-winning) account of life as a child growing up hippie in 1970s Kauai. (Spoiler alert: it's like the Glass Castle, but Hawaii.)

In case all that wasn't enough, here's a complete list of all of my 50+ books. Yes, I write a lot! And I hope you keep reading. *As long as you do, I'll be writing.*

ACKNOWLEDGMENTS

Aloha dear readers!

Thanks so much for joining me, Kat, Keone, Lei, Ilima, Aunt Fae, Pearl, Elle, Artie, Opal, all the Red Hatters, and most of all TIKI! for this latest adventure crime solving in paradise. I continue to love to escape to the imaginary and wonderful town of Ohia on Maui, with its tiny microcosm of the greater island of Maui.

You, yes, YOU! Are the wind beneath my writing wings. If a book is never read, is it even a book?

Special thanks go out to Angie Lail, the "Keeper of Secrets" of the entire Paradise Crime World. She is not only my copyeditor, but the one I count on to create a library of spreadsheets that track all the character names, quirks, characteristics. She catches so many things, like the fact that there's no Buddist temple in Iao Valley, and that Maui Beach Hotel doesn't have room service, so Kat and Keone have to stay at the Hampton Inn.

As with all my books, I make sure you know they are fiction, but I am inspired by the events of history and current social and environmental issues. I hope you come away from even this lighthearted read with a little more knowledge of the Islands and their unique challenges and joys. If so, would you leave a review? They mean more than you know, and help others find the books.

Without your support I'd just be a middle-aged redheaded honorary Red Hat wandering the beach, telling stories to my dog. Thanks for saving me from that lonely fate.

Until next time, I'll be writing!

Much aloha,
Toby Neal

ABOUT THE AUTHOR

Kirkus Reviews calls Neal's writing, "*persistently riveting. Masterly.*"

Award-winning, USA Today bestselling social worker turned author Toby Neal grew up on the island of Kaua`i in Hawaii. Neal's mental health career has informed the depth and complexity of her stories. Fans call her writing, "*Immersive, addicting, and the next best thing to being there.*" Neal also pens romance as Toby Jane and writes memoir/nonfiction under TW Neal.

Sign up for her email newsletter HERE at tobyneal.net, and get a free, full length book!

You can also follow her writing and books LIVE AS THEY HAPPEN on her Substack newsletter HERE.